created by

created by

Richard Christian Matheson

BANTAM BOOKS

New York Toronto London Sydney Auckland

Grateful acknowledgment is made for permission to reprint the excerpt from "EVERYONE'S GONE TO THE MOVIES." Words and Music by WALTER BECKER and DONALD FAGEN. © Copyright 1973 by WINGATE MUSIC CORP. All Rights Controlled and Administered by MCA MUSIC PUBLISHING, A Division of MCA INC, New York, NY 10019. USED BY PERMISSION. ALL RIGHTS RESERVED.

CREATED BY
A Bantam Book / October 1993

Library of Congress Cataloging-in-Publication Data

Matheson, Richard Christian.
    Created by / Richard Christian Matheson.
        p.   cm.
    ISBN 0-553-09543-9
    I. Title.
PS3563.A8356C7   1993
813'.54—dc20   93-3693
                                                      CIP

Published simultaneously in the United States and Canada

PRINTED IN THE UNITED STATES OF AMERICA
BVG   0 9 8 7 6 5 4 3 2 1

For my father, Richard.
My remarkable teacher and friend.
My brilliant inspiration.
I love you.

ACKNOWLEDGMENTS

Deep appreciation to Pat LoBrutto, whose passion helped bring this book to life. Thanks, pal. Many thanks to my editor, Lou Aronica, for a highly perceptive eye and abundant humor. More to Jennifer Hershey for patience, taste and thoughtfulness. And to Binky Urban and Heather Schroder for impeccable instincts, all the way around.

A final thanks is in order. I'd like to acknowledge some of the writers I worked with in television who shared a gift: Thomas Szollosi, Kenneth Johnson, Oliver and Elizabeth Hailey, George Kirgo, Nick Corea, Donald Bellisario, Andrew Schneider, Dinah and Julie Kirgo, Jerry Davis, Tony and Nancy Lawrence, Babs Greyhosky, Harve Bennett, Renee and Harry Longstreet, Karen Harris, Bill Sandefur, Herb Wright, Steven E. DeSouza, David Frankel, Sid Ellis, James Hirsch, Frank Lupo, Patrick Hasburgh, Gy Waldron, Lynn Montgomery, Norman Steinberg, Steven Spielberg, Aaron Spelling, and most of all Stephen J. Cannell.

"The adage in television is that the fluke is the hit."
Brandon Tartikoff,
Former President of NBC

"One does not become enlightened by imagining figures of light, but by making the darkness conscious."
C. G. Jung

"Everyone's gone to the movies, now we're alone at last . . ."
Steely Dan

Q. With "Hill Street" and "L.A. Law" you have really pushed the line as far as what you can do on network television.

A. We're going to go farther.

Q. You don't think that you've already gone further than any other show?

A. Yeah. But not enough. I want more. I think that you're going to see all kinds of things in the next half-dozen years on television that you can't even imagine today.

> Excerpt from interview with producer/writer Steven Bochco, July-August 1988 *American Film*

teaser

May 12
Los Angeles

~~~~~~~~~~~~~~~~~~~~~~~~~~~~~~What is it? I'm getting some-thing?"

Alan smiled. Maybe she was as incredible as everyone had said. He'd been sitting with her for five minutes and it was happening: the top-hat-zap.

"I'm not sure. The new pilot, I suppose." Alan made a nervous face. It was borderline creepy hanging out with this broad. The way she sat there, staring.

Watching.

The trappings weren't much, sure. Just a hold-it-in-your-hand condo in a so-so part of town. The whole dinky place had a blown-up Vegas swap-meet look and there was velvet everything. Cruddy art, too. Piles and piles of that ultrabrocade, Liberace nightmare stuff. As they talked, Alan couldn't ignore a swag lamp that hung overhead, golden cupids encaged by cat gut that dripped glycerine in slo-mo. Sort of the tacky tears of time trickling into schmaltzy eternity. Nearby, the electric Elvis air freshener hummed.

Not at all the right setting for a famous psychic. Rich oil sheiks

~~~~~~~~

sought out this woman. Incredibly wealthy celebrities. Major league ball players having bad seasons. Lovers who feared defection. Terminal disease sufferers. Gamblers. They all came. Filled with wonder and hope. Lots of hope.

All the guys at Paramount who'd gone told Alan they swore by her. Absolutely fucking swore. As in the Holy Virgin or even J.C. himself. The faith ran that deep. Maybe even deeper when you got right down to it.

Shows that were going to have legs or ones that were fated to be flushed. It didn't matter. She *knew*. She could pin it just like the gas man reads your meter. That's how weird it really was. One felt more than vaguely naked.

And her specialty was picking shows. She'd even been on big salary with one of the networks to do that very thing. They sat her every day in a hidden little office and let her look at pilot proposals, pilot scripts, casting ideas, you name it. And, man, she had the fucking touch.

She'd seen Bell's pilot "Mike and Pooky" two seasons back and loved it. Watched the whole half-inch cassette in her office at the network H.Q. in L.A. and laughed her head off. Loved it. Dialogue. Pacing. Acting. Action. It was all there, ready to roar like a rocket.

And when the suits marched in with tasseled feet and asked her what she thought, she said it didn't have a chance in hell. Three and out. Maybe four.

Her visions had been a kindness.

"Mike and Pooky" got creamed first two weeks against some old Sly movies the other networks put in America's face.

After a month, the network pulled the plug. No chance to catch on. Find its audience. Bell had freaked. All his Emmys, Humanitas, and WGA chrome, brass, and crystal didn't make a bit of difference. That's what was so fucking crazy. Didn't matter if you had a star that tested out better than sex. Didn't matter if you had a premise that was plated at the mint. None of it mattered.

And there was that goddamned psychic pulling down twenty-five large and calling them like some pointy-hatted diety.

The network had poured god knows how much into the promotion of "Mike and Pooky" and they were as frazzed as Bell. Over lunch last week, at Lorimar, some gay line producer swore up and down the network had dropped at least five million. Double truck spreads in *Newsweek, The Stone, Time, TV Guide.* Radio and television spots. Talk show jibber-jabber with the groins who played Mike and Pooky, charming Jay, walking on the comedy sun-surface with Dave, doing a Pearl Jam ballad with Paul and the band.

But it didn't help. The pilot got a fourteen share and it just wasn't enough. Bye-bye, Mike. Bye-bye, Pooky. Turn in your wax figurines to be melted down. Back to potato chip commercials and method workshops.

And she'd done the same thing for the last six years, employed by the network. She'd only missed a few times. She even claimed she could get 80 percent accuracy. Time had proven her right.

"What about the new pilot?" Her eyes were somehow very sad. Too much despair. Too much everything. But then how would anyone look who knew what was coming tomorrow. And the day after. And next week. And five years from now. And could see you dying in some hospital ward. Or maybe worse.

"What do you see?" Alan's fingers braided, nervously. "Will I do well with it?"

She closed her eyes, took several deep breaths, polished toes tugging at blue shag. Her body faintly vibrated, curled in the chair as if she watched a favorite movie on TV. All she needed was buttered popcorn and a kitty.

"Write down the name of the show . . ." Her eyes opened a bit; shutters. She gestured to some writing implements on the desk. Then, her stare was petitioned back by the trance and heavy lids sealed, again.

Alan picked up a felt pen and scrawled THE MERCENARY on a sheet of white paper. It looked great, he thought. Bold and gutsy. The kind of title that made you want to go out on a midnight raid and slit villagers' throats.

He slid the paper back to her and she didn't move. The strange, hammocked eyes were restive. A minute passed.

More.

Alan needed to cough but drowned it with some Hires she'd given him. It was warm, tasted like the skull soda they give lunatics so they can dress themselves.

She stirred a little, opened eyes. Traced her finger over Alan's words. Slowly, again and again. It was eerie. Maybe ten times from the *T* to the *Y*. Then, she stopped, froze; peered up at him, from her little writing desk. Smiled. "I see a great deal of money . . . you're going to be successful."

She stared off, as if savoring an evocative painting, she alone saw.

"It's going to be a huge hit. I love the whole thing. I love all the *E*'s in the title. *E* is very good for you. People or places with that letter . . ."

Alan's smile fanned. It was a rush. Like your best friend in high school telling you he'd talked to the girl you had a crush on and finding out she didn't sleep at night thinking about you.

But it was a lot more. He'd been totally balls-out nuts working on this pilot idea for "The Mercenary" and the outline bible was the best thing he'd ever done. It had all the colors, textures. He knew it would make America insane and spin on the meanest, biggest ceiling fan they ever saw.

Mimi was still trancing, surfing the solar system. Jesus, thought Alan as he watched her, this lady might be the wall and the plug. And she was sparking to *his* idea.

She'd told Franky his sitcom for the Fox Network, "Let's Get Serious," was going to pull numbers and yank a fat pickup for a full twenty-two, first three out. And that's what happened. One year ago, today.

That was Mimi.

Like you wind a clock and it ticks. That's what she did. Franky had explained the whole thing this way: your life was a book and as Mimi sat with you, she zonked into some starry, forever place, sat on a rock, skimmed a few chapters, then galaxied back, opened her eyes, and abra-fucking-cadabra she's in her tacky little condo smiling up at you and the Elvis air freshener.

At least you hope she's smiling.

Tell that one to Bell, Alan thought. No smiles on that clog in his bloodstream. Just a ten-million-dollar cancelled albatross winging over a traumatized brain.

"Any problems? Delays?" Alan had to know. The network hadn't even heard the idea yet. And those clawhammer smiles could smash your head.

Mimi sighed.

But it wasn't weariness. It was just giving the channel some room to breathe and stretch and feel good about doing the reading; making the timeless data feel at home so it would stay awhile.

He needed some coffee. He always needed coffee.

All day, at Paramount or Universal or Columbia or wherever somebody was renting his thought process, he'd drink as much head diesel as he could hold. Fucking stuff was probably eating everything inside. Take an X-ray, get a big blank. "Sorry, Mr. White, you don't appear to have any internal organs left. You really should consider a nondairy creamer."

"No delays. But it's . . ."—she took his hand like a mother—"it's going to be very difficult, Alan." She grasped his hand more tightly. "This show of yours. It's extremely special. I want to be here for you if you need me. Do you understand what I'm saying?"

He said nothing. It was the way she was looking at him, the way she was gripping his fingers harder than she needed to. The fear that seemed to flash across her face, a REM death mask.

"Maybe not," he confessed.

"Success can be . . . very dangerous."

He felt the bromides slinking near; Dear Abby thongs rounding the corner, out for a stroll. Thanks, lady, but I'll put up garlic and mirrors if it really gets . . .

". . . religion may not help."

Alan stared. Spoke softly. "Did you just read my mind?" He was more uneasy than he sounded.

She didn't reply. Looked away in private travail.

"Right," he muttered. "So, what's going to go wrong? Am I going to have a heart attack or something? Go bankrupt?" His eyes twinkled. "Get stuck on a bad cruise?"

She didn't smile.

Alan sensed the crystal ball going black. He wanted to leave.

"Could just be . . . challenges." She gestured without detail.

"I . . . is there something you're not—"

"Alan . . ."

The two locked in an uncomfortable stare. Those eyes, lost in miserable giftedness, were aflame. She was being scarier than shit, again.

"I'm right, aren't I? There's something you want to say to me." He'd kill for a cup of coffee. Something to do with his hands. Something to make him forget. His eyes had the shifting-crawlies: left, right, up, down; like Beaver Cleaver caught jerking off.

"Your show is going to be very powerful."

Alan didn't exactly feel shook up by that one. He'd figured she was going to tell him something really horrible. Something monstrous that psychics tell doomed souls. Some cursing finality.

But this was good news. Why the dread?

Then, it hit him the way the punch line of a complicated joke suddenly goes from gas to solid in your thoughts—ka-boom: the genie appears with subtitles. He realized everyone in L.A. was too damn melodramatic, that was why. They all wanted the kleig-rub, and Mimi was just stroking the histrionic gloom.

The ones who weren't trying to act were trying to model. The ones who weren't trying to model were trying to write screenplays. Or produce. Or write jingles. Or produce jingles. Or act in jingles. Or be a jingle. People talked about pilots not feelings, unless it was how they felt about pilots. The box-office bloodstreamers were leaking everywhere you went. Ideas or creative notions were regarded as signals from deep space if they were good. If they were bad, they were treated like bad dogs.

L.A. didn't need a mayor. It needed a director.

"Then I really don't have anything to worry about . . ."

Mimi stood in the cramped bedroom-converted-to office, went to her bookshelf. Squeezed fingertips along books, found a musty hardcover. Slid it out, undusted a semicircle on the cover. Handed it to Alan.

"Depends." She'd lowered her voice and Alan tried not to feel her sawing him in half.

"I want you to have this. Keep it, Alan. Read it if you need to. If not, it's still yours."

He glanced at the book, accepted it. Grimaced at the odor: old bookstore smell.

He rested it on the lap of his blue jeans, cleared a bit more of the semicircle of dust. The title looked him in the eye.

Mind Potentials.

Written by some guy named Seth Lawrence. First chapter, "Dwellers in the Mirage." Second chapter, "Shadows Move." Third, "Man as Slave." Fourth, "The Divine Terror." Fifth, "No Way Out." Sixth and final chapter—"One Way Out."

I love it, thought Alan. Big laughs.

"Thank you," he said, politely.

Mimi nodded, looked at her watch. Another appointment outside. They could hear him, in the living room, popping his ballpoint.

"Alan, do you understand when I say your show is going to be powerful?"

"I'm comfortable with the idea of success if that's what you mean."

She shook her head sternly, suddenly angry. "Not success. *Power.* Incredible power. You have to be cautious."

"I don't plan to let it go to my head. I'm not a kid." He was thirty-four. He *was* a kid.

The other appointment coughed.

Mimi took Alan's hand, gripped it tightly. But something was different. Her hands were cold.

"Be careful. The next six months are going to change your life. Money. Power. And something else . . ." She shook her head, troubled beyond words. ". . . not sure. I see two—no, three people. The third is very bad for you. Very bad. You must . . ."

Her breath stopped, face drained white.

"Am I going to be all right?"

Mimi made a groaning sound, pressed nails into his palm so hard he tried to pull away, seeing bloody slits. "Say the title to me, again. I need to hear it."

He spoke in a tense whisper, repeated it three times. She seemed to be crying yet no sounds issued, no tears. She saw the blood on his palm, quickly wiped it with her sleeve.

"Stay in touch with me, Alan."

Oh, yeah, I'll stay in touch with you, he thought. Every morning I'll give you a buzz and—

"Don't make this into a joke."

Fuck. She was reading his mind again.

"Well, what do you suggest? I let it keep me up nights?"

"I have no doubt it will."

"What will? What are you talking about?"

"Something inside you. Something that . . . wants out." She looked off, trying to describe the borders of a grotesque Rorschach. "It will come out." She seemed confused by more disconnected images. Lost but continuing to try, stricken, swirling in some awful place. ". . . it will live in both places. Inside . . . outside." She suddenly saw it and jerked back from him.

"Mimi . . ."

She became calm, like the victim of an air disaster, sitting in stunned agony on a bloody runway, waiting for ambulances.

"It's a . . . monster," she said. "He will bring tragedy. Murder. Pain." Her heart flooded with psychotic impressions and Alan stood to go.

"He'll come out. He'll find a way."

It was the last thing he heard as he left and ended up in the bar at Spago's, drinking until it closed.

act one

the pitch

Smog covered L.A. like thin, concentration camp smoke.

"Andy, great to see you. I know this season's been a circus with all the cancellations and strikes. How you been?"

Alan could barely make eye contact with Andy Singer. All he kept seeing was Cleo's imbecilic smile supcrimposed on Andy's conceited face.

Andy stretched, his iridescent Bijan shirt doing a trout shimmer. "Well, you know, 'Cleo' has been very good to us again this season."

Really? thought Alan. Got news for you, pal; if Cleo had been good to you, she would've cut your heart out and fed it to you.

"Oh, yeah?" Alan smiled a little. But not enough to give it away. "Well, I'm not surprised. That show just really hits people."

Yeah, he thought. Like the bubonic stupids it hits people. Andy was delighted and giggled a bit. Alan stared at him, trying to imagine how so profound an injustice could've occurred.

Andy was all of twenty-five years old and had been promoted to junior V.P. of programming for the network one year earlier. But regardless of whatever the hell it was he did for a living, he was fucking good at his job. Alan couldn't deny it. No one could.

The list went on and on.

"Surgeons." Forty-two share after the second week, up against the Super Bowl . . . there was no way, but Andy picked it.

"A House for All." Sweeps Week didn't even make a dent. The other two networks threw-up *Lethal Weapon 3* and a two-hour, tear-jerk cabala with Barbara Walters interviewing seriously maimed celebrities to try and stop it. And the goddamn thing cleaned their clocks like fucking napalm. Stupid? Sure, it was stupid. Serious faces, talking over serious family "drama" and crying at every break. But incest cuts into the veins. Mel and Barbara didn't even get a chance to pull their pants down.

"Cleo."

Well . . . what could you say? What could you actually *call* it? It sure wasn't no comedy, Jack. But try to tell that to the rating's points that were hugging that sucker like a beam of golden light.

There wasn't a writer in town who could stand to even watch the teaser. But they all wanted to write for it. Resids, kids. That show was going to ride into the sunset like Mighty Mouse, with a hundred zeroes between his furry little legs. Even if some guy got cut off at story and the script got finished in-house, he knew he'd pull down endless checks from syndie bread; foreign, domestic. Eventually the fucking Solar System would be bouncing "Cleo" into black holes. Even subfungi life-forms would sit around eating Doritos, watching.

And Andy with his Shirley Temple hair, lame jokes, and vapid taste was responsible. Some said he'd disfigured the cosmic order. After all, "Cleo" was his "baby." His "concept." His guiding hand was there, every excruciating inch of the way.

It was hard to decide which made one ulcerate more, the part about a castrating hag and her defiant cat Mr. Pink Nose, or the part about how the two insinuated themselves into the life of her merry, brain-dead son-in-law who resembled a more masculine Pat Sajak.

"Dad" was trying to raise two daughters after his wife left him for some gonk Richard Belzer somehow got talked into playing, to much publicized regret. That's when "Dad's" former mother-in-law, the sarcastic, festering horror, Cleo, had decided to drop in and help him get along, with her agonizing homilies and fat, grotesque cat.

Mr. Pink Nose had become quite the tasteless phenomenon after Andy suggested the hateful creature be given an opportunity to take a leak on someone in each week's episode. As the laugh track shrieked, the editors would cut to a close up of Mr. Pink Nose's furry face. Then, as the sound of feline urine trickled hilariously, Mr. Pink Nose would make his trademark hiss.

America was in love.

But there was more. The character of Cleo's grand-daughter, Poppy-Sue, was especially odious and the producers had attempted to recruit her endlessly over used line of dialogue, "I've never seen a butt with legs," into mainstream venacular. T-shirts, pull-string dolls, posters of people with butts where their heads would normally be. This was whoring at an epic level, and by any decent measure, a total nightmare.

To say the show was widely despised would be putting you up for a Humanitas. It sucked. The lines were indescribably unfunny. The plots embarrassing. The actors couldn't've gotten work in claymation. The theme song, as rendered by accordion, snare drum and strip-show cymbal plus some unnerving guy from a beer hall singing, was twenty-five seconds of sheer agony.

    OH CLEO, WHY DO YOU LAUGH SO MUCH? (BOOM,
      SPLASH)
    OH CLEO, IT'S YOU WHO BRINGS US SUCH (SPLASH)
    JOY! SUCH (SPLASH) JOY!!
    (SPLASH, SPLASH, BOOM)
    OH, CLEO, YOU MUST HAVE DROPPED FROM A CLOUD
    OF GOLD (BOOM, BOOM, BOOM).

ONE DAY WITH YOU (SPLASH, SPLASH) AND THE WORLD
WOULD NEVER GET (SPLASH, BOOM, SPLASH)
OOOOOLLLLLDDDD!

How could Andy live with himself? Creating that kind of Alz-
heimer drivel; airing it every week.

And he was rich!

"Cleo" was a prospering corporation. It wasn't a show. It was
U.S. Steel with sets and punch lines.

And this twenty-five-year-old Flintstone vitamin was behind
the whole thing. He'd been on the covers of *Vanity Fair* and
Newsweek. And the network loved him like they loved few persons
or things in the universe. He had brought great riches to their
barren souls. He had brought a smile to their disheartened faces.
And last but not least, he'd helped them gross an extra eighty
million in fiscal '92.

And he could barely write his name.

They'd yanked him out of MGM when he was a reader for a big
Italian producer and given him a shot because he'd discovered
some good properties for the Italian guy and made several purely
accidental moves that resulted in mushroom profits for Metro
during an otherwise bad year.

So, they give him an office and he picks a couple more properties that switch swill to box office and it's another promotion. This
time right into the sagging TV division. Then, he hits a homerun
with lips. Movie of the Week. Three nuns out in the desert with an
escaped-con-rapist-psycho: "Sisters and Brother."

Bad doesn't cover it.

Reviewers are in pale stupors they hate it so much. Even the
Catholic Church decries it. The Pope was rumored to have switched
over to "Who's the Boss?" Cardinals are calling the dreckish extrav-
aganza "an abuse of human values as well as fundamental tenets."
Angry telegrams are beyond earth math. Hallmark doesn't make
cards for this level of outrage.

And the goddamn show *cleans* up.

Forty-two share. Even though he couldn't figure out how to work a book of matches, Andy had invented fire.

"So, what do you have for me?" Andy gestured in fast little circles with his right hand, its nails chewed to gross nubs." I haven't seen you for a while. Geez, you do some episodes for Bochco and all of a sudden I can't get a call once in awhile?"

Andy stared, nodding with amusement. Alan nodded back, smiling. Andy's minions, lined on the couch, nodded equal amusement; intestinally blocked Kewpies. They were there to round out the meeting and served no identifiable purpose; full grown people, living complex lives in L.A., sitting pleasantly in this room, exuding nothingness for a living.

"I've got something in mind for an hour show. Not really cop genre. But it's action," began Alan, seated on the rattan Kreiss chair before Andy's huge, glass desk. The desk was so big, it resembled a sliding glass door, supported by thick travertine legs. Designer stuff. And Andy looked right at home behind it. The frizzy-headed video sultan, lost in the immense regality of his own success, surrounded by plants that looked like they came from a designer jungle.

Everything was right. Like a perfect alibi.

"What's the direction?" asked one of the Kewpies, a good-looking black woman, never changing expression or tone of voice. Her blazer looked just like Andy's, her pants silky and balloonish.

Andy glared discreetly at the assistant. Don't steal my fire, was the look. Don't ask my questions. The assistant crossed arms, self-consciously. Andy's sulky glare was enough to bring on jitters. It's why his office was called the Nut-Cracker Suite.

"I think what Diane means," interpreted Andy, "is . . . we're all intrigued."

All nodded, looking intrigued.

"It's the story of the return of the real individual," said Alan. "The individual who can fight for himself." He took a dramatic pause. "The kind we don't have anymore. The kind we all want to be."

Andy stared at him. Lit a cigarette. Silence.

"His name is A. E. Barek. A mercenary. That's the name of the show I'd like to sell you guys: 'The Mercenary.' " Alan knew it by heart. "He's say thirty, thirty-five. Handsome. Powerful. Smart. Hero in small wars. Big ones. Gulf time, whatever. Comes home from one to a situation that has no use for him. Wife remarried. Parents and kids don't understand him. He's angry. Alone ..."

Andy snuffed out his cigarette.

"What's this angry guy's franchise, Alan?" He held up a soft hand, palm forward. "Sorry to interrupt but that's essential this season. Character pilots aren't happening for us. People can rent *Driving Miss Angst*. We gotta give them a lasarium show ... for a price."

"Affiliates," explained one of the other Kewpies, nodding at Alan as if having just explained the theory of relativity.

"Well, like I say, he's a mercenary," answered Alan. "A gun for hire."

Andy sighed and it made Alan nervous. Guys like Andy spoke in elliptical Morse code: enigmatic semi-nods and *hmm* sounds, when assembled in proper sequence, forming messages of rejection.

"Well, of course so much hinges on how it's written, Alan. Everyone in this room knows your talent." He shrugged a little. "But frankly, the thing doesn't really feel ..." he struggled, "it feels, I don't know," he made a put-off, just-watched-a-cat-run-over face. "It feels ... passé. Nobody's watching that delayed stress, Viet Nam stuff much anymore. I mean, sure, if Oliver Stone wants to develop *Platoon* into a goddamn variety show, I could give him thirteen guaranteed."

There were scattered chuckles. The Kewpie beside Alan indicated a desire to talk. Andy nodded.

"Just thought I'd mention Carsey-Werner is doing a pilot about a gay soldier division."

"Yeah, I know, 'Pinks,' " said Andy, uninterested.

"It does have a military backdrop."

Andy acknowledged the information, returned his stare to Alan.

"Anyway, Alan, you know I hate to tinkle on anybody's parade but . . . I mean, look, I pride myself on being one of the few people in this town who'll green light in the room and I gotta tell you, it doesn't make me crazy."

That's because you're already crazy, thought Alan. He smiled at Andy. "Can't have that, can we?"

Andy was amused. You could tell because one side of his mouth rose a tiny bit and he spun slowly in his Roche-Bobois chair to face an infinite view to the ocean, far above L.A. congestion and swelter. Sort of like God.

Then, he turned back. Then, he said: "Funny."

No actual laughter. Just, "Funny." That's how you knew you'd amused Andy Singer. He told you.

"I left out one thing, " Alan added, quietly, knowing the effect his tone of voice had. "I think I know how we can make this thing the biggest hit on the air."

Andy stared like he'd heard this rap many times in his illustrious five-minute career. "Yeah?" he asked, politely, hoping he was wrong.

Alan stated the idea, plain as day. "We play the violence for real and we do frontal nudity. Sex, four-letter words . . . whole bit."

The little sultan didn't flinch.

"I mean, guys, let's face fucking facts. Your audience is down fifty percent. Cable and cassettes are taking too big a bite. Not to mention whatever Diller's litter is planning next over at FOX to kick you around, and four labor strikes in three years. Craft unions, DGA, SAG, WGA. You guys lost, what? Fifty million? Seventy-five?"

The room was listening.

"Your programming can't compete. People wanna see more. See what they wanna see. And what the networks are programming ain't it."

Andy was amused again. But he wanted to hear more.

"You gotta understand where people are at today. Out there." Alan pointed through the huge window. "On the street."

Andy steepled chewed fingers. "And what are they saying?" He got up, walked to the window. Didn't turn to face the room.

"That they're on a yawn drip feed with the network schedule." There were tiny snickers. "But really . . . that they're scared to death to leave their houses because crime on the street has gotten so bad." He was speaking to Andy's back. "Gangs. Drive-bys. Crack. Fucking psychotics every two blocks, looking to slice'n dice you 'cause they don't like the color of your Reeboks, or 'cause your Rolex ticks too loud. How about aquitted cops with little temper problems and big batons. How about the fucking riots?"

Andy stared into nowhere. "And your show?"

"My show, 'The Mercenary,' entertains the hell out of them with enough action and blood to compete with Segal, Norris, Schwarzenegger. They don't have to rent *Die Hard 7*, 'cause they can watch better every week. My guy doesn't take shit, doesn't take prisoners, and this show is gonna get 'em outta the theaters and VCR rental joints, back in front of the goddamn set where they belong."

Alan moved eyes from face-to-face. Andy's buzzer sounded and he turned from the window.

"Hold all calls."

Andy stared at Alan, saying nothing; mind lining up crosshairs. "Alan . . . I gotta tell you, I don't know, man. You're making some real good points and all that and what you're talking about might—I stress *might*—pull an audience away from our competition." Andy sounded sincere for the first time in the last ten minutes. "But we haven't got a chance with the direction you wanna take. I mean, we aren't doing features. You're talking Joel Silver time. FCC would close us down."

"Let them sue you. Tie 'em up in court for ten years waiting for a trial. If the affiliates are happy, you're making money. I'd rather be in litigation than broke, wouldn't you?" Alan stared out the window, again. "Andy, I've seen the annual reports on your profits.

You guys need something other than a Jim Brooks syndication package. Getting grim."

Andy said nothing. The Kewpie who looked like a nose in clothes cleared his throat; offered wisdom.

"He's right, Andy. Last year was a . . . fall-off."

Andy didn't glare. No repudiatory sulk. No arrogant pout. No power-tripping sarcasm. No argument of any kind. He knew it was the truth. The network was hanging by a finger. So were the other two networks. Maybe FOX, too, with or without Bart Simpson. Cable had cut off everybody's balls and left them to slowly bleed to death, ratings pooling; a hemorrhaging attention span.

They needed something.

All the programmers talked about it among trusted advisers and friends. It was time to start taking huge risks. Blow the lid. Stop firing rubber bullets. Something that would hit like a fucking Amtrak crashing through your forehead at three in the morning and didn't cost a fortune. And if the sponsors didn't like it, get new ones. Besides, thought Alan, all *Variety* ever talked about was the sponsors moving to off-network. They had no fucking loyalty. They had abandoned the networks, forcing them to unravel the whole mess.

How many were leaving?

Enough to wipe the chalk right off the scheduling board. Millions of dollars invested in pilot episodes. Presentations. Holding deals with stars. Staged readings. Preproduction costs. Post-production costs. You-name-it-it-costs-something costs. It wasn't home movies they were discussing here. It was enough money to run a country.

And the awareness of that made Andy's face a tight drumhead; tension stretching his features flat. He tapped half-digested nails against the desk. It was impossible to imagine what might be coursing through that strangely empty mind. The Kewpies shifted restlessly. Alan said nothing, swallowed by his big chair. Andy liked all the silence. It gave him the leisure seconds to formulate his closing thoughts. Which were most often identical to his opening thoughts.

"How much do you have?" It was a tone Alan knew; the sound of scented blood, of Andy's interest in a state of growing erection.

"The characters, basic bible. Ten or fifteen springboards. Pretty clear direction for a two-hour pilot."

Alan knew he only had half that but it wouldn't be hard to fill it in. He was already playing with an opening sequence for the pilot that involved a crashed British Airways 747, on the bottom of the Atlantic, filled with trapped passengers; entombed, screaming. Exactly the kind of hypnotic trauma that should become the show's insignia.

He was starting to get a twinge of something.

Even the Kewpies were looking into his eyes every second or so. They did that when they felt their boss responding. It gave them the freedom to look at you, with the confidence they weren't staring at failure. They hated that. Failure was worse than death. Worse than original sin. And when they saw maybe you weren't a sinner, they wanted to get a good look at you. They wanted to see what living forever looked like.

And when a show stayed on, that's what happened. If it could survive sixty-six episodes, enough to syndicate, not only did everybody including the creator get crazy rich, the show could run forever. They said that somewhere in the world Richie and Fonzie were sucking malts, twenty-four hours a day. With the right show, you never had to die.

"Alan . . . I think our chances are like a hundred million to one . . . and we may all be sharing a plug-in chair . . . but I don't know. It's real different."

Alan smiled. "I can play with the tone a little. But I wanna make it hard-core. Make what Mann was doing with "Miami Vice" look like *Police Academy,* you know?"

"It's weird," said Andy. "I haven't felt this—whatever I feel— since I heard the pitch for 'Cleo.' I'm getting that . . . it's hard to describe."

Lettuce is hard for you to describe, thought Alan.

"Anyway, I'll take it to Greg and Scot, see what kind of reaction

I get. I mean, with the FCC thing . . . I'd say we're dead meat. But it might crack 'em up."

"We'll certainly get an interesting reaction," said one of the Kewpies with robust participation.

The black lady Kewpie also spoke.

"This kind of an idea could be a real breakthrough, Andy. If done right, of course."

Andy nodded half interest at their contributions; he looked off. "You know, ever since 'Cleo,' it's hard to get excited with ideas. You get spoiled." He sighed, then brightened. "Hey, Alan, how's your raquetball game these days?"

"Good as ever. Terrible."

As soon as Andy chuckled, everyone else did. It was strange, thought Alan. Hearing sounds of happiness issuing from Andy's denuded soul. As if he were some kind of satanic muppet. Andy stood and everyone did.

"Look forward to hearing from you." Alan was shaking hands.

"Right," said Andy. "I'll call Jordan or Anna, if I can't get you. I like them, by the way. Terrific agents."

Alan nodded, knowing the network was in bed with half his agency's projects. Everything was packaged so far ahead of time, the agent/network Siamese twin fusion was the thumb-screw carbu ration that made stuff go. It was simple greed-math; half charm, half ransom note. When the agency wanted the networks to buy a pilot script they represented, the script was positioned to include one or more of the agency's stars, producers, and directors. In an ideal scenario, it had everything the networks wanted and became an irresistible juggernaut the agency controlled; like the names of powerful johns in a madam's scheduling book.

Then, the bully pulpit made two really big fists; if the network wanted to be first in line to bid on the project, they had to give the agency a decent order and time slot. It was more than mere mutualism. It was chic blackmail.

They were at the door.

"See much of Eddy anymore?" asked Andy.

Alan didn't think Andy even knew Eddy. He'd been Alan's writing mentor and one of the best all-around writer-producers Alan ever knew. But he pissed all over his own fire with too much Jack Daniel's and Llama talc. Missed deadlines, got in too many fights. Threw it all away. Now he was in Cedars basically waiting for his remaining healthy cells to up and hit the high road. It was inevitable and Eddy knew it.

Alan called as often as possible, saw him at least once a week. But it was getting harder. The drugs they chlorinated him with made him crazy. Even though they stunned the pain, chemo had sculpted him down to a sickly Lincoln doll and Alan could barely handle it. A guy's hero deserved better. A guy's enemy deserved better.

"You two ever work together?" Alan asked.

"Once. He fucked-up an M.O.W. we worked on together when I was at Metro," said Andy. "I hear he's dying. Too bad. We all get cancelled sooner or later."

Yeah, thought Alan as he left and walked around on Melrose to clear his head.

Sooner or later.

setting

The house drowsed above sea, groggy perfection.

It had been built in the fifties and the real estate agent, a blond bayonet, bloused in Claiborne, told Alan previous owners had included a neurosurgeon, a famous mystery novelist, a feminist lawyer who once punched Dick Cavett in the nuts, and a witless, top-forty-hit-derrick who wrote a song called "Sunshine Lady."

The current owner had been aboard the brain trust that invented those big cardboard things you put in your windshield to block the sun. He was currently in the T-shirt racket and worth over twenty million give or take a cotton blend.

Alan walked around admiring the breathtaking view, hearing waves sledge shore. He passed leather sofas, carved African masks, and framed T-shirt business awards. Started humming "Sunshine Lady," a cloying, kindergarten melody he'd always hated. It was about a perfect girl, with a perfect "sunrise smile" and how she was mysteriously abducted by an exquisite sunset that just couldn't resist her shiny teeth. It had made the top ten in '82 but got bumped by Melanie's "I've Got a Brand New Pair of Roller Skates"—a more complex achievment.

The place was exactly what Alan was looking for. Big, airy rooms, light-flooded, accented with white-washed trim. Huge decks off the living room and master, overlooking blueberry sea. There was a fireplace you could look through from both the living and dining rooms, a sandblasted ceiling. Glass blocks that stacked sunlight. It was tasteful, easy to be in. Almost a million. But the way things could go with the pilot, the new deal at Universal, money was coming fast. And he wanted a new place. A new atmosphere. Something different.

Something he couldn't put his finger on.

"You like?" she was following Alan around. Lifting big sunglasses.

He didn't answer, starting to remember something. An article he'd read, years ago. An item that evaded detail, tucked away in the back of *Variety*. About the . . . but it couldn't've been this house. This house was too cheerful. If something like that had happened in a place, you'd still feel it. There would be a feeling; a nausea. The white walls would have a telltale pinkness here and there where the paint didn't quite—

"Nice."

"Gorgeous." She had a lung-cancer laugh; struggling for sufficient oxygen. Lit a Virginia Slim, took out her calculator, and opened the sliding door, seeking deck sun. A refuge to do math.

Alan followed, leaned on the deck railing, instinctively smiled at the view. A family of porpoises was doing a smiley, slo-mo cruise through waves, yards off shore. As they traveled north, Alan kept staring, eyes losing focus. His mouth went dry as he imagined them being harpooned, silver skin bleeding, mouths screaming. The ocean turned to blood in his mind, an awful burgundy, crashing on sand.

"There may be another offer coming in this afternoon. Just so you know." Her right foot tapped air.

Alan watched the dolphins writhing as the whalers laughed,

pulling them closer to small boats. The young dolphins tried to stay with their parents, though the older ones frantically nosed them away to save them. The men had no faces, just smooth flat skin; slits for mouths. The mouths grinned, as arm muscles pulled harpoon ropes, and the porpoises were dragged through plasma, clubbed on the head. They struggled, making a horrible noise, and the sea churned, red foam.

Alan turned to her. Looked back at the perfect blue Pacific. A windsurfer scalpeling currents.

"The one who was a song writer . . ."

She looked up, sharply. Down again at her calculator. Flicked an ash into a potted cactus.

"Did he live here in the seventies?"

Then, all at once, he remembered. The article, buried deep. The murders. The man and his wife tortured in a two-hour attack by a former band member he'd fired when "Sunshine Lady" hit. Alan remembered hearing about the details at a party, where the host, a famous TV star, was tight with LAPD.

The guy described detectives saying the couple was beaten, stripped naked, and nailed by ankles and palms to the bleached, wooden floor. The killer had taken two hours to crush their heads, ball-peening the skulls progressively harder until bone under bruised skin began to give.

The murderer later admitted that while they were still alive, begging him to call an ambulance, he'd found an electric knife in the kitchen.

He'd sawed all the way down the man's sternum, slitting open skin and muscle, making crude scrimshaw on bone before moving the humming blade across to her. As her head shook from side to side, nipples were circled; cut off.

Then, more cutting and sectioning, finally sledding to legs, thighs, and tendons which were sawed into ruin. The murderer had testified later that it took half an hour to trash both bodies. The screaming had slowed things until he realized by cutting their larynxes he could work in relative peace.

When he was done, he took the desecrated bodies, placed them side-by-side on the master bed, resting on Ralph Lauren pillow shams, staring forward, waiting for the police.

"A murder . . ."

She said nothing.

She was lying; could tell Alan knew it. She looked at sun doing cut-crystal on ocean. "I think someone in the office mentioned there was a break-in at one point but that's all I know. I got the impression it was years ago." She smiled useless comfort. "Anyway, in L.A. hard to buy a nice house that hasn't had something. That's why they invented alarms, right?"

Alan watched the porpoises steer around the small peninsula, continue north toward Malibu pier.

"I have a feeling they'll let this go for nine twenty-five. The owner just bought in New York and he needs to be there full-time for business."

He looked through the dining room window, at the wood floor. Tried to detect nail marks: holes or nicks, spaced far enough apart; spread-eagled scars on hardwood.

"I remember hearing about a murder," he said, not looking at her. Drawn once again to the floor; the sacrificial trauma sponged in cracks and grooves.

"Would you rather look at something else? I have a couple listings up on Broad Beach that are to die for."

To die for. He folded the phrase into smaller and smaller sizes until it disappeared.

"But I remember you saying anything beyond Zuma was too far north."

He went back inside, trying to decide if he could live in a house where something so ghastly had happened. His mind saw things; that was always the danger. His feelings and perceptions could shift for no reason and inexplicably imagine terrible prospects in anything.

A mother pushing her baby on a sunny park day could suddenly change, in his mind, to a crying woman whose selfish husband was leaving to take the baby to another state, where it would be molested; murdered.

A smiling cashier at McDonald's would become a crumpled statistic, victim of a gang drive-by which would strike exactly at the moment Alan was being handed his McNuggets. Exploding blood would puddle on the shiny metal counter.

The times he imagined people pulling alongside his own Porsche and shooting him. Or the times a windy night sounded like footsteps. Or the moment a neutral face at a mall became an abhorring glare that would follow him out to the parking lot and beat the shit out of him until he was bloody, begging for his life.

It was everywhere.

A voice on the phone, soliciting for Vets of Nam, who didn't like him saying no, he "already gave six months ago." The way he could see the voice break in to his apartment and wait, and he would open a closet late one night and it would plunge a knife into him.

The mention of his mother making him imagine her alone, inside her casket, pounding to get out, ripping at puffy satin, screaming helplessly, nails torn off as she struggled to claw free.

"Broad Beach is too far," he said.

"Well, we can keep looking. There's always new stuff coming out in listings." She was looking at Alan like he scared her a little. Like something about him was changing. She was studiously measuring what he needed to hear, watching carefully for reaction.

He looked at her.

Saw her getting old. More desperate than she already was. Saw diseases rooting. Saw all those who ever cared about her, pulling away and despising her frantic demands as she sat alone in a corridor in a depressing nursing home. Saw the sheet being pulled over her face, covering carefully bleached hair.

"Can I tell you something . . . don't buy if it doesn't feel right." She smiled, teeth pressing brown lipstick. "We'll find you something you'll love."

Alan watched waves spread champagne on sand, as the sun

passed out. He felt overwhelmed, knew somehow, despite the house's nightmare history, this was home.

Where he could create.

The wind came up, strumming chimes that hung on the deck, and he told her he wanted the house. It was the right atmosphere. He could be himself here. Was somehow even fascinated by residues of terror and helplessness that stared up at him from the floor. He didn't know why. But he imagined himself kneeling on the wood, staring at it until blood seeped from the peg and groove; surfacing welcome. He imagined placing an ear to the dented wood, hearing tiny pleas.

She seemed surprised Alan wanted to go ahead with it and smiled quickly. "That's wonderful," she said. "I'm sure we can get this." She touched his arm; financial foreplay. "We better write this before someone beats us to it."

He said nothing, moving onto the deck, sounds of torture drenching his mind.

character
motivation

Paramount was tripping on adrenal fluid; a frantic operating room, filled with a fresh shipment of hopeful wounded: writers, actors, directors.

Projects.

Five shows in production, plus Jonathan Demme huddling with Eddie Murphy; the black interferon. Robin Williams and Kevin Costner were shooting a new John Hughes script about the discovery of cheese, or some such high-security rumor, and the whole lot was doing the Cape Kennedy, pre launch rumble; Pachinko-hyper.

CAA and ICM agents roved; Armani hammerheads. Stars scarfed in the private room, in the commissary, shielded from earth contact. Development executives campaigned and pleaded. Over lunch. On 560 SEC cellulars. Anywhere talent would listen and commit. Anywhere red lights could be bribed or stroked green.

Alan crossed the lot in a complimentary golf cart, on the way to his office; a junior Bob Hope. He stopped at Frank's office and found him, in his chair, spinning slow, nasty circles, rolling a bomber. He'd been given Lucy's old office, the one she ruled before she'd moved to Desilu in 1807. She'd inherited it from Howard Hughes after he dropped bra research in favor of alphabetizing his urine. Further along, it got passed to Pica Lancelot Stephen J. Cannell. It was one of Hollywood's priceless hand-me-downs.

The office was a three-room suite, complete with bar, blazing fireplace, and furniture that looked like it came from the mansion of one of Balzac's mistresses; even the pillows seemed carved. Frank kept his Harley knucklehead parked inside, leaned against the calfskin sofa. It leaked chain oil on the Berber but that was okay with the studio. Frank's show was number one and his pilot just pulled a thirty share. He was royalty.

Def Leppard's "Adrenalize" was coming through the Bang and Olufsen system with garden shears. Frank was practically yelling, complaining.

". . . this star of mine is worse than the soundtrack to *Torch Song Trilogy* injected directly into your colon."

"He's still driving you crazy?"

Frank gathered his thoughts; beyond gone. Turned down the ear-throb.

"I'm bleeding seventy grand a week for this guy, right? Man spent two months working in a soap before the network jams him down my pilot. Show makes him a star, right?"

"Right."

"Does he extend appreciation?" Frank pivoted his head in a slow no. "What he does is—now get this, it's seminal—the Minnesota state fair decides to fly him in for a special promotional gig. God only knows, okay? He's gonna fuck a hen in front of forty thousand people far as I know, 'cause he's the star of a weekly show and that's valuable." He held up the joint. "You want some of this?"

Alan passed, scanning the litter of compact discs everywhere; loitering like little flying saucers. He wasn't in the mood to get high. He'd been writing all morning and took a cart ride to clear the numbing procession of eight-by-ten glossy, Prell-heads that had been sent in envelopes for the part of the Mercenary, though Andy Singer hadn't ordered the pilot. But rumors did the carcinoma seep and agents wanted the jump.

Only one guy had been vaguely interesting. But the pink galaxy of freckles on his face was so visually alarming you could barely look at him without feeling like Margaret Mead seeing the Canary chain from a plane for the first time.

Frank got up to fuck with the fireplace he kept going for atmosphere though it was summer. Alan glanced at him and knew "Let's Get Serious" was driving Frank nuts, as usual. Frank took a swig on the burning sausage of dope, flung booted legs over the couch and landed in eleven grand of tufted red cow. Covered his eyes with a hairy forearm, thinking colitis thoughts. Sometimes Alan saw his future in Frank and it unnerved him.

Alan went to the beveled window and watched two fat executive producers who bulged out of their Bally's, quietly arguing with a troubled director who was shooting an episode of their series, on the lot. The parklike courtyard outside Frank's office had been dressed to resemble a mental institution yard and extras with narcotized faces did the prefrontal lobe crisscross; dim guppies.

But to achieve the gritty appearance of a genuine head-farm, all the set decorator had done was place a sign which read EARLEVILLE SANITARIUM AND MENTAL FACILITY in a prominent spot. Alan realized everything else had been left unchanged and was about to comment when Frank screamed out "Fuck!"

He asked Alan if he wanted to hear the rest of the story. Alan was ready to listen to anything to take his mind off casting.

Frank paced, cracking knuckles.

"Okay . . . so this slide-of-smegma has his agent call me up and tell me we have a 'star explosion' on our hands. A supernova is born, right? Our goat-fucker is 'exploding' because he sang 'Born in the U.S.A.' in front of forty thousand farmers and assorted 4-H wildlife and this agent thinks he's repping goddamn Elvis's corpse risen from the grave."

Frank looked at Alan and cracked up, zigzagged into madness. The orange spot glowed bright between Frank's smirking lips and the smoke vacuumed in.

"So, what're you gonna do?" asked Alan.

Frank got buzzed on his com line. "Yeah?"

"It's Wayne," said the secretary, flat-voiced.

"I'm in Melbourne getting a head transplant," Frank barked. Alan smiled.

"Tellin' ya' Al, these guys are 150-watt assholes. They should shoot guys in the streets if they catch 'em carrying an SAG card. Turns people into fuckin' vampires."

Alan nodded, knowing this would pass. And knowing it would be back, stronger. "Wanna catch a screening next week? New Rohmer film? Singleton has a new one out next Tuesday, too."

"Call me."

"Right."

"Hey, by the way . . . I heard about the pilot you pitched from my agent. What the fuck is it? Mercenaries on Metamucil, something like that?"

"One guy. The Mercenary. Gonna take it to the edge if I get a go-ahead."

"That's what I hear. Good luck, man. Andy Singer is a fuckin' pain to sell a show to. You get a nibble, you did good . . . you're in the pink tunnel."

Alan smiled. Frank knew him from way back when they were staff drones for "Tits 'n Trans-Am" shows at Universal; he knew how many nerve endings got shoved into pencil sharpeners and lost forever working the prime-time mines, listening to your brain crave oxygen. He knew what selling a pilot meant if it took off. Not just success and recognition.

It meant a way out, with fifty million waiting on the other side of the guarded wall, sitting in a gold convertible.

"Alan . . ."

Alan turned, heading out the door. Frank pointed a chubby

finger. "Keep one hand on the rip cord, huh? It's gonna get heavy if it pulls numbers. Trust me."

Alan said nothing, starting to get nervous. He was about to leave Paramount and start a new contract at Universal, and they'd agreed to pick up negative costs in exchange for a piece of syndication, if it made it to sixty-six episodes. But he was still nervous.

If Andy green-lighted "The Mercenary," Alan would have to move fast. He had no star, only a partial pilot story. It could all evaporate if he didn't pull the pieces together. He began to realize he was afraid of failing.

And more afraid of being a hit.

casting

The guy had a tic. I'm tellin' you. His fuckin' cheekbones were doing the Jane Fonda tape through the whole reading."

Marty made a face. Producers all had that "antacid commercial" look about them; pained and squirmy.

"Alan, he's the best so far. That guy who was the semiregular on 'Wiseguy' was like a fuckin' nightmare. I think he had a sock in his pants." Marty chiseled a fingernail over shiny psoriasis; nerve mica.

Alan tilted the coffee into his mouth and washed it over his teeth; a miniature hydroelectric dam gushing brown water. Then, he swallowed it down.

"I don't know. Maybe he didn't have a tic. Maybe he was winking at me. Maybe he wanted a new friend. We got more people coming in?"

Marty nodded, stood. Went over to the shutters and played with them, opening and closing the slanting lids as he rubbed the back of his neck. He wore a flannel shirt and hiking boots, and his front teeth were so prominent, he looked like a Bugs Bunny lumberjack. Being the nuts-and-bolts guy, making sure all the technical crap stayed on track, making sure the set ran efficiently was his personal leukemia; he wasn't dead yet, but it was only a matter of time.

"The network called me again. They're having this blood-pressure problem."

"I know," said Alan.

"Do you? We're facing some real prep-time problems here. They want this thing in two months." Marty turned, pointing to the empty, video cassette shelf above the studio-type monitor. "We got zip. They don't like zip."

"Hey, whattya want me to do, pour Doug Henning outta my dick? It's gotta be right. I wanna get the pilot story and everything right. I mean what's the point? If they're that desperate . . . I mean, Christ."

Alan looked depressed and Marty gave him a compassionate nod; a soothing, rabbi backpacker. Marty smiled. "Hey, how about Art Garfunkel as the Mercenary? He'd be great." He looked at Alan, landed his glance on amused eyes. They were both exhausted.

"This is getting extremely ridiculous. A whole town full of guys who'd kill to be this guy and so far we've read a bunch of golf clubs." Alan rubbed tired eyes.

"You didn't like that guy yesterday? 'Tech'?"

"That was really his name?"

"Comes very highly recommended by MTM. He was second in line to play Arnold Becker on 'L.A. Law.' Done a lot of great stuff."

Alan paced. "Love the name."

"Not his idea. It was his agent. Told me he thought it would set him apart."

"Yeah. But not get him one." Alan popped a Trident, leaned against the wall.

Marty glanced at his watch, scowled. "Gotta get to Citrus. My ex is bringing her attorney and I'm bringing mine. She wants an extra sixpack of my blood every month."

"Who's her guy?"

"Marvin Roth . . ."

"Roth? Guy's a fuckin' weasel. Wear steel mesh."

"My guy's good."

"Roth's better. He's the attorney represented that eleven year old who said Jim Croce's remains raped her." No reaction. "Marty? I'm kidding . . ." Marty didn't react and Alan hummed "Operator" to annoy him.

Marty pressed on. ". . . I gotta split. Do something about this, will ya? I don't want to go back to producing game shows."

"Game shows are great. Be a guy."

Marty was at the door, grabbing the knob.

"Remember . . . two months. You don't make a decision, they'll make it for us."

He slammed the door and Alan sighed, staring at the glossy of Tech and grabbing his Bic disposable. He lit the corner of Tech's chin and the flames crept to lips and nose. Alan tabbed a Diet Coke open and watched Tech's face burning beyond recognition as he emptied the can.

"Thanks for coming in," he said, feeling the Ganges rising in his brain. He closed red eyes. Slumped.

Listened to the air conditioner humming Alaska sounds. Tried to imagine himself in a cool lake, floating. Spinning; a wet second hand. Tried to feel the chill water holding him in a clear hand. Tried to stay there forever.

He heard his door open and close.

When he opened his eyes, a man was seated before his desk staring at him. His skin was rough, like he'd worked oil rigs or construction. His eyes were subzero; executioner remote. Hair black. Longish. Alan could imagine him stabbing children and listening for the tiny screams like it was Beethoven. He was no more than forty but the years clearly came hard, with pain. He stared at Alan.

"Who are you?" asked Alan, unnerved by the way the man swallowed him whole with a direct look.

"Somebody told me about an opening . . ."

"Opening?"

"A part." His voice was low. Dominant. "Name's Corea. Jake."

"How did you get in here?" Alan didn't like this at all.

"Snuck onto the lot. Fucked with some old guard's head. Called your secretary, got her out of the office with some bullshit."

Alan was about to throw him out. But something in the man's face stopped him. He looked as if he'd just murdered a family of eight, then fixed himself a sandwich, ignoring the mutilated bodies. He looked unstable. Dangerous. Alan couldn't take his eyes off him.

"Do you have an agent? Are you an actor?"

The man made a sour face. "Fuck agents. I'm what's gonna sell tickets."

They locked eyes. There was something frightening about him. Something not right.

"What kind of experience have you had?"

He grinned. "Whattya need?"

Alan laughed a little. Corea froze an uncomprehending stare. It was like, "What the fuck is so funny, asshole?" Afternoon shadows were shifting through the shutters and Alan could see, all at once, the man's terrible skin. Pocked. Uneven. He wondered if it were a childhood disease? Acid thrown by a lover. He couldn't be sure. But it added to the septic menace.

"So you want ratings—or whatever the fuck it is you guys want?"

Alan nodded. That's what he wanted.

"Then that's what you're looking at. Ratings." Again, that arrogant, fuck-you hardness. That contemptuous, pained anger at an Evian pussy.

Alan just watched him.

"So you are an actor? You've worked in things?"

"Wherever I was, I knew my lines."

Alan nodded. Ooookay. . . .

"You're a pretty unfriendly guy. Anybody ever tell you that?"

"Everybody," said Corea. "And you're a charming phony. Anybody ever tell you that?" A torturer's smile.

"You don't believe in flattering a potential employer."

"Planning on employing me?"

"Who knows," answered Alan, wondering if this guy could deliver anything a coach could sculpt into decent work.

"Then you're a stupider fuck than I already thought." He got up. "I'll be watching for the cancellation."

Alan stared after him, not believing this. His secretary, Lauren, buzzed him as Corea slammed the door. "Geez, who was that? You tell him he couldn't act or something? He stormed out of here ready to kill somebody."

"How'd you know he was an actor?"

"I just assumed. The guy has presence."

Alan told her he wanted to talk. She came in, looked at the burned photograph of Tech. Made a face, ran a palm edge on the desktop to sweep blackened fragments.

"What do you think?"

"That guy? Sexy. Reminds me of like Oliver Reed in a really bad mood."

"Oliver Reed is always in a bad mood."

"He's incredible. Can he act?"

"Don't know. Didn't read him."

"What were you doing in here?"

Alan didn't answer. Still shaken by the odd behavior. Lauren came behind, massaged his shoulders. "You like him, don't you?"

Alan said he didn't.

"You like him."

"No. He's not what I want."

She nodded; unconvinced.

Alan thought more and called to her as she walked to the door. "Call the gate. See if you can catch him before he splits. Try and get a phone number on the guy."

She nodded, closed the door. Alan didn't feel good. His head ached. And Corea gave him the creeps.

A "charming phony."

Fuck him.

back story

To get to Palm Springs from L.A., you stroked your armpits with surfboard wax, poured your car its favorite beverage, and tried to go into a trance for a couple hours. The drive during July was a bad, sticky drag that made people want to punch little kids in the mouth just because they asked for an ice cream.

The freeway went through weird, spectral places like Cucamonga or Azusa and smog wiped grimy hands over everything, making the trip like a ride through a muffler. For geeks into bug organs on glass, it was major.

Every weekend, people in the business flocked to the "Springs"; solar lemmings. It was hot and dry and easy to score; coke, cock, cunt. Control. In forty-eight hours, players big and small could make the round trip. Brown in the sun. Have drinks. Set up deals. Make connections. Play tennis.

Lie.

Business didn't stop in Hollywood on weekends. It just moved and used a net. The Tijuana wristwatch hustle kept rolling 125 miles south under a welding sun. But really it was another workday. The sun beat down on the crazies, an interrogation lamp, and deals sweated along with everything else.

Alan downshifted his 928S as a bunch of Big Mac hyenas in a rowdy Trans Am cut him off, laughing mindlessly, dragging an unleaded tail. Two sixteen-year-old girls in back smiled through ghoul makeup and lifted blouses. Their dumpling breasts shook, mimicking the road; D-cup toys. Then, the car vanished.

Alan pushed his CD player on and cranked the volume on Concrete Blonde's "BLOODLETTING" to ten. Another hour to go. He hoped his father was in a good mood.

Or at least not a bad one.

He roared in front of La Petite Gallerie about noon. The Springs was already on broil and the sun speared him the second he snuffed the engine and got out. He stretched a cello spine, reached back in, tossed his CD and cassette box behind the seat, in shade. Big mistake leaving tapes in an obvious spot. He'd done it once and come back to find a Dolby sundae.

No different from what this place did to its population, he thought, starting to sweat. Took fine people with good brains, treated them like butter in a frying pan. "Sssssszzzzzzzzzz . . . honey, I don't feel so good." Too long on the fairway, your brain is running down your tie.

Alan grabbed the gift he'd brought for his dad's birthday and headed in the fancy front door. Much cooler inside; a meat locker. He straightened his hair, strolled through, taking note of inventory that had come in since his visit a month back.

Magrittes. Two of them. *This Is Not a Pipe.* One of Alan's favorites. Magritte would've been a trip to have a Heineken with. The bottle would drink him.

At the curving, teak counter, Alan's father, Burt, was chatting with a woman in her seventies who looked very rich. She dressed Town and Country summer chic, with emerald-and-diamond bracelets cuffing wrinkled wrists, hair pulled Grace Kelly tight. Burt always had Broadway show music playing in the gallery; never got all those years he'd directed in New York off the turntable.

Give me a break, Dad, thought Alan. We're in the fuckin' nineties here, this isn't Brigadoon; get used to it.

"Alan!"

"Dad! Listen, don't let me interrupt. Looks like you got a live one here." He was talking loud enough for Grace Kelly's hair to hear and she smiled tautly.

Burt raised a smile that kept a polite distance. It had always been that way, thought Alan, and it seemed things never changed. Never got easier.

Never got more personal.

Alan realized it had been the challenge of his childhood to seek his effect on his father by trying to surpass himself. Jokes. Gifts. Accomplishments. Money. Anything that could be measured. Admired. Objectified. All to get enthusiasm from a man he sensed deep down wasn't capable of it. But Alan knew he'd always keep trying anyway.

It wasn't that his father withheld love. Or had none. It was trickier. The love was all there. Just that Burt wasn't. He was lost, preoccupied, pointing his telescope away from earth, at topics and issues, not human intimacy.

Since he'd retired from Broadway, and come to the Springs, it seemed to Alan it had gotten worse. Burt railed about lofty ideals but never spoke about personal stuff. It was always "the integrity of art" kind of shit. Life in the pauperized culture. Alan's mother, Dee, had managed to keep Burt at sixes and sevens with it all. But since she was gone and Burt had remarried to Wanda, he'd become a bad Breslin column; half soapbox, half water balloon.

Wanda, not exactly Ariel Durant, wasn't able to give Burt much perspective since she had the depth of a serving platter. Alan had never felt she was good enough for his father, but Burt had few complaints. She was his twenty-eight-year-old doll and made him happy no matter how much of a snipped kite she was. The word *dip* came to mind when contemplating Wanda. So did the word *user*. But Alan could never allow himself to say that to his father. It would've stabbed what little communication they'd managed over the years. It just wasn't worth unscrewing the bulb over a woman who couldn't understand peanut butter.

And it didn't help that Alan was hormonally thrilled by the sight of her. When the sun hit her just right, like a crew of overhead lighting techs, he could see himself in bed with her. Lost in tight little muscle caves. Sometimes he thought it would be so easy to just—

Burt grabbed Alan's shoulders.

"Hey, you made great time. Played Pac-Man with your radar gun, huh?"

The two laughed. But it was that strained sound that doesn't make you think either person is that happy about things. Burt's grape-green eyes blinked, waiting for Alan to fill in the blank. Alan was feeling it again; the way his dad always put him in that position. Waiting for Alan to do something. Expecting him to say something. Perform for him. Please the director. It was these moments Alan could see himself loading the chamber and pressing the barrel against Burt's—

". . . happy birthday, Dad." Alan walked closer, gave his father a big hug. Burt smiled, hugged back.

See, it was things like that that drove Alan into the wall. Burt would hug like some big, loving, Italian father, then let go and stare. Not say a word. "Zorba goes zombie," Dee used to say.

"Hungry?" Alan asked, even though what he really wanted to say was, "Dad, I'm uncomfortable in your company, but I love you and I wish maybe together we could work on it and make it better. What do you say?"

But he couldn't. He'd opted for the safe topic. The habit. Anyway, he was only down for the day. How do you fix thirty-four years of being politely estranged from someone who gave you life and can barely see you, in an afternoon?

"Starved. I was thinking you'd be getting here around now, so

I skipped breakfast. Wanda went shopping . . . picking me up something at the last second, no doubt."

They walked toward the front door.

"How is Wanda, Dad?"

"Looks younger everyday. I think her next birthday she'll be what . . . ?"

"Twelve?"

"Hey! I got a crazy idea for lunch. Little different than we planned. Okay with you?"

Alan shrugged. Smiled. It was nice to be with his dad.

The tram car tipped from the platform and groaned free, suspended by arm-thick cables. It had been made by the same firm that rigged the ones in Switzerland, which crept up snow-frosted mountains, snail-shuttling wool caps; red noses.

Burt was moving from side to side, staring out the window, acting like Mr. Gyroscope.

Alan felt sick.

"Ever been up this thing? You'll love it. It's a kick. Goes from the desert floor, thousands of feet up. Snow up there, too. Believe it? We're going to eat in the snow. Crazy place to live."

Alan acknowledged the wonder of it all by closing his eyes, trying to plug a cold sweat. Don't pass out, you fucker, he told himself. It's your Dad's fucking birthday. Don't be an asshole. Stay calm.

"Hey." Burt was pointing. "Over there. Mountain goat."

He ran a tanned hand over the railing under the window. "I mention your sister sent me a card? Cute message. The marriage must be wobbling, though. Loren didn't sign it. Just her and the kids." Burt gestured philosophically.

Alan always dug Loren. But when he and Marie had this garlic/vampire effect on each other, it was hard to like either one. Good was quickly pleated into anger and destruction when they got around each other. But the kids were gorgeous. They made beautiful children together.

"Yeah, I don't talk to them too much. Owe them a call I think." Had to be four months. Alan and Marie had little in common. He'd tried. She'd tried. They just couldn't get the horizontal and vertical right.

Father and son nodded in a way that moated off further discussion. Alan's sister wasn't an area for pleasant conversation. Burt and Marie were as different as there and gone and the future dimmed when you considered the stuff that comprised their basic cores. Forget it, thought Alan. That relationship just washed up on shore one day and headed off onto the island of life in two separate directions.

"Just too independent for her own good. Never did get with her outlook." Burt looked over the retreating Springs. "But one hell of a cute card. Real sweet. Hey, you still living in that house at the beach? That murder place? Why don't you move?"

"It was a great deal. Told you. And it's an incredible spot."

"I couldn't live there."

"You don't have to."

"Violent death clings to things."

"Nice phrase. Junior college?"

A competing smile.

"Anyway, I never think about what happened." It was a lie.

"I think it's very weird you don't think it's weird. I couldn't live there. Upset me too much."

"What're you talking about? Palm Springs is fucking death row. Everybody listening to their Grecian Formula dry. Waiting to kick."

"Oh, that's a nice thought . . ."

Alan felt his colon trapeze as the tram car hitched over one of the towers that guided it up the mountain. He gripped the handrail. Burt noticed.

"Afraid of heights? Shoulda told me."

Alan managed a smile. "Falling. Afraid of falling. Different."

Burt laughed, silver, Sinatra hair shimmering. He steadied Alan, wanted to talk about a film Warner's was thinking about offering him to direct. He told Alan it would be a joint production between a French financier and Warner's and would star Julie Naughton.

"She's still alive?" Alan remembered Julie from when he was a kid and his dad almost killed her with his bare hands.

Julie had been an impossibly gifted, anorexic nightingale, and basic renaissance loon, with so much scar tissue on her wrists, her hands seemed attached by skin-zippers. She was egotistical and demanding; a *Bell Jar* Mary Martin.

Eight years back, when Alan was still at 20th, executive story editing a *G.Q.* cop show, and his dad was between musicals, Burt had directed Julie and Dru Simone, an annoyingly moody ex-model and recovered heroin addict, in a two-woman *Grand Guignol* three-act for a Central Park summer festival. The play was about two sarcastic lesbians who shared clitoral intimacy up to the moment one, armed with scissors she'd been using to snip tampon coupons, reduced the other to entrails, then committed suicide, gulping a Smith and Wesson.

The play, titled *East Infection,* had been written by a bitter but witty androgyn who later put his/her head in an oven and died as a slightly confused roast. Opening night, it had sickened theater critic Frank Rich, who closed the show.

Burt had been cited in all major criticisms, and *Newsweek* had referred to him as a former footlight wunderkind whose every good instinct had simply "dropped dead."

One thankfully brief *Esquire* blurb had said the play was a "drill with no bit which still managed to bore. No one was sorry when the lesbian murder-suicide was over and the single regret was the play hadn't opened with it."

Still, Burt and Julie had mostly gotten along and always sworn they'd find a project, up the line, to do together. Mademoiselle Simone had retired from performing altogether, after two badly received, excessively cheery films she'd done in Australia lost huge money. She eventually opened a chain of croissant-themed sandwich places which sprang up all over America like poppies.

"Howard the Dyke . . ." was all Alan said, teasing Burt with his usual joke about *East Infection*'s reviews.

Burt smiled tightly. "Got your mom's sense of humor, telling you. If you'd taken after me, they'd've thrown you out of TV a long time ago. I'm too damn serious. Can't do humor. Different mindset. Lighter, I suppose." He coughed. "Hey, I ever ask you if you know Norman Lear?"

A hundred times.

Alan spilled a little of his vodka and tonic onto Norman's arm at the bar at a Writers Guild strike meeting once. Norman was decent about it.

"Yeah. Great guy."

"Gotta hand it to him. Guy takes prejudice, turns it into an entertainment empire. It's impressive."

Alan waited for the fatherly advice that always followed the question about Norman Lear.

"You know, that's what you oughta start thinking about with your writing." It never failed. "I mean, long as you're doing something other than selling deodorant from eight to eleven every night." He tried to clarify but Alan was already upset. "I'm talking about the limits of television . . . not your talent. You understand what I mean."

Alan said nothing. His father never realized what a fucking elitist he was and there would be no point in Alan telling him. He hated the way Burt always made him feel small and trivial for being in TV. Like he put toy whistles in Cracker Jack boxes for a living.

Mr. Broadway. Mr. Lime-fucking-light. Mr. I'm-fucking-better.

"Having fun?" Burt was smiling.

Alan said nothing, staring out at a goat.

There was snow.

A giant Georgia O'Keeffe desert way down there and up here,

all this cold, white stuff. The tram car docked drunkenly at the top and doors slid open.

The restaurant perched, as if some avalanche lookout station in Grenoble, complete with blond behemoths walking around like Robert Shaw in *From Russia with Love;* Third Reich knights.

It was deserted. Chairs turned upside down on redwood plank tables, making the whole place a warehouse full of reverse gravity picnic sets.

Alan dipped chicken chunks in teriyaki sauce as he and Burt stared out over the desert, seated on the balcony. Tall pines swayed and wind dropped cones on the roof. *Clonk.*

"So . . . how's your novel coming along?" Burt tried so hard to make decent conversation, to Alan it always sounded like it was learned from a bad article on improving human relations in some retiree's magazine.

"Okay. I mean, it's a first novel." He laughed a little. Spread lost hands. "I basically have no damn idea what I'm doing. Not like writing scripts at all. It's all about internal, not external." He took a sip of espresso; a giant's hand holding a doll cup. "Anyway, it's tough making the time."

Burt pointed with his fork, gobbling fettucine.

"Gotta make the time. Always more you can do." He slid back slightly from the table, expanding his pulpit. "When I was doing Broadway, I always thought . . . you know, I'm maxed-out, time wise, energy wise. But you find a way when you care."

"Television is a little different. The pace . . ."

Burt waved his hand in wordless agreement; a Helen Keller comment. Wiped his mouth of Alfredo. "I understand. Not comparing the two. You know, I'm not questioning what you do as a way of life . . . even an art form."

Bullshit, thought Alan. He meant every fucking word.

"Look, Alan . . . you know how highly I think of what you can do with your writing." He burped, softly. "Sometimes I just feel TV can't capture what you have to offer as an artist. It's inveterate to the medium. That's my point."

Alan could never be sure exactly what his point was. But it always made him uncomfortable and ill at ease. Like his father was knocking it all under there somewhere; under the pretty words.

"Maybe we should change the subject."

Burt agreed. Then, couldn't.

"Alan, you're too good. I know you hate it when I remind you, but you are. You've got more talent in your little finger than a hundred Norman Lears or Bochcos or . . . who's that damn heroin addict that did that Miami thing with Don Johnson . . . ?"

"Michael Mann. 'Miami Vice.' He's not a heroin addict. He wrote about drugs."

"Good-looking show. Great production values. But what are the damn characters saying to each other? Too esoteric. That's what I like about what you're trying for with your stuff." He played with the salt shaker, screwing, unscrewing. "You're never afraid of your own voice. You know, you were always a fearful boy . . . afraid to confront, afraid of so many things. It's good you don't do that in your work."

Burt tried to remember, face doing a quiet flashback. "Maybe your fear early on . . . I don't know . . . maybe it's because of Mom. Guilt, maybe? Possible, I suppose."

Alan didn't like the way his father's thoughts were facing; didn't want to be in another plane crash together.

"Dad, it's your birthday remember? We didn't climb fifty miles above the earth's surface to discuss what I do for a living, or what happened to Mom. Maybe I should give you your present."

"What is it?"

"A blue sweater."

"Great idea!"

"Should be. You've been asking me for seven months." He mocked Burt's low voice. "I want a blue sweater. Hey, I'd love a blue sweater. Know what I don't have? A—"

"Okay, okay." When Burt laughed, he was handsome the way Newman was. He sipped some cappuccino and lit his pipe. A cloud of Chart Well lounged between them.

"So . . . how's the new place in Malibu where the people were murdered in cold blood?"

Alan chuckled, patiently.

"Tell you what, I'd rather talk about my career and get lectured than answer questions about my house."

Burt's eyes twinkled; an opening blade on a pocket knife.

"I got a question for you. You think television is real?"

"Real?"

"In your mind? Does it really exist? Or is it a lot of craft, however heartfelt?"

Alan was right. Dad was moving in for the kill.

"You mean, of course, like the stage has heart and soul? Something like that?"

Burt said nothing but it was clearly something like that. Alan went back to his julienne fries, holding their yellow heads under ketchup. Burt kept puffing, thinking.

"I don't know too many writers . . . true writers . . . who wouldn't agree the stage has more life. I mean, shit, Alan . . . it's right up there, pumping away like crazy. Reaching out. Grabbing you by the ears and saying 'hey, motherfucker, I'm *here*. I *exist*. And I will leave you a different person when you leave this theater.' "

Alan felt his stomach tightening.

"And television is what? Some . . . I don't know . . . mindless contrivance that just sands corners till you can't feel them?"

"Can you feel them? I can't."

"Dad, with all due respect, you're full of it. Maybe it's time for the blue sweater portion of the show?"

Burt wasn't interested.

"How about we go for a walk, then?"

"Just let me finish the point." Burt sat higher; passionate. "C'mon, let's face it, in TV they sweeten the audience reaction with laugh tracks. They hose migraine music all over sequences that don't work. Actors are picked by demographics. *Demographics*. You know what that means?"

Alan knew.

"It means," explained Burt, "a goddamned computer picks 'em for you. 'TV-Q.' Now if that's soul . . ." He was tamping the pipe, slowly shaking his head.

Alan realized he was going to have to fight back if this meal wasn't going to turn into the lunch from hell. "And you didn't think about audience reaction when you directed a Plummer or a Preston? Elizabeth Ashley? Pacino? Gimme a break. What you're saying is supercilious and condescending."

"Do you *have* to use such big words?" Burt was smiling.

Alan hated it when his father teased him but continued. "Listen, Dad . . . I *remember*. I was there. I heard you bitching at the dinner table back in the Gramercy Park apartment when I was a kid. You used to *suffer* over the casting. If you didn't get a major name, you practically had to be peeled off the roof, and things for Mom and Marie and me were lousy till you cheered up and got somebody you could splash on the marquee." Alan was breathing hard. "Your memory is playing games with you."

"Casting stage isn't the same thing."

Alan placed his water glass down, irritably. "Exactly the same thing! You think because it's put on film it's not *real*? It has no substance? What're you talking about?"

"Ah, ah, ah, . . . hold it. Film isn't the issue. Lotta fine films have come down the pike. But they were the expression of a single artistic vision . . ."

"Right, sure. And the studio had *nothing* to say about it."

". . . those visions were not preprogrammed, clinically manipulated, and analyzed. They were not paint-by-the-number regurgitations of a bunch of fucking TV executives. Suits who know *nothing*, not one goddamn thing, about art. They're in the business of programming Mars bars for a nation of *brain-dead*."

Alan hated Burt when he got like this. It had driven his mother crazy. Maybe it was part of what happened. Made as much sense as anything else. Burt always assumed people found this behavior stimulating. But one by one, they backed away, put off by his exhaust in their face.

But Alan was stuck up on a mountain. A lonely citadel in the clouds where old St. Bernards came to die. He couldn't leave and wondered if his dad had chosen this place deliberately. It was getting chilly and Alan crossed his arms.

The two were suddenly surrounded by singing waiters carrying a burning cake. They sang "Happy Birthday" and Burt blew out the sixty-one candles that were sunk to the waist in frosting. The waiters cut two pieces and left proudly, feeling they'd spread Alpine cheer.

"Musta been Wanda's idea," said Burt, delighted by the surprise. "She amazes me. Always puts me first. Even after the life she's had . . ." He pressed lips; philosophical sadness.

Alan nodded, properly grave; tried to feel bad. But it was impossible. Every time he ran it through his head, it always struck him as absurd she was so fucked up. How bad could it be? She'd been a top sandal model with perfect feet and as if that weren't dumb enough, she'd had a vapid-eye-movement marriage to a guy who did lighting for huge New York stage productions. The bulb-hubby was booted after Wanda met Burt, who was directing one of the productions.

According to giggly legend, as told by an always breathless Wanda, she'd been backstage, giving herself a pedicure, waiting for her husband to finish work, and Burt, taking a note break, had been instantly struck by her; the uncoaxed smiles, radiant curiosity. Her inordinate level of health. They fell in love and she'd only told him after the marriage about the epilepsy. She hadn't wanted to scare him off, knowing he'd been living with an ill woman.

But Wanda had two siezures on the honeymoon, in Acapulco, the worst during waterskiing, when her ski binding had refused to release, as her tongue flushed into her throat, and she'd shorn off three perfect toes. Her modeling agency had been compassionate but the phone instantly died. And the seizures timeshared her world.

Over years, the epilepsy had gotten worse and any little upset seemed to make Wanda stop breathing for seconds, waiting for her throat to form hands and strangle her. She drank teas, visited acupuncturists. Wore sandals with hundreds of rubber nubs, to calm her nervous system. But seven toes just weren't providing enough surface and every couple of weeks, she'd go wolfman, foaming, snarling.

As father and son licked frosting from forks and Burt tried on the blue sweater, Alan chose his words carefully.

"Dad . . . I wanted to tell you, I may have sold a series."

"Oh?"

"Still waiting for network go-ahead. But if I can get it on, it's going to be a breakthrough show . . . that's what they're all saying."

Burt was nibbling on a frosting-flower like a big bee.

"Well, can I say congratulations?"

"Yeah. But not yet."

"Your creation?" Alan nodded and Burt looked at him, proudly. "Well, I hope you win those bastards. Get something good on the air."

Alan watched his father, chomping on the birthday cake like a six-year-old. He was so damn cute sometimes. With blue frosting on his chin and matching blue sweater, he looked like a child model in a Kodak commercial; fucking adorable.

On the drive home at dusk, Alan thought he could feel his father's cells moving inside him. The sun was a bloody gunshot wound over L.A. and he swore every gene his father passed him was playing Chutes and Ladders under his skin; roaming, hiding behind nerves and muscles.

Crouching. Murmuring.

Scheming for a way to take over, in tiny blue sweaters.

dissolve

Mirror on closet door, eyes staring back. Lamp shades tilted; lights glare. He squeezes the razor.

The hooker stirs, bruises laking. He glares, goes back to mirror. Begins to cut himself, razor across sternum, down at an angle, to navel; two sides of a blood triangle.

Decides to leave no note. His body will be the message. Raw scrawls; how he wants out. How nothing works worth shit. Everybody promises everything. Lies. Nothing comes true. He should've killed his agent. Make the world better.

She starts to cry. He tells her to *shut the fuck up*. She won't stop. It feels like everything. Nothing he says matters. He's furious. Watches blood run, skin drain white. Years of training; expectation. Now just anger. Feels himself go nowhere.

She opens the door. Runs.

He lets her.

The motel room is crap. It's enough. He doesn't miss the apartment. Tampa. His wife. Workshops; résumés. Dead nights of Neil Simon, equity-waiver tombs. Special abilities: horseback riding, akido, hypnosis. He sits on the bed, stares at bureau mirror, watching blood roam.

The phone rings. Her. Wanting to know how it goes. How interviews are coming. Callbacks. He lets it ring. Hates her. She's infection. Her love is greed.

The cuts give off heat. The A.C. rattles. Hollywood Boulevard pisses desperate sewage past his window. He turns on TV, watches a soap. Pouty mannerisms; a doll show.

Eyes close. Cold.

Angry black voices next door. Tempers shove accusations. AC rattle. Tourists laughing; diving in the tiny pool, lunging up into poison air; mindless *fucks*. Blood slips past ribs, onto sheets. Staring at roof shadows; drape leaks. Tired. Car horns fade. Heat thins. Poolside voices; gone.

Sleep.

Sleep . . .

A knock.

Again. Twice. Footsteps; gone. Eyes opening. Listening to blood; sheet's soft suction. Crawling to door. Listen. Reach up, open a crack. A manila envelope. Delivered. A studio. Tear it open.

The pilot script. A note clipped.

"Jake: I was serious. Read this and call me." *A. White*

messages

Alan's Porsche howled-up Pacific Coast Highway; a Kraut missile. The CD player blistered Stevie Ray's heat-seek blues. It was nine-fifteen. He'd just left seeing Eddy at Cedars and felt awful; sad, lost.

The 928S skimmed alongside burnt-orange surf, roaring for Malibu, and he tried hard not to think about the hospital visit. The mangled emotions that had fallen from a thousand-story building, sitting with Eddy, trying to let him know he was loved.

Alan tried instead to think of Bart's hairy *Tyrannosaurus rex* smile. His happy, black wiggle when Alan came in the front door. Bart's dreamy look when the two would hammock on the balcony, together, overlooking the warm sea, swinging slowly.

He shot past where Sunset Boulevard punched its fist into Pacific Coast Highway and couldn't get the evening out of his head. Every thought drew him back to the Lysol gloom of the huge hospital. The lima-green surgical slippers everywhere. Knife-leprechauns walking around, exhausted, speaking to haunted families in quiet reassurances, green slippers like blood snowshoes.

Alan hated the visits. Hated seeing Eddy that way. Hated the echoey scent of broken bodies moving up in the checkout line. His agent, Jordan, had told him he didn't mind hospitals, even liked them. Thought of them as "hi-tech greenhouses, tilling the flesh and watering bulbs of good health. Like human rhododendron."

Alan told him he was certifiable. But then Jordan had problems; his own, plus 10 percent of everybody else's.

The visits were always difficult. Unsettling, *Dr. Strangelove* realities with Eddy telling Alan about the world, while his own was shrinking to a pinprick.

But tonight it had been especially troubling. Alan had walked nervously down the carpeted hall in the cancer ward, toward Eddy's room, on the third floor. He felt the wetness of the carnations coming through the waxy tissue, onto his hand. He'd been glared at by hairy orderlies who were wheeling some miserable wretch along the hall, on a gurney. The blanched face was sunken and rivered with fat, silky veins that looked as if they tied the meatless head to the pillow; ropes steadying an old ship.

The guy looked like he had about a minute left and had pivoted his head to look at Alan as they'd coasted him by. He'd winked, as if sharing a lewd gag with a fellow perv, then struggled a bit against the canvas belts that pinned him at the chest, waist, and legs. Indicated for the orderlies to stop. He'd coughed and Alan stopped to spend a moment with him.

"I'm not here for my health, y'know. I'm here because they *need* me." Then he'd glared angrily. "Okay?!"

Alan nodded. Trying to be calm, not upset him.

The old man had bared decayed teeth, spit at him. Alan pulled back and the old man hissed. ". . . you're in much deeper than you think, asshole. You went too far this time."

The orderlies had quickly rolled him away. But he looked back at Alan, forcing his neck at an angle that looked broken. He grinned a dead-man smile.

"I wouldn't want to be you, asshole. You're a"—then he said the word that had chilled Alan—"fuckin *monster*. How did you get out?" He grinned ugly again, then went white as milk. Looked horrified. And he was gone, around a corner, like a sick rumor.

It had disturbed Alan a lot. He'd realized to a dying old man, everybody probably looked like monsters. That they could live, and he couldn't, made *them* the hideous. The deformed. But still, the way he'd said "monster" . . . it had reminded Alan of how Mimi had said it. Even the way she'd looked. The deadness in her eyes when she said it. The same deadness in the man's eyes.

At least Alan had felt that.

But the day had been too long, too stressful. And visits to Cedars were always hard; painful.

One night, on the way home from visiting Eddy, Alan thought somebody was in the back seat of the Porsche, waiting to kill him. Another time, he thought he'd heard his dead mother, Dee, beckon to him from one of the hospital rooms to the side of Eddy's. He thought he'd heard her say she was cold and afraid where she was and would Alan please come and get her, take her where she could be safe; warm.

But he figured it was bound to happen when a mind like his was under pressure. Run a hundred-million-dollar submarine too deep and the weight of all that water compresssed it into a door-knob. What the fuck did he expect? There was a lot going on. No wonder he was upset; seeing meaning in things. Susceptible to empty detail.

He raced past Topanga Beach, rolled down windows, giving his hair a ride. He still couldn't get it out of his head that that old guy was some kid's dad. Some mother's son. The larger progression hit him. Just like it usually did every time he'd said goodbye to Eddy. Quietly took a last look at his dying friend after tucking him in and kissing him gently on the forehead.

The facts of pain. The unnegotiable truth of hurt. He lost track of it sometimes. Then, some inconsequential asterisk on the reality paragraph would remind him. Maybe it was passing a motorcycle accident and seeing a red form pried off chain-link by cops in bloody uniforms.

Or some horrible item in the news that forced you to read it twice, despite its cruelty, its impossibility. The human race could get very real, very fast. Sometimes Alan thought working in television could make you forget where the lines of reality started and ended. Where you came from.

Where you didn't want to go.

He'd been home an hour when he and Bart wandered in from the deck, hungry. It was a bit after ten and the two sat on the kitchen floor, sharing a bowl of pesto tortellini Alan warmed in the microwave. Bart dug a gourmand muzzle into his personalized bowl, tongue a single, pink chopstick.

He stared up at Alan with moody brown eyes and Alan nodded. "Okay. I hear you." He stood, grabbed a Kirin from the fridge, and poured half in Bart's bowl, the rest in his own glass.

"Gotta check my messages, bud. I'll ask if anybody called you. Okay?"

It was okay with Bart.

Alan hit the Panasonic autodialer and the little Disney-flea-beeps sang a three-second overture. He stuck it on speakerphone and settled in on the floor with Bart, cross-legged.

"Hello, Mr. White's residence? May I help you?" It was a new voice. A little bored, a little interested. Intelligent. Like just maybe it knew what the hell was coming down.

"Yeah, hello ... this is Mr. White. Uh ... anybody, you know ..." The Kirin was scraping paint off his skull.

"Call?"

"Call. Right." He was exhausted. Even Bart sensed it, wagging a counselor's tail.

"I'll check." He heard paper shifting, as if she was making an origami crow. "By the way, Mr. White. I just wanted to say hi. My name is Kimmy."

Kimmy. It's what people named their mice.

"Yeah, hi. How're you doin'?"

"Well, it's my first night. But pretty good considering. Mind if I ask you kind of a personal question?"

He sipped more beer, felt things scaling his stomach walls. "Depends . . ."

"Well, if I'm not mistaken, you did that sitcom 'Stacked Plates' couple of seasons ago, didn't you?" She cleared her throat. "Those waitresses with the big tits?"

Yeah, that was me, he thought.

"Don't remember." His head felt crooked.

"Oh, you'd remember something like that. My sister says it was probably just displaced anger toward women. She's sort of a gender analyst. But not a dog or a lesbian or anything. But I thought the show was funny. You were producer or something?"

Yeah.

"No . . . listen, my messages?"

"Right. Well, let's see . . . Jordan called at eight-fifteen. Said the network was showing signs of budging but not to count on anything. He'll call you in the morning. Wow. Sounds provocative."

Alan was starting to find her mildly irritating.

"That it?"

"Hold on . . . I'm getting there. Your business manager Ed called at seven-forty. A bunch of foreign-run residuals came in. Said to call him in the morning. Gonna be a busy morning, I guess, huh?"

"Yeah. Anything else?"

"Your mechanic called, said to bring the Porsche in on Monday. He's booked through the week. Summer. Whole world is overheating."

Thank you, Carl Sagan.

"And a last one from Erica at ten-ten. Said just to say she was thinking about you. Call her back no matter how late. Sounds like a sweet person."

Alan said nothing, staring at his foot, half-asleep.

"Is she?"

"Sorry?" he was getting drunk.

"A sweet person. Is Erica a sweet person?"

Ask her three ex-husbands, thought Alan. One tried to shoot

her, one tried to destroy her life, one burrowed into Scientology and became obsessed with John Travolta and hidden meanings in the meaningless. She was a nice girl who seemed to trigger exaggerated reactions in guys, other than himself. Alan asked her about it once and she told him she was baffled; she gave men all the room in the world. She swore she did nothing to drive her husbands to lunatic behavior. But it just kept happening.

It was somehow suspect.

"Yeah . . . she's great. I mean, it's not like we're married or something. Sure . . . she's great." God, he was telling his life story to a girl who folded paper birds.

Bart wanted more beer.

"Well, that's good. Is she pretty?"

"Pretty?"

"Yeah, you know . . . sexy? Don't men like that?" She was lowering her voice like a neckline.

Alan looked off, smiling. Christ, she was coming on to him. It was weird. And after the Hard Day's Night he'd been sucked through, it felt good.

"What's your name again?"

She told him. He said it a few times to her, using his nicest voice. After a minute, she told him he sounded sad and if he wanted, she could come over after she got off and keep him company.

"I work out a lot and I give great back massages. Do you like blondes or brunettes?"

Alan couldn't recall the difference but managed some answer that made her laugh and told her where he lived. She said she'd definitely be there. Asked if he were serious with Erica. He said it was more the other way around and Kimmy made a happy, cat-toy noise.

"I really admire your talent," she said. "And that isn't coming from some naive place. I'm taking the David Berg comedy writing class at the *Fade-In Scriptwriters' Academy.* Have you heard of him? He's really an exceptional instructor."

Berg was the biggest hack in the business, thought Alan, now lying sideways on the floor with Bart, cradling the ambitious voice that was charming him; saying the perfect words it hoped would open Ali Baba's cave.

He stared closely at a hole in the wood floor that looked like it had been made by a nail. A blemish of darker grain under his feeling fingertip seemed like a sleeping bloodstain; death rust. He could faintly hear an electric knife humming, screaming voices.

"So anyway, what do you look like, Alan? I'm medium height and everyone says I have a great figure. I grew up back East? You know, one of those 'so what do you wanna do?' towns?"

When she got to the part about a spec feature script she'd like him to read and produce, Alan told her maybe they should make it some other time, managed to get off pleasantly, and stumbled out onto the deck to get some fresh air. He sagged in his hammock with Bart, staring out at the slow, sweeping tide as it rolled and foamed, making its way toward land. He began to unbutton his shirt, after tossing off shoes and hearing one slide off the deck into water. But he never finished and his sleeping form lolled in salt mist under moonlight.

His dreams were violent and bloody.

The Mercenary was knifing someone's chest open, and just as the blade seamed upward, about to carve out the throat, Alan jerked awake. He scared Bart, asleep between his legs, head in Alan's lap; a whiskered anvil.

The two went inside but Alan couldn't fall asleep.

He kept the light on, holding onto Bart as waves crashed like angry beasts, pounding down his world.

subtext

〰〰〰〰〰〰〰〰〰〰〰〰 I got my first ulcer when I was fourteen. It felt like a helicopter crashed inside me."

Throat cleared. Fingers of both hands welded together. Separating; a tearing zipper.

"My father's a director. Stage. Very famous. Great guy. Brilliant. Brain a little bigger than his heart. But . . . lots of talent. I'm a writer."

A Cessna divebombs outside; Pearl Harbor noises. A gardener trims, five stories down.

"My mother?"

Face put on pause. Reverse. Stopping at a year.

"I don't know. She was very kind. An actress. Her emotions . . . I don't know . . . mix was too rich, maybe. She was on antidepressants. Used to paint when she'd be at home recovering at the beach house we had in Sag Harbor. That's back East. I'm good with directions if you ever need a map or anything. Is it okay to make jokes?"

A meerschaum pumping smoke signals; comfort.

〰〰〰〰〰〰

"Nothing really to say about my sister. Pretty normal stuff. We fought, we got along. Sometimes we still talk. I don't know."

Feeling in a womb.

"I was married. Maybe it was a mistake. The divorce, I mean. But I wanted a big career. I started getting into a lot of success thinking. My ex-wife, her name is Cynthia. I guess I didn't say that."

Confession lingering. An impression in fresh, wet thought.

"I think my ambition scared her. I got married when I was twenty-three. Divorced three years later."

Discomfort.

"I was reading a lot of books about how to make things happen. Make dreams come true, manifest the extraordinary . . . that kind of thing. Bothered her. She thought I should stick with more concrete approaches. I told her concrete was for sinking dead bodies."

Restless, percussive mannerisms.

"We never had children or anything. I wasn't ready. I'm still not. I don't understand them. To me, they're one step up from clay. It's weird. She married some fucking gauze-head named Dave who leads self-realization workshops. Guess she was getting revenge."

Dark shrug.

"My writing is my contribution. My creation of life, I guess you could say. Is that bullshit? Can you test for bullshit? I'm strong on the essay part."

Glancing at watch. Mind searching for a rope ladder. A way to escape sieged thoughts.

"I've been having nightmares. Violent, bloody images. I came to you because I—I'm under a lot of pressure these days. I've created a TV series and it's taking up all my time working on the pilot. Did I already say I'm a writer/producer?"

Acid glance.

"I actually have my own slash. That's how you know you've made it in television. You're two people."

Eyes forcing amusement; sad bellows.

"Anyway, I'm under a tremendous amount of pressure with this new pilot and moving into an expensive house and having these weird nightmares and ... I don't know what they mean. Maybe what I need to find out is it means nothing. I guess that would be interesting. If it means nothing, do I still have to pay you?"

Smiles. New question.

"The marriage breakup? I don't know. Sex was routine after a while. You hand me this, I'll hand you that. Start a fire, put out a fire."

Mood weeds.

"She used to tell me I was incapable of expressing rage."

Avoidance.

"I've had fantasies about my father's new wife. Is that *weird*? It's weird, right?"

Dimples clenching; retreating.

"I feel embarrassed. I mean, I think it's a little ... but she's young and totally gorgeous. Every time I'm around them, I have to hide my reaction. I should be put in like Freud prison and have a giant salami for a cellmate. I even think my father knows sometimes. But it isn't like she's really my mother."

The pipe considering; smoke thoughts. A glance at the wall clock. Minutes left.

"Maybe I hate her because she's alive and my real mother is dead and the wrong one is still around. The one who thinks art deco is a guy who owns a deli."

Nothing.

"I don't know that I'm really all that bad off. I mean, I've got a friend in the hospital dying and that bothers me a lot. Overall I'm okay. It's just I don't sleep well and I worry about things."

Long pause.

"You know, they say the reason writers write is that they're fucked up about life having no form. And writing is about controlling ... you know, what we wish it was. Am I rambling?"

Arms and legs crossed; flesh armor.

"I get scared sometimes. I don't know who I am. I get so depressed. Angry. I don't want to end up like my mother. I don't want to . . . have that happen."

The hour was up.

outline

FADE-IN:

8:04 A.M. Fifty miles off the English coast.

A. E. Barek hovers over storming sea. Huey blades gust craters on steel water. The cable is lowered. He firms mask against unshaven face. Looks at the chill expanse of Atlantic.

The British Airways 747 is down there. Full of people who were watching a movie, having a snack when the missile amputated half a wing.

Americans. Red-blooded innocents.

Only half an hour ago.

Maybe some are still alive. Managing on overhead masks. Struggling to live. Screaming under thousands of feet of icy water.

Waiting for someone like Barek; an angel in tanks and fins to descend, bring salvation.

He lets go of swinging cable, presses mask to face, drops into white-cap pewter.

In VOICE-OVER, we HEAR his thoughts; an unsparing venom. General Garris had called. Asked for help. Army couldn't be involved. No soldiers; only an independant. Someone with no ties to anything; anyone. Someone terrorists couldn't get to; leverage.

He swims deeper, the water aches; frigid gravity.

When he gets these defenseless civilian pawns out, the next move is simple. He'll go to whatever terrorist group did this and "rip their throats out. Hang them upside down and peel one foot of skin for every passenger who doesn't get out alive."

He swims on, lower and lower, searchlight a glowing spear.

Finally, sees it.

A faintly blinking beacon.

He swims toward it. Closer. Begins to make out enormous, dinosaur curves. The doomed shimmer of metal. The little windows with people behind; a horrid aquarium.

Faces seem dead inside, hair floating in currents.

Barek enters the drowning fuselage through a shorn emergency hatch. Inside, cabin lights still glow and passengers sit, held by seat belts. Magazines and food float. A little girl's doll does a slow-motion cartwheel.

All are dead.

Barek's VOICE-OVER takes in the saltwater morgue, as he slowly swims toward the rear of the 747, passing dead travelers who stare ahead; features puffy, skin clay-white.

Barek's professionalism corrodes.

"I hate this fucking job. The stupid, needless death I have to see. Greed and politics turn people into goddamned animals."

He stops, braking with palms.

A little dead boy, clutching his mother, is seated beside the aisle. Barek looks at the little boy. Brings thickly gloved fingers, wrapped in insulating rubber, to the child's eyes. Closes them. Then, notices the boy's throat has been cut. The mother's, too. The blood has been cleansed by sea. Barek doesn't understand.

Swims on.

Shines his beam on other faces; necks. Many have been cut, violently slashed. Dangling masks have been sliced away from air hoses; beheaded.

"What the fuck happened here?" we HEAR him say. "Mass suicide?"

He swims on, hands pushing aside millions of gallons of sea. The beam zigzags from death mask to death mask, as he creeps toward the rear.

He passes on old priest, who seems to be staring at him, and Barek gasps as the man's arms reach out, grab him! Barek stares in shock as the man looks at him pleadingly, body filled with water, oxygen mask expired.

Barek quickly offers his own mouthpiece and the priest's gulping features suckle.

"Breathe!" Barek screams, in VOICE-OVER.

The man looks at him with terrified eyes, gripping Barek's hand. But his grip weakens, his eyes seek rest.

"No!" Barek shakes the man, forcing him to breathe, not giving up. But the eyes shut, the mouthpiece slips out; jerking, writing nonsense on water.

Barek finds the man's Bible tucked in the elasticized seatback pouch, places it in the man's jacket, near his heart. Closes the priest's eyes.

Drifts on, toward the jet's rear.

Near the galley, he struggles to open the bathroom door that's squeezed in its jam by water pressure.

Stops.

Hears bubbles from inside; a faint seepage.

"Someone's alive," we HEAR him whisper, listening hard for secretions of life; a trapped survivor.

He pulls harder; it feels welded.

He begins to pry with his survival knife, shiny serrations chewing door edge. Finally, the lock breaks and it opens.

Inside, a man dressed in deep-water scuba lunges at underwater half-speed toward Barek! The man clutches an upraised knife; struggles to cut Barek's air hose.

Now Barek gets it. "They sent down a diver to kill whoever survived . . . sons of *bitches*."

Barek pulls at the man's mask. Manages to get his own knife gripped, cutting the man's suit.

Frantic bubbles.

Then, blood, as the knife razors open rubber and flesh. The man leaks red into the sunken carrier as they fight.

Barek holds the terrorist's forearm and cutting hard, sinks the blade into wrist, sawing through meat and bone. As the man's face contorts, mouth screaming inaudibly, the hand separates, floating away, fingers still jerking in spasm; a macabre wave.

Barek waves back in deadly parody, stares into the man's suffering face, and immediately plunges the knife into the man's ear, twisting the upturned tip deeper, cutting cartilege, piercing eardrum.

The man's mouth stretches in agony.

Bubbles chain.

Barek isn't done.

He pulls the knife out. Watches reaction, as the man's hand clamps over the useless ear and more crimson fluid escapes, thins in water.

Barek opens an automated fuselage hatch; the generator still alive. It slides up two feet and Barek forces the terrorist into the opening, halfway through.

As the man struggles, Barek brings the door down until it meets pliant skin under thick wet suit. The man's eyes roll into his skull as his ribs are crushed. Barek watches as the door sections the terrorist into grisly bookends.

The torso and screaming head float away outside. The bottom half remains trapped; bleeding Wicked Witch legs, under a fallen house.

A. E. Barek swims on through the horror-gloom, expressionless faces watching him go.

Alan leaned back, sipping at espresso. Reread the pages.

Would Andy Singer abide by any of this expense and carnage, he wondered. A man who emotionally responded to Cher albums. This sequence and what came after would come as a major shock.

Alan reread it, again.

It felt like the right tone for the opening sequence in the pilot. Jim Cameron meets De Sade.

But still . . . a fucking Catholic priest dying in close-up. Children with slashed throats. Waving goodbye to the hand, as it moved off, a five-fingered man-o-war. Then, poking out the guy's eardrum. Pretty fucking cold, folks. But it was exactly what he'd promised the network, bless their massive fear zones.

A. E. Barek.

The independent agent. The warrior for hire.

There were holes you could use for a landfill but the network wanted it lurid; violent. Bigger than life, however illogical. Alan had asked them about why the terrorists or the government would send a diver when the people couldn't have survived.

Because it was entertaining, they said.

Why make the priest live? Why a priest?

To add ethical presence, they said.

Plus, as Andy Singer reasoned, on the phone, when Alan told him some of the moves from the opening, ". . . people love religious figures who die heroically. Whole Joseph Campbell thing. Have you seen the tapes? You know what to do. And make some of the stewardesses attractive. Even if they're dead, don't make them look sickening."

As usual, Andy's advice was impeccably worthless.

Alan finished the espresso and walked to his kitchen, which overlooked La Cosa Beach Club. Fat children rode waves like vulgar pool floats and teenage girls gathered in gossiping squads, stuck to towels.

Alan rinsed out his baby mug. Chuckled a bit. It was strange writing this stuff. Odd how easily it came. He just stared at the sand-blasted ceiling and watched the parade of gore fuming from his mind; then wrote it down.

Cutting a guy in half. Sawing off a guy's hand. *Christ.* He was amused by it, yet it all struck him as perverse. For a guy who never raised his voice, or beat any kind of drum you could hear, this pilot was a torture chamber in thousand-point Helvetica.

But A. E. Barek didn't fucking care.

Alan was starting to get a kick out of this soldier of fortune who did whatever he felt like; used violence and brutality to solve everything.

It was fascinating.

transition

xxxxxxxxxxxxxxxxxxxx0000000fffffffffffff
coa . . d . aaa
dar kk . ppppppppppppppppppppxxcoal . . dd
mt . . .
zxeeetddd . . . hongrr . xxxxxxxxxxxxxxxzzzzzz hngrr
coal . . ddddd.
sha xxxkee0xxxxxxxxxxxxxx
ng.xxxxxxxxxxxxxxxxxxxxxxxxxxxvvvvvvvvvvvvvvttttt
Al . . . xoannnnnnnnnnnnnnnnnnnnnnnnnnn.
000000000000Hngrrxxxxxxxxxxxxxxxx00000.
alon.
. . . . darkkk. m-t . . . mtmtmtmtmtmtmtmtmtmtmt.
mtmtmtmtmtmtmtmtmtmtmtmtmtmtmtmtmtmtmtmtmtmtmt
mtmtmtmtmtmtmtmtmtmtmtmtmtmtmtmtmtmtmtmtmtmtmt

~~~~~~~~

lunch

Le Dome was filling up for lunch with fever and dread.

Method-trained food-stamps in red vests bustled, handing parking tickets to the lithium royalty who smiled and entered.

The restaurant held court on Sunset, just west of La Cienega, and was a preferred Vatican for deals and meals. Poseurs, profiteers, and sleek warheads came to suture deals that were stillborn, bleeding to death, or worse. They came to eat, to sell; to hang upside down in the cave, looking for blood.

The whole place had a shadowy, well-bred virulence and every glance hunted for something. Every nod collected rumor. Expiring starlets, nibbling on angel hair, made Down's syndrome conversation with their managers, trying to grasp why they'd made the ugly, gunshot collapse from features to miniseries to guest shots on daytime. They would softly wipe Mattel faces and not see their lives oozing into the mausoleum as their managers listened sympathetically, scanning for new flesh and bones who sat at the bar, fresh in from nowhere. In time, the managers would carve their initials in virgin bones, use them up, and walk away, crunching through the sediment.

"Anyway, she tells me she can't have oral sex because she's got bulimia." Jordan acted it out like a grim Mummenschanz routine. "Seriously. Not making this up. So, I say what's the matter 'cause she's just . . . staring at it like it's junk mail and out of the blue she bites the head. So, I say, are you kidding me? And she gets so upset, she sticks her finger down her throat and launches a lovely evening at Spago onto the couch."

Jordan sighed, surgically disassembling a plate of ahi; a fish bypass. ". . . now it looks like a piece of sectional vomit."

He dumped some Pellegrino into his stomach. Let the bubbles punch pink lining. Shrugged with disappointment. "I don't think the relationship is happening. How's your lunch?"

Jordan sniffled, rubbed his nose with a napkin. The repaired septum was making him sound wrong.

"I tell you I just signed a gang? Bunch of real motherfuckers. Crips from south central. Some ex-Cannell guy is over at 20th doing a cop pilot, using street gangs."

"Yeah, yeah. What is that? 'Bad Blood'?"

Jordan nodded, pronging more dead fish.

"Anyway, he wanted the real flavor, so he was gonna hire this paroled gang member to give him input, right? So, I said, fuck that, and I signed another whole gang. Crips. These guys like whack white people on their day off just for a fucking goof. Anyway, I negotiated with Twentieth and the whole gang is under contract as consultants on the series."

"Weird . . ."

"Pretty okay guys. For fucking cannibals with Uzis. I have 'em out to the house and they just hang on the sand, bring their 'ho's' and get high. They're about danger and anger . . . but they actually have a story sense."

Jordan tensed, gestured with his eyes, changing the subject. A gay studio head, with Joan Collins's skin, stepped politely to the table and Jordan traded quick hugs. They bartered gossip. Launched distortions. The older man wanted to be introduced.

"Victor, Alan White. Just sold a series to Andy Singer. *Total fucking missile.*"

"Well, consider us a target. We're looking to get into the hour business, again." The cashmere smile grew and he shoulder-squeezed Jordan goodbye, whispering something in his ear. Victor moved on, working the room; roaming for tactical blips.

Jordan sighed. ". . . guy's a fuckin' vulva. Been trying to get in my pants for a year. Got no respect for that . . ."

Alan knew that meant Jordan would find ways to make projects inaccessible to the guy unless the deals were huge. He could feel it; see it in his edgy expression. It was how Jordan manipulated people; punishing and rewarding. Among the devices of torture were unreturned phone calls and hot spec scripts withheld from voracious career hunger pangs; thrust under control-freak cuticles by omission. Top agents like Jordan were experts in mind control; B. F. Skinner Wise Guys.

"Tell you I'm thinking about leaving the agency? Maybe going back to Vermont. Make syrup for a living. I don't know. Agents don't talk film or life. They don't talk art. Higher values. It's all deals and pussy."

"Uh-huh." Alan pointed. "Jord . . . butter."

"I mentioned Bertrand Russell to this guy in TV packaging the other day and he wanted to know if Russell worked in half hour or long form. Acidophilus has more live culture than this city. Sometimes I feel like I've been seduced and eroded by L.A."

"Maybe you should start carrying tanks of oxygen."

Jordan glanced at his Piaget. "So, he should be here any minute. He's having some trouble with his kid, had to put her in a de-tox ranch up in Santa Barbara."

"Oh yeah?" Alan found it interesting. Sad; odd. He wanted more detail.

"Kid's thirteen and drilling both arms. Place costs ten a month. Hector's ready to work. Timing's good."

Alan watched Jordan eating, ahi sacrificing perfect Hawaiian contours to his quick mouth. He gathered perfectly measured califlower to one side of the plate and poked it like a cage of POWs. He looked good tormenting things.

He'd started with ICM, right out of running a comedy club in Cancún that had been demolished in a storm, killing sixteen Mexican comics who were buried under rubble; the final 120-mile-an-hour heckle.

Within two years, by the time he was twenty-eight, he'd grafted PAC-TEL to his ear and packaged four successful sitcoms that in a better world would have been declared felonies. "Chunky Bill," "Robot Dad," "No Way, Jay," and "Sayonara" strangled everything that came near without having to use both hands.

Jordan quickly did a multizero skip to CAA when Ovitz started hearing about the stealth-savant who was restless for bigger body counts; bloodier waters.

When CAA moved to their new I. M. Pei building on Wilshire, Jordan was given a chamber in the clout hive. He repped only the top directors and writer/producers. Anyone not leaving major smoke damage with their gifts was left out; Jordan was looking for asteroid momentum. By only signing a fleet of rising stars and transfer students from Andromeda, he could do little wrong.

At the age of twenty-nine, he was a legendary deal-boa, renowned for being oversexed, charming, aggressive, tasteless, and generally undeterred by conscience. Everyone knew it was only a matter of time before Jordan was the major player in the business. People were afraid of him. People had contempt for him. But everybody wanted to be on his phone sheet.

It had been his suggestion Alan meet with Hector Lee.

Alan had fallen silent and stared at Jordan incredulously when the name came up. He'd heard Hector had committed suicide with his ever-present pistol, or was a carrot in some mental institution. But he wasn't. Jordan was still representing him.

Him and the Crips.

ugly gossip

Hector had a mixed track record. A few hits: mostly cheap action pictures. A few films that were total body bags. The look was always there. But some of the nihilistic stuff was unendurable. Dreary, Bergmanesque two-hour funerals with doomed lovers and gray moods. Voices with rainy weather in them; Auschwitz faces.

Critics had said *The Deer Hunter* was *Paint Your Wagon* compared to Hector's third film, *Sea Level,* in which a self-loathing juggler/clown jumped off a building onto a schoolyard full of retarded children, crushing several, including a charming little brain-damaged imp and his kitten Booboo, a sweet calico that was all the child lived for.

It was a cheap, opaque manipulation and *The New Yorker* said deveining shrimp was more entertaining. Hector was demolished and disappeared from the L.A. film scene for six years, finally resurfacing in Recife, Brazil, in 1981.

There, he'd commenced a mostly unrewarding homosexual affair with a young pinhead cabana-boy named Sergio Cunha, who was both a curse and a blessing, ultimately lifting Hector's mag-goted career back into reasonable levels of opportunity.

But the personal toll was excruciating on Hector who fre-quently found Sergio cheating on him. And to make matters worse, in response to Hector's jealous fits, Sergio would often throw tantrums, ripping Hector's clothes to shreds. There were rumors Hector bought over thirty pairs of shorts the first year of the rela-tionship.

Hector's ideas were also lifted by Sergio at dinner parties where Sergio's tiny brain would suckle at whatever wells of thought or viewpoint Hector had, and deftly represent them as his own. It would always infuriate Hector and when they got home, arguments would go on for hours until Sergio pulled the scissors out and cut up more bermuda shorts, driving Hector to great levels of emo-tional upset.

Then, just as Hector had hired a young thug to kill Sergio, as he tanned, and get him out of his thinning hair, Sergio sprinted up from the beach, where he'd been hard at work on some secret project for weeks, and showed Hector something in a binder, writ-ten in a sloppy, vacant hand.

A screenplay.

And though it lacked thought, originality, literacy, and grace, it was the lottery number Hector had been waiting for his whole life.

It was called *Yesterday Isn't Tomorrow* and was the sort of dreck that tends to make a reader dizzy with stunned, wordless shock. It was the worst thing Hector had ever read, including a two-part "Bewitched" his former business manager had written on spec years back in which Samantha's mother, Endora, implies to Darin that she would actually give him a blowjob if he'd accompany her to a warlock's ball.

It made no sense, had no identifiable plot, wandered blindly for forty pages at a time, and drew with extravagant creative bur-glary from every well-known film Sergio had ever seen, which numbered under ten.

There were shreds of *The Good, the Bad and the Ugly* beside pathetically copied dollops of *Deliverance*. It was everything a script shouldn't be and achieved its vacuous state so confidently that when Hector first read it, he'd had three Coronas and passed out.

When he came to, on the veranda overlooking the samba bay outside their apartment, he knew he could make the film. He knew exactly how to rescue it from the inertia and deadness soaking its every cell. With the right bulldozing and ruthless editing it could work.

Though Sergio had done nothing more than two or three functional circus chimps could have managed, Hector saw a comeback. Reentry. His long-forgotten body rising from the bossa nova grave, wearing a new pair of shorts.

Sergio, so rumors went, was predictably rhapsodic; the imbecilic script had forged a new identity he would go on about for hours, his perfect coffee skin shellacked in tan lotion like a person with waxy buildup. At times, he would stare up at the ceiling with a conceited grin, forever retelling the evolution of *Yesterday Isn't Tomorrow,* which Hector had, by that point, begun to secretly refer to as *Sergio Is Brain Dead.*

But Sergio was beyond pride.

Beyond self-esteem.

His ego pigment only grew darker. To hear him tell it, which occurred almost hourly, he was Orson Welles. He was Woody Allen. He was the new voice cinema was starved for, its desperate ribs beginning to show until Sergio started writing. Though he had the intellectual depth of a parakeet, he was in love with himself anew and his superego swelled into an offensive, Boeing-like thing.

Ultimately, through Hector's remaining connections, the film managed financing through a group of Mexican dentists, looking for a tax shelter.

It was hastily filmed in three weeks and the final product, in which Sergio starred (he'd demanded to star or the script wasn't for sale) as an enigmatic character named Señor Samu, was decried by animal rights activists everywhere for including footage in which hundreds of sheep and chickens were burned alive, in a sequence of indulgent surrealism, when Samu burned the farm of a cartel greaser, located on the pampas.

There, amid the lanolin and feather-scented carnage, a jubilee of yelping, expiring animals, the hero, played frozenly by the former cabana-boy from Recife, wept.

His stoic, imbecile's expression bored critics internationally but Hector began to think Sergio could be the next David Hasselhoff, minus the range. And though Sergio's expression never changed, he looked excellent in clothes, and the two ended up making six lucrative films together in a joint venture with the Peruvian government, who adored Sergio's on-screen persona.

In each successive film, Sergio, as Señor Samu, seemed impossibly more mummified than the film before, his nostrils barely registering the awareness of odor, his lips faintly twitching at the sight of bodies skinned alive by his sworn enemy in every film, Eumir Puma.

As nimbly written by Sergio, Puma was a fat, sadistic, nauseating slob. He always played a merry debaser of the little people and Sergio was always cast as Senor Samu, the fearless force of justice; or as Hector saw it, basically a cadaver with a fag mustache.

Sergio wrote all the scripts, such as they were, and in one of his more profligate acts of bad thinking decided to include voice-over narration, in all the Samu films. In each picture, he droned in a nearly falsetto Portuguese about how much he hated Puma, sounding like a pissed Debby Boone.

In Sergio and Hector's third film, *The Dead Cannot Live,* Sergio was particularly proud of the scene in which he was tied to the back of a Jeep and dragged over three miles of bad Lima road, in an insensitive attempt on Puma's part to extract information. Sergio never flinched and thus his inability to act and a scene which demanded a face devoid of any expressive range, had merged into the ideal filmic lie in which he actually appeared to have some talent.

The Samu films got Hector back on his feet and when he

finally got an offer from Paramount, in 1988, to direct a picture, he instantly walked out on Sergio, whom he'd come to loathe. The ex-cabana-boy and former Speedo model had been devastated and committed suicide by cutting off his hand and bleeding to death, signing a blurry GOODBYE with his wet stump on their white leather couch.

Hector, so the story went, had said Sergio's writing was unclear to the end.

lunch two

Anyway, we'll be lucky to get him," said Jordan, gulping a cappuccino, throat bulbing. Le Dome was beginning to empty and he waved to exiting faces, memorizing which smiles deceived him.

"From everything I've heard, sounds like he's out of his mind." Alan gestured at the waiter to refill his iced coffee. "Can the guy still direct? I mean, have you seen any of those *Samu* films? Scary fuckin' stuff, Jordan."

"Low period. He's still got the magic. I've been talking him up around the network and the buzz on this guy is palpable."

Alan paused. When Jordan said things like "palpable," it made him nervous.

"Hector's gonna be bigger than ever. He paints with Dali images. And actors love him. Nicholson calls me once a week to see if they can do something."

"Jack Nicholson?"

Jordan hadn't even heard the joke. Alan could sense him going into his bonfire-coercion mode. The stream of ideas got faster, annoyingly ridden with incomplete references Jordan had picked up from reading too many film magazines; glittering fragments.

"But he doesn't bring that mescaline bullshit look. It's more Coppola. Bertolucci. Very rich, very textured. And he plays billiards with the camera. His shots always have something on their mind. His stuff makes Ken Russell look like Opie directing *Splash*."

". . . if this guy had directed *Splash*, he'd have cut off the fucking mermaid's head and boned her on camera." Alan was dabbing at mouth corners.

Something caught Jordan's eye and he excused himself to visit a corner table where Meryl Streep was having soup with a twenty-one-year-old microtwat director.

As Alan watched Jordan cross the room, his mind paced in a distressed circle. He remembered reading a *Vanity Fair* article about Hector in which he was described as being "The Nervous Breakdown King of British Film": a heroin addict who always wore black and spent time in and out of psychiatric facilities for years. He'd counted among his friends, the Stones, the Beatles, various Pythons, and several royals, one of whom had a cousin Hector had dated and was rumored to have had bizarre sexual parties with.

The *Vanity Fair* piece said, at one point, years back, Hector had made the front page of the Brit rags, getting caught in Madame Tussaud's, after hours, where he, all his friends, and royal gal-pal had broken in and were Polaroiding themselves fucking famous wax figures.

The article went on to describe midnight boar hunts, in the nude, which Hector organized on his five-hundred-acre estate outside London. Sometimes, groupies were dressed as pigs and Hector's many guests would hunt them down, tie them to fallen logs, and . . . they didn't elaborate.

Among the stranger allegations in the piece was that Hector was a cannibal, and indeed the accompanying photos in the article showed an intense smile, complete with teeth that seemed almost sharpened. It was too fucking strange.

Further inglorious acts, the article implied, included Hector stabbing his wife, causing her death by massive infection days later. Ultimately, it was ruled involuntary manslaughter with extenuating circumstances and commonly viewed as a miscarriage of justice owing to his links to the palace. From there, Hector had directed a rumored snuff film for a royal to enjoy.

In the video, an oriental girl had been murdered after being tied up and brutally raped by a group of men wearing masks. In the finale of the maniac gem, a bottle had been broken over her soft, young forehead, then used to cut her up, inside and out. The article went to pains to say it was unconfirmed Hector had directed it. But many of the angles and camera moves bore striking resemblance to his idiosyncratic style: the entire video screamed Hector. It was allegedly titled "Broken Bottle," and a popular underground classic. The article's version of Hector's filmic evolution opted to refer to earlier films as profitable "misjudgments."

As Alan let the waiter take his plate away, a large man with a Vandyke and shoulder-length hair lumbered across the dining room, led by the maitre d'. He was dressed in black and extended a multiringed hand.

"Alan," said the man, in a breathless Ringo growl, "my god, I'm so sorry. Hector Lee. I feel absolutely awful. Got tied up coming down from Montecito. Big car accident, terrible traffic." He gestured embarrassment. "Were you waiting long? Please say you just got here, I don't think my heart could take it. It's a huge pleasure to meet you . . ."

He lifted a warm smile and sat, rolling his sleeves up, then down; a nervous mannerism. Alan quickly noticed a nose softened to a red ottoman by Dewar's and battery dust. Hector dabbed his forehead with a cloth napkin and grinned; a corroded survivor. He ordered a tomato juice and looked Alan in the eye, happily. His hair was tangled and flecked with gray and he forked it from his eyes.

"My god, we've got so much to talk about. This pilot you've written is fucking brilliant! Let me just pick something here and we'll get right to it."

Alan watched Hector absorb the menu and sensed something decent about him. He liked the passionate eyes. The warm zeal he used for conversation. Even felt himself wanting to forgive him, for all his storming adventures and strange choices, if they were true. He wanted to believe this troubled, recovering man wasn't responsible for a girl being murdered on camera and even agreed to share a small bowl of raspberries with Hector, who said he was a vegetarian.

By the time Jordan had returned, Alan and Hector were laughing. Hector told Alan he loved the pilot script for "The Mercenary" more than anything he'd read in ten years. His notes were well presented, thoughtful, and made Alan realize Hector understood his vision.

Hector suggested they find a strong second-unit director to do the action stuff so Hector could concentrate on the character shades and Alan agreed. Hector alluded to several small changes. They were perceptive and positive. Alan instantly agreed to them all.

". . . the trick to making this pilot genuinely overwhelming, is to play it *absolutely* real," said Hector with massive enthusiasm.

Alan nodded. "And it should have a kind of moral ambivalence . . . the audience must question their own morals about violence and sexual frankness . . ."

"Oh, absolutely! Absolutely!" Hector was nearly yelling. "This has to be tough. But it must explore values and social assumptions about violence. If it's a stunt show . . . or a bloodbath . . . it becomes dim-witted . . . becomes, I don't know . . . sort of pornography. Same with the sexuality, don't you think?"

". . . no, that's right. It really has to look and sound and feel dangerous. But it must comment all along . . . have an editorial conscience, just as the script does."

Yes. Hector agreed. He even said he thought Alan was a brilliant talent and that didn't hurt relations. At one point, as Jordan caught Alan's eye and winked, liking the way things were going, Hector used Visine and shut his own eyes, tightly.

He rubbed them hard and they remained shut for a minute or so. As the closed lids trembled, Alan sensed Hector was thinking about odd things. Things Alan didn't even want to imagine. But despite himself, he liked Hector.

For so brief a meeting, things felt unusually good. Except with everything Alan knew about his background, he didn't really trust him.

Maybe it was the faintly sharpened teeth.

z o o m

Alan locked his door, gripped the wheel.

What was the fucking problem? He'd accidentally cut him off and this nut was jacked, flipping him off; a six-pack jammed in a Stetson. Alan took a breath; scared. Looked into his rearview; the huge pickup was on him, lights flashing angrily. A signal ahead changed and Alan ran the red. The truck followed, primered body tanking through intersection, ignoring horns.

Alan raced through Malibu Canyon, toward the beach and the truck hung tight; filling mirror. It moved to pass, ran alongside him. The fat face looked over, grinning I-really-want-to-hurt-you deadness. He tried to swerve into Alan's Porsche and Alan turned the wheel to the right, dodging. The face looked over, furiously, teeth bared. Tried again. Alan floored it, raced ahead, scared.

The canyon tunnel was just beyond the next curve and he could see it as the big tires of the truck wailed alongside. It pressed closer, bullying the Porsche to the shoulder, wanting him to go over the side.

"... *suck* me," Alan hissed.

What next? Was the guy ready to whack him over a mistake? Alan tried to dial 911 to get a cop, trying to watch the road. Fast busy signal. Canyon; a coffin.

The tunnel was ahead and Alan was out of shoulder, road, time. He slammed on the brakes, skidded through dirt. Sat in exhaust and dust; a gas chamber. Frantic bootsteps. A sweating face at his window.

Alan stared forward, didn't move, trembling. He could jam the 928 in reverse, floor it; maybe there was room, maybe he—

"Get out!" Pounding window.

The engine died. Wouldn't start.

The man came around, peered in through windshield. Alan looked down, avoiding, afraid. The man tapped with false calm; fingertip rain.

"Now."

"Go away." Mouth dry.

The man became furious. Grabbed a big rock, smashed the driver's window, reached through, opened the door. Yanked Alan out. Alan stood before him, paralyzed. Tried to get mad but couldn't. Tried to fight back, resist; handle it. Wanted to talk reason; somehow be friends. But he couldn't move, a terrified child.

"Don't like the way you drive, asshole!"

A shaking voice. "... it was a mistake. I'm sorry. Please, let's just—"

The man threw Alan against the hood, then dragged him over to the truck. Made him look into the truck cabin.

"Apologize to my girlfriend, you sonofabitch!"

A girl, nineteen, sat on the torn seat, nervous; embarrassed. Alan apologized but could see in her eyes how afraid she, too, felt. How impotent. He saw in her eyes what he knew she saw in his.

She looked like she might try to say something to make the guy stop, but Alan was suddenly punched in the gut, and stared up from ground at cowboy boots, coming closer. A boot was on his throat, the face started to put weight on it. Grinned, enjoying, glancing at his girlfriend for a praising look. But she had turned away, hating this. Alan couldn't breathe; began to black out.

Alan's eyes opened.

His body ached. He tasted blood and stared at a black wall with little raised words on it. Focused, realized it was his front tire. He rolled over, slow pain. Traffic whooshed in and out of the nearby tunnel. Horns echoed; teenagers.

He tried to get up, suddenly saw the truck was still there. Jerked back. Eyes searching. Was the Stetson waiting for a second attack? Went to take a leak? Come back and shove him over the side? Tie him to his steering wheel, cram a gas-soaked rag in his mouth, light it; push the car over the cliff? Alan crawled toward his Porsche, terror rising. Wanting to escape. Then, he heard it. Soft crying.

He stopped, stunned. Swallowed blood.

Legs protruded from bushes, beside the Porsche. Pants torn, red oozing onto boot embroidery. Alan slid toward him. He was bloody, unconscious. Clumps of his hair had been ripped out. Several fingers were bloated blue; snapped. Eyelids swollen. One ear hung partially from the head. There were bite marks.

The girl sat cross-legged in dirt, cradling him.

Alan stared in confusion; didn't remember a fight. Had she tried to stop it and the guy hit her? Did she stagger back to the truck and take a tire iron, fight back; totally lose it? He couldn't think straight. Could only remember being knocked out.

He tried to say something to her and she looked up. Began to scream. She told him to stay away; threw a rock at him. She said he'd almost killed her boyfriend. Alan didn't understand, then looked at his own hands; knuckles bloody. Skin and hair under nails. He felt sick; lost. It was impossible.

He'd never been in a fight in his life.

subtext two

~~~~~~~~~~~~~~~~~~~~~~~~ Stare glazed.

Fingers plucking sofa fabric. Voice trying to water down deep fires.

". . . you know, these network people . . . they just sit there and expect you to solve every problem they've created for themselves. Their crops wilt and you're the savior who'll reverse their dead schedule. Correct their bad choices. It just offends me. But you can't tell them. They'll punish you . . . politically fuck you."

A sip of water. Feeling dust crawl over tongue and gums. Feeling irritable. Sounding calm.

"I try so hard to be fair, you know? But what's the point? It's like . . . I mean, Andy Singer is a barely fertilized *egg* and he hasn't got clue one about innovation or quality. I mean, he's ten fucking years old."

An amused note taken.

"I'm only exaggerating a little. These are people who should be worried exclusively about clearing up their complexions and they're running fucking networks. And I just act very friendly . . .

~~~~~~~~~~

but inside I've got this constant, running commentary going about which mind near me is most vacant."

Silence. Two men, in a two-man church.

"Some of the things that little prick said in the pitch meeting the other day. When he said my friend Eddy, who's dying, was nothing to him. Like he never existed. Like his whole life never happened."

Face flushing. Fingers pointing; guns.

"I wanted to just . . ."

Styrofoam cup torn; skinned alive. A quick glance.

"I tell you my dad called me? It was strange . . ."

A haunted distance.

"Everything is strange . . ."

A lost smile.

two months later

creative
differences

~~~~~~~~~~~~~~~~~~~~~~ The room was dim, padded like a psychiatric observation chamber. Five rows of thickly upholstered living-room chairs faced a huge screen, and the projectionist remained in the room behind, taking orders by intercom.

Two network panzers sat in the middle row, sipping coffee and talking about the latest gossip trickling in from CAA's annual confront weekend, in Palm Springs, where all the agents spent two days telling each other the truth, in a way that sounded good.

Alan sat beside Marty and "The Mercenary's" pilot second-unit director, Bo Bixby, a muscular, former stuntman who looked like a Norwegian Norman Mailer. Bo favored dressing in a smoky gray flight suit; a stoic obelisk. Alan called him "the line you draw between madness and fearlessness," and Bo loved that.

He'd quit working as a stuntman after turning both knees to cheap hinges in a high fall off the Century Plaza Hotel for an episode of "Knight Rider" where Kitt the talking car got infected gaskets or some inspired twist a nation hungered to see.

~~~~~~~~~~

Bo was famous for helicopter falls into airbags and always spoke very softly, as if his larynx was turned to 1. He'd become a second-unit director, handling the stunts and action the first-unit guys didn't want to bother with for reasons of time or esthetics. Bo had done a million big action pictures and was one of the best. His footage got in your face with urgent realism.

A row in front of him, sat the two editors, Jack and Jackie, a married couple, who listened for which takes the producers preferred, so a fast first assembly could be managed and the network could see an early cut ASAP.

They were all there to see the first set of dailies and waited for Hector, who was late.

"Let's run 'em for you guys," Alan suggested. "I'll run 'em again for Hector when he shows."

"He must've stopped off to hallucinate somewhere," cracked Greg Gunnar, network liaison number two, to Scot Bloom, network liaison number one. They both had happy little Montessori faces and were twenty-four and twenty-six.

"Yeah, exactly . . ." added Scot.

Alan buzzed the projectionist. "Brace yourselves, boys and girls," he said.

Scot squooshed down into the chair, feet on the chairback in front of him, loafers kneading. The lights came down and the screen was suddenly filled with huge underwater closeups of dead faces, eyes staring.

The camera did a slow creep through harsh glare, from one corpse to the next, and 747 windows could be seen in backgound, ghostly ovals. Glassy eyes and drowned stares anchored floating hair.

"Love scene . . . ?" Gunnar delivered it just right and scattered chuckles rumbled in darkness.

". . . very eerie, Alan." Scot was watching, tilting his head in a troubled posture, repelled; drawn.

". . . little camera jiggle there," said Marty, jotting notes onto a clipboard with a tiny light attached. "Second take should be better."

Alan nodded. Liked what he was seeing.

He and Hector had been arguing about the look of this scene two days earlier and though Bo offered to shoot it, Hector wanted first crack. Bo agreed to set up the big tank on the back lot, gather stunt people who'd descend into the sunken fuselage cutaway, in passenger clothes, be seat-belted in, then wait for the divers with oxygen until the camera tracked past. Finding a kid actor who was a qualified diver to play the dead boy and getting parental sanction had been a bitch.

But now that his ex-wife was financially colostomizing him, Marty was motivated.

Alan watched, startled by the effect.

The white faces, slightly plumped by death, were exactly what he'd imagined when he'd written the scene. The crashed tomb with bottom-of-the-ocean lighting, filled with vacant, executed faces was stunning. More upsetting than he'd imagined it would be.

It was working and he was relieved. He'd been afraid Hector was going to take it his own way, if not outright fuck it up the ass with some bullshit approach, heavy on unmotivated zooms, bombast angles. He'd even considered firing him when he finally, actually realized how difficult Hector really could be; with or without coke.

When he'd told Hector in their first conceptual meeting about "The Mercenary" pilot that he wanted Corea to look cut-off and let it all play in the eyes, Hector, the ever-defensive child, had taken a long pause and Alan sensed the legendary wrecking ball of peevishness swinging. Hector fell silent and merely glared for two or three minutes as Alan explained his original vision, as creator.

Hector, rather obviously, couldn't've cared less.

They'd argued for a long time, and though Alan never directly threatened to let Hector go, the implication was there. Especially when Hector told Alan about how he'd been tinkering with the script to get it "up to speed" and Alan smothered that fast.

When you boiled it right down, the more Alan got to know him, the less he wanted to. He was, true to all accounts, a lunatic. He was also a potentially grave liability and Alan had to watch him every step of the way for fear he'd go amuck and jackhammer the whole project into ego-rubble.

The underwater footage was over and the reels changed to a scene where A. E. Barek first meets his Army contact and old friend, General Jack Garris. In the pilot script, as written, the two had served together, as Black Berets, lived in trenches filled with corpses, and belly-crawled over their own dead men to slaughter enemies all over the globe. They'd hidden in treetops, killed together with bare hands. Garris was one of Alan's favorite characters in the series.

Garris had become a general after escaping from a POW camp they'd both been held in while Barek wasted away in a hanging bamboo cage, after being captured, trying to make sure Garris made it. Thanks to Barek, Garris got away and he didn't.

In the POW camp, where Alan had written graphic scenes of pain and degradation, Barek was tortured daily until Garris, working from the outside, helped him to escape.

The two-hundred-thousand-dollar escape scene included a helicopter armada and a shocking massacre at the guerilla guard village near the POW camp. Several teenage village girls would be filmed naked, bathing in a river, as Garris's soldiers snaked through jungle, near shore, slitting throats.

The scene on screen, right now, was set in a red-light bar in Saigon, where two girls danced topless, and the actor playing Garris, Simon Buss, looked nonplussed about the reunion, drinking a Sapporo. It was the wrong performance and Alan hated it. Corea, face scarred by years of deadly missions, was animated and happy to see Garris and it couldn't have been more wrong. Barek should've been weak and scathed by what he'd been through. Smiling was completely off. Things were emotionally backwards.

Alan was about to try and get Hector on his carphone when the door opened and light plunged in; a yellow King Kong arm. Hector entered, mumbled apology for being late, slumped into a chair in the front row, hair belted by a bandana. He sniffed like a Dristan commerical and Alan wondered if he was fucked-up.

"Hey, Hector . . ." said Bo.

Hector lifted his arm straight up, then dropped it. Greg Gunnar turned in his seat and whispered something to Scot who nodded. Scot faced Alan, spoke low.

"Alan, isn't Barek a little big here?"

Alan tried to decide if he wanted to take the rap or just bust Hector in front of everybody.

"I don't agree . . ." said Hector, loudly, overhearing. "I think the man is emotionally moved to be out of the camp and a bit joyous at this—" he waved fingers around, searching, "momentous re-bonding with his old pal."

No one said anything and the scene continued to play, all wrong; false and strained. Simon, though he'd won two Emmys and stewed with fierce presence, wasn't coming across. And Corea's performance was dissonant; smiles and grimaces in search of a focus.

Hector had missed the point.

Marty discreetly bent his mouth to Alan's ear. "What do you want to do? We can't use any of this bar stuff. All needs to be re-shot."

Alan whispered back. "I'll have to get him to do it over. We're already overbudget . . . we're only into our third day. We're all over the road if Hector doesn't get our act together . . ."

Gunnar and Bloom had fallen conspicuously silent and the room went dense with wordless disapproval. Fear. Hector chuckled to himself at the scene and at one point called out with a confident, bemused voice.

"So, Alan . . . do you love it?"

Bloom, unable to miss the terrible awkwardness, tried to save the moment. He'd even planned for something like this, having told Alan confidentially, that morning, that if things got unworkable with Hector, the network would play bad guy and beat him up. Alan said he thought Hector would do a great job but listened appreciatively, wanting network support, especially if re-shooting was required.

"Hector . . . wasn't the tone supposed to be more restrained in Barek's performance?" Bloom sounded reasonable. Gunnar backed him up, saying that was how he'd read it, too. They both said the network, and particularly Andy Singer, had been "looking forward to that."

Hector said nothing.

The room didn't move. Alan and Bo exchanged looks.

Bloom took another stab. "Look, Hector, this isn't . . . really the feeling we want with this guy."

"Right. Or with Garris, either," added Gunnar, to underline.

Hector didn't turn his head. Just continued watching the dailies. "I see," was all he said.

Alan cleared his throat, not anxious for an argument that would Jim Jones the whole production. Hector had done this too many times to too many other films. Alan wasn't going to let him blow his first big pilot.

"Hector, we're just talking about a readjustment. Not a new show."

"Absolutely," added Marty, looking right at Alan, trying to help.

Bloom picked up on the thought. "Look, maybe later in the year we can do an episode where Barek shows some bigger emotions. But for now, we wanna shoot for a certain feel."

Silence.

". . . so what are you saying?" asked Hector, staring dead-ahead, hair suffocated by the bandana.

"We'll need to re-shoot," said Bloom.

Hector said nothing. No amuck threats. No steaming tantrum. After several seconds of coffin-still, he simply stood, blocking the projection beam. Then, as his silhouette clung to the screen, he withdrew the .38 from his shoulder holster, turned to face them all, and shot Scot Bloom. The bullet went into Scot's boyish chest and blood geysered from his monogrammed pocket.

Gunnar was in shock but managed to comfort the young

programmer's slumped form, like Jackie, when she held Jack in the limo, in Dallas.

Bo tried to lunge for Hector and was shot in the thigh, as all looked on in horror. Bo fell to the floor, hissing in pain, bleeding on carpet.

Then, as if he hadn't planned it at all, and was being forced into the decision by some outside force, Hector turned the pistol's barrel to his own open mouth. He looked puzzled and made a stunned sound as he pulled the trigger and his troubled mind exploded, flocking walls, chairs, and Armani blends.

Bits of his tormented head even sprayed the screen and the nearly hysterical Greg Gunnar, who'd just joined the network, after graduating from Yale. This was the closest Greg had ever come to being touched by original thought and he screamed, face covered with Hector's schizophrenic pulp.

Alan quickly moved everyone out of the projection room and called studio security. Marty went to the bathroom to throw up. Both editors were pale. One passed out. As they waited for an ambulance, Bo tourniqueted his own leg and talked about a "fag costume guy" he'd worked with on a huge feature who'd become depressed and completely severed his penis on location with a knife. The anecdote only made things worse. Alan went into the screening room to help Greg comfort Scot Bloom who was dying, losing blood, calling out for his mother.

When Jordan heard what had happened, an hour later, he called from his XJS and expressed shock. Then, just as he was about to enter a tunnel, he told Alan there was another guy he represented who'd become available and made Hector's directing look hackneyed.

He said Hector was a moody guy and things like this happened sometimes. Alan was moved by the insight and as Jordan went into a tunnel, he broke up and vanished.

Alan went home early that afternoon and stared out at the Pacific. The bluish water looked like blood in a body and when it struck the sand, it was a wound that went up the coastline; a vast, never healing cut. He tried to comprehend how many things had gone wrong in a few hours. His director had shot lousy footage, a network liaison, a second unit director, and himself.

Alan smoked a joint, stared into space, and pet Bart until the sun went down.

demands

When Alan was asked who should direct the remainder of "The Mercenary" pilot, which by now was eliciting unhappy attention from the network's Zeus fleet, his mind stalled.

Then, the words left his head and pulled in front of an idea he'd never seen. "I wanna do it," he told Jordan. "I know what I want. I can bring in the look and the budget. The network loves the dialogue and the attitudes and the whole approach. Tell Andy I wanna take a crack."

He didn't know where the words were coming from. He'd never wanted to direct before. Why now? All he knew was he wanted to protect his creation, as a mother would her unborn child; to keep the pilot away from the meddlesome Xeroxes most pilot directors called "style."

Even Jordan, in his usual esthetic trough, had warned that for-hire, "astigmatic hack" types would make "The Mercenary" look dreary and narcotic. And the new breed of film-school poseurs was as bad. Pimply auteurs with their wet streets and sultry colors, fiberglassing every frame; drowning the pilot in narcissistic gem-shades.

It was just shinier crap.

Either way, Alan figured critics kicked you in the balls and no one watched. He knew it needed more.

But knowing all that and being able to explain why he'd thought to direct were different. The words felt like foreign places; ideas you needed shots to get to. Yet something was pushing him to demand his chance behind the camera.

To everyone's surprise, when Andy heard Alan wouldn't stay with the show unless he directed the pilot, he agreed. He viewed the work Hector finished, felt all the underwater footage was usable, and that some of the wide shots of the red-light bar could be cut into a new sequence between Barek and Garris.

He also felt Alan should get a single credit, in order to keep Hector's suicide a nontainting presence on the pilot. The press would eat it up if they got hold of the whole blood-soaked mess. He told Alan he'd pull some strings with Hector's attorney who owed Andy "favors."

"What kind of favors?" Alan had asked and Andy's dimples darkened.

"And don't worry. Hector messed with every film he ever directed. It just caught up with him." Andy played with the words, deluded into thinking he'd coined a new idea. "Or . . . maybe he caught up with him."

Alan thanked him and wondered aloud why Hector had committed suicide in such a horrible, public way.

Andy thought it over. Yawned a little and nibbled on fresh, office popcorn. "Well," he said, loving to speculate on the maca-bre, "if you know his work, Hector never could stage a scene without going over the top. Good news is public will eat this up. Whole perverse aura about the show now. Can't buy P.R. this strong. Guess Hector finally did us a favor."

And then he had to take a call from Judd Hirsch.

Alan hung up and closed his eyes, not able to forget the look on Hector's face when the gun garaged in his mouth. The second or two before he fired, he'd looked right at Alan. At that exact moment, Alan had instantly seen Hector's wounding of Bloom as coming from rage, and the wounding of Bo Bixby from a simple desire to protect himself. But firing a bullet into his own brain . . .

The way Hector had looked at Alan as he squeezed the trigger for the final time . . . something about it was very weird.

Like it hadn't been his idea.

p . o . v .

Alan watched orchestrated explosions below, match-heading on Mexican jungle.

As he peered through the camera lens, the fictive Viet Nam burned prebudgeted, perfectly arranged annihilation and palm trees went up like bombs. Smoke ballooned into sky, and rented choppers dropped movie napalm as Alan had his director of photography zoom in, slowly, on flaming huts and frightened oxen.

He stared down at earth, aflame, day-scale villagers scattering and screaming, his helicopter vista craning higher. Then, he gestured for the pilot to swoop lower and yelled into his own walkie-talkie, telling his assistant director, on the ground, to tell the extras what to do.

As they did exactly what he said, delayed in their response time by mere seconds, Alan was aware of becoming calm. He was in the helicopter, photographing A. E. Barek's P.O.V. shots of jungle assault and strangely, all memories and sensations of mortal limit were gone.

Lifted.

He felt peace; transcendance. Putting together a life for Barek calmed him. Getting the authentic contours just right. The textured history. Experiences. Scarred emotions; triumphs and traumas. Details of a life that didn't even exist. Yet, as he filmed, committing it all to emulsion, he realized it was almost no different from the real thing.

Except for genuine danger, lurking near, everything at this moment looked and felt identical. The shame and glory were living things. Though he was on location, just south of Puerto Vallarta, and the whole cast and crew were staying at a beachfront Hilton, he felt he was in a helicopter, over Viet Nam, on a search-and-destroy, the enemy burning and screaming below.

The physical and visual sensations of it all were so close to being real, he was beginning to understand what directors were talking about; setting the vision. Sculpting reality. Getting lost in the dream.

Control.

A. E. Barek's highly specific, imaginary world was everywhere Alan looked and he smiled to himself, unprepared for the impact it was having on him.

It was like he'd created life.

act two

ten weeks later

reviews

LOS ANGELES TIMES

Folks, bear with me here. This will be slightly more than my usual review and a bit less than Kant's *Critique of Pure Reason*.

I'll try not to sound like my head is about to explode off my neck, but I'll be honest with you, I can't hold in lava this hot any longer. They pay me to be objective but beyond a certain point, and today I'm there, a thermometer couldn't be objective.

Basic truth, so let's get it out of the way: TV ain't Bach. Never was. I'll swear on my two-year-old-daughter's healthy future, it never will be. It's just rock and roll, I guess, one way or the other. Just a glow-riff.

Our adored morphine-boxes are the only tubes we have in our homes that squeeze us, and indeed recent findings, according to a 13-year study, are that the more you watch TV, the worse you feel. It sort of cremates your reason for wanting to go on, you know? Am I getting through or has your head turned into a test pattern with hair? I can relate. I just keep sinking deeper into my Barcalounger, praying my goddamn Sony will blow up and be taken away while I still have an original thought left it hasn't hawked a major lugie on.

Want to feel your piles swell? Try this one on:

The study found identifiable relationships between changes in a viewer's mood and the number of hours they spend watching. It further discovered that the longer a person watched the hell-square the more drowsy, bored, sad, lonely, and hostile the viewer would become.

Bottom line, Faustkateers? How about something like it can be argued using TV habitually is no worse than or, importantly, no better than habitually using alcohol or other mood-altering substances. And they didn't even factor in the newest obscenity to roar into the currents of American viewing. We won't even mention the network, but suffice to say it is three simple little letters. Emphasis on simple.

I'm talking about "The Mercenary," kids.

Have you seen this one?

Forget the "A-Team." It was Othello.

Scratch "Hunter." "Hunter" was *My Left Foot*.

This new, recently debuting series is quite literally the worst thing I have ever seen, been degraded by, had to review, or felt depressed and horrified by in my entire career as a critic and/or human being, depending on your opinion of my actual lineage.

I wish I could just say it's more bad, stun-gun television and leave it at that. I wish I could just say it is the most horrible thing I have ever witnessed and then politely call a cab and get out of your hair. But it ain't Christmas, I don't owe anybody powerful enough to fire me a favor and my parents raised me to call 'em like I see 'em. Especially when what I'm calling doesn't just elicit contempt but actually drops about fifty pounds of nausea into your gut and leaves you writhing.

Creator Alan White can only be thankful he didn't grow up in Salem or he would currently be speaking to us while tied to a very firm stake, going up in flames. How this man, who has been involved in other, classier projects over the years and who I once favorably reviewed prior to what can only be viewed as a complete nervous breakdown, could attach his name to this inhumane, sadistic horror is beyond me.

This isn't just embarrassing. This is the death of taste in America. This is organized, professionally broadcast hatred, ugliness and simple-minded thinking at its most base and unimaginative.

Did I say unimaginative?

Maybe I'm being too hard on "The Mercenary."

They have managed to figure out immensely clever, if not painfully obvious, ways to show women in states of undress and/or to splash blood on almost every square inch of this unendurable hour of sensationalistic sewage.

But I speak before I think. Let us reevaluate. This isn't sewage. It's different. Sewage is going somewhere.

If this series is allowed to continue, I question how decent values can remain undrowned by the blood and vicious poison Alan White and his "breakthrough" series are dispensing like so much tampered Kool-Aid.

I'm gonna try and kill this one, dear readers. Because if I don't, the next series that will follow on the wastrel coat tails of this one will be the end of civilized life. And you gotta draw the line somewhere.

Consider this a line, Mr. White.

HOUSTON DAILY PILOT

While I admit to a certain shame in admitting it, the latest action/ adventure offering to hit the air, Alan White's "The Mercenary," is a guilty pleasure.

There's no denying its self-conscious efforts to resemble the tough violence and sexuality of its bigger brother feature films, which have been doing this kind of thing for a decade. There's no denying the harsh ferocity either. It's there. You can't miss it, even if you're in the other room, outside, or even down the block visiting friends.

This one is so overwhelming in production values and genuine power, you can probably hear it when you're watching a whole other channel.

The lead, played by Jake Corea, is so disturbingly alienated and savage in the role of A. E. Barek, a nearly sociopathic soldier of fortune, we only scantly suspect his pathos when he stares at the ceiling of his little hotel room, in the dingy gloom of Black's Hotel, and flashes back to when he had some semblance of a life. A wife. A child. Now long gone. He is a deserted island, floating in a sea of despairing emptiness. He helps others, when hired, and as his defenders say, "does the job. Whatever the cost."

But this isn't Stallone puppet opera.

There's something more here. Genuine angst. A darkness and intelligence that seeps between the extraordinary violence and shocking carnality.

This is blood and nudity like it's never been seen on television. There is little in the way of compromise or discretion. It all hangs out and it feels real.

And that's what I'm responding to.

A frankness and a candid potency.

Make no mistake, "The Mercenary" is a jolting, almost inconceiveably tough step for series television. But like the best drama and the most memorable tales of history, this one has substance under all the flesh and explosions. There seems to be true suffering here. We can only assume Mr. White has known this world. These feelings. This sort of suffering. To his credit, he allows it to resonate and keep us fascinated at the same time.

This one is going to redefine controversy, I suspect. But it's the kind of controversy I welcome.

SEATTLE TRIBUNE

Beyond any level of crap the English language can accommodate. It extinguishes everything worth living for and celebrates pain. I enjoyed the commercials.

FT. WORTH OBSERVER

Indefensible drivel. Don't bother. Tune it out. Turn it off. Unplug the set and get a life.

NEW YORK POST

This one is impossible to categorize.

There's so much wrong and evil about it, it's hard to simply dismiss. The networks are obviously so disoriented and frightened by the loss of their audience to cable, they've reached the stage of absolute vertigo. This series should never have been allowed where children might happen upon it.

Had it remained a feature film or a made-for-cable project, perhaps it could be discussed on its own terms. But it is so wrongly positioned, available on network television, whoever's watching the store is now willing to sell anything. However coarse. However debasing. However meticulous in its cruelty. Heaven forbid it does well.

They should all be arrested for allowing this one. And by the way, where's the FCC in all this? This is not just bad TV, it's bad kharma. For god's sake, don't let your children see it. The world is terrible enough as is. We don't need more converts.

FAIRBANKS WATCHER

Hey, maybe I'm a moron but I love this thing.

It moves like a damn rocket. There's babes wearing barely enough to floss with and pretty darn accurate sexual activity. I mean, what more could you ask for, other than some beer that isn't imported and a good signal.

Don't miss it. History is getting made here. And it's a lot more fun than the boring stuff they made us study in high school.

NEW HAVEN DAILY

Has America lost it's mind?

What next? Snuff movies? The "Dr. Mengele Variety Hour"? I thought you had to watch the news to see the terrible things going on out there.

Well, now you have a second choice.

Every Tuesday at ten o'clock. It's called "The Mercenary" and it is beyond pitiful. It tries to pawn off a concept with so much mileage on it they should just pull it over and tow it away. But I wish I could report it as just one more hackneyed act of desperation on the part of the network.

It's too mean-spirited for that. It's violent, gratuitously ridden with nudity and nearly explicit sexuality and the whole effort has a seedy, money-grubbing, sordid smell about it. I think the networks have finally lost it. They're losing their audience and it's making them all bend over a toilet to come up with new ideas.

So, here's the latest in a batch of vile junk whose single distinction is that it easily surpasses previous seasons of vile junk to the tune of a thousand.

How the FCC can go along with this is the biggest mystery.

If you like pornography, hang in there. They probably have something up their grimy sleeve for midseason replacements.

God bless America.

SARASOTA JOURNAL

Finally something on TV we can sink our teeth into.

The newest effort at a mix of reality TV and out-and-out entertainment is a doozy that won't leave you asking for much except some bottled oxygen. This one will take your breath away.

From the moment its throbbing titles begin, to the way the violence and bloodshed cannonade in peyote colors and angry camera angles, the whole show simply overpowers the senses. While there is admittedly much nudity and perhaps the argument could be made that it is an audience lure, it never feels wrong, false, or kite-tailed.

Also it should be emphasized that not all the bodies shown are beautiful or perfect. Amid a fair share of Coppertone figures are hunched and crippled villagers, torn by shrapnel, clothing burned to reveal full frontal nudity. But anyone who finds this prurient or vaguely sexual is the one with the problem, not the series.

I particularly admire the way creator and executive producer

Alan White has woven in character eccentricity and a showman's eye for wonderful scenes, commingling vulnerability of heart, with frayed and wounded spirits, against fiercely funny people.

This may not be as good as it gets. But it's getting there.

Mr. White, I predict you are going to be a very rich man once this thing catches on. It's simply wonderful.

Five stars.

CHICAGO TIMES

Forget your antacids and aspirins, somebody is going to have to hit you with a tranquilizer dart to get you through this one. Pretty bleak going here, America. Maybe there's a rerun of "Three's Company." If so, do yourself a favor and see how John Ritter's crotch is faring.

overnights

The Don Ho sun shone over the sleepy bay and everywhere you looked somebody was going into a coma.

"You may as well spread pâté on me and throw me to the damn sharks . . . I'm dying here. I have no pulse. Go ahead, feel. Afraid to aren't you?"

Erica lanced Alan with a loving smile and he sighed, looking into burning sky. He was coming out of his skin.

"Hey, how do you think it's gonna do? But really . . . no bull-shit." His lids were shut, and he watched single cells canoe across his eyeballs. For a fleeting second, he could see Hector's mind dripping down the screen; angry red wax.

Erica's sunglasses lifted, meaningfully. "It's gonna be bigger than God, himself. Bigger than God's furniture. All right? Will you stop?"

Alan looked between his toes and watched green-blue water spreading like Italian ice over the black sand. It frothed and sizzled, then backed away, trailing itsy-bitsy bubbles. Miles off, Molokai stood, knee-deep in sparkling water; a post-leprous Eden.

Maui was hot and breezy. Palms swayed like slow dancers and sailboats paced, rainbow cheeks billowing, yelping maniacs hanging off the side at self-destructive angles.

At the sand's edge, the Sheraton had a trio gargling Hawaiian ballads, skin like damp Cadbury bars. As the brochures swore, with ukelele adjectives, it was wall-to-wall perfection.

Alan moaned, sounding food-poisoned.

"God, I hate this fucking place."

"You always say 'fucking' a lot when you're tense, dear." She calmly rubbed Coppertone on his face, as if preparing a death mask. He peeked up at her knowing she was right for him. Smart. Pretty. Quick. No pressure to marry. No pressure to get too close; put her before his work. No pressure to love or be loved. The fully accommodating, stimulating dead end.

Last time he asked, anyway.

"It's the fucking pits."

"Honey, we're in Hawaii. Hawaii is not the fucking pits. Hollywood is the fucking pits. If you'll recall, that's why we came."

"To escape its purgatorial nature?" The trauma of Hector was a lodged bullet fragment.

"Correct. Now relax." She always sounded too much like a lawyer, even though she was. And when she smiled, the gums were a bit too evident. But she made him laugh. After the last thirty days, it was penicillin.

He sighed through a nervous stomach, wishing he hadn't eaten the Continental breakfast. "Y'know, I never used to say things like 'fucking.' Show business has made me a cheap person." He shifted. "I think my spine is melting. Is that possible? From the stress? I mean . . . seriously."

She turned onto her stomach, as if on an invisible rotisserie. Her back was creviced in puffy red and white where the towel had crinkled and softly carved her. Alan watched the indentations fade away, semifascinated, actually counting the seconds it took, hoping it would extract the hatchet splitting his head.

"I keep thinking maybe there's something I forgot to do. Some detail. A piece of business in a scene I should've covered better. Performances. Dialogue I should've punched up a little. More inserts. I don't know. I didn't have much time to step into the directing . . . maybe I fucked it up. Maybe I should've handed the reins to somebody else. Damn . . ."

He was rambling.

Erica listened, took his hand. "How about a drink? Something that'll take your mind off waiting to hear." She meant the overnight ratings but didn't say it, to avoid upsetting him.

Alan checked his watch. "God, someone should've called me with the numbers by now. Marty, Jordan, Andy, Crosby, Stills, Nash . . . somebody." He drummed fingers in sand. ". . . Jordan is probably out robbing twenty-four-hour markets with his Crips to release tension. Shit."

She was looking at him, waiting.

"Okay, okay . . . I'll take a drink. I'm actually thirsty. My entire system has dried up from stress. Tell you what . . . see what they have in an arsenic. You know, something with a cute little parasol so I can shade my nose as I slip away . . ."

She looked at him, square-on. A glint of amusement.

He looked at her, deadpan. "It's a pressure being festive."

She kissed his fingertips, strolled off toward the outdoor cabana bar that rose from the beach like a big, square palm tree. Alan watched her go and got a little harder as she hitched up her bikini bottoms, tossing permed, blond hair. She disappeared into the crowd like some Daryl Hannah mirage.

Cute, he thought. Unless you cared.

Ask those three ex-husbands. Casualties, all. *Some*thing pissed them off. But it was subtle; nearly invisible. She was one of those great women you always hear some other guy landed. Charming, self-effacing, beautiful. She had good taste in nearly everything including witty asides, astute silences, and expressions of empathy.

But beyond the three perfectly punched holes that bound her, Alan found her essentially selfish. She showered him with adoration and happy mischief, but it seemed suspiciously like a means to measure herself; keep track of how she was doing.

After a couple of months around her, Alan realized her jokes weren't intrinsically for others' benefit. They were to remind herself how amusing she was. Her praise and support assured her how giving she was. Her kindness was evidence of wisdom. Even her orgasms were movie-perfect; humid, Kabuki storms that made a man feel he was the best.

It was her proof she was.

Alan figured it was that basic behavioral distortion that her three former husbands detected, somewhere in their confused reaction.

Though they could never point to anything she'd ever done that didn't qualify as loving, it all felt somehow specious. And it enraged them, and they went out and bought guns, or froze into bugshit stares, or came to find Dianetics fascinating.

Alan looked around at the sea of prone bodies who wore sunglasses and nursed drinks that resembled primary paints with straws. He realized Maui was assembly-line relaxation at maxi-tweak when you stayed at these chain places. Sort of like McDonald's; over fifty million tanned and blitzed. He sneezed as some furry, Quarter-Pounder in trunks walked by in the sand, singing "Muskrat Love" in a Greek accent.

Alan sat crossed-legged and stared out at the ocean, watching surfers hook waves, wondering how "The Mercenary" had done. The other two networks and FOX had thrown their best against it and with the volcanic reviews he was getting, if he'd been creamed it wouldn't shock him. The show had tons going against it. Exploding flesh. Explicit suffering. Alan as a first-time director. And whatever negative press had leaked about Hector's currently missing head wasn't going to help. The overall violence and nudity were a harrowing cerviche that might rivet the whole world. Then again, the world might pop in an Eddie Murphy cassette.

Weirder shit had happened.

Look at the "A-Team." Nobody believed that one. It just took off and kept going to number one, nearly every country in the world. No one could've called it. Rumor was even NBC hated it, when they first saw the pilot. Thought Mr. T looked like a moody toilet brush. And it was their idea. None of it made any sense. You just hoped it took off for you.

Alan scratched a small scab off his knee and watched it bleed. Dug his feet in the sand, leaning back, trying to relax; take his mind off the show. The fuzzy swelter was pressing tighter and he began to sweat; drift.

He shut his eyes more tightly, getting that vein-trance as the fainting waves crashed wet hypnosis. He felt himself walking into a spinning, entreating time tunnel as hang gliders turned radiant circles, far overhead; sunbirds.

College . . .

It's where everything had fallen apart. Or collected into an acceptable puddle. All those aspirations to do something serious and make what his fraternity brothers called a "dent." The problem with making dents was that they could be pounded out, Alan had always told them. And they had always laughed and called him a caustic bastard who was destined for big success. Caustic in college meant success in life. That was the cosmic algebra. But no one predicted he'd choose writing. Despite his high grades and amusing, running commentaries about everything.

It had caught him off-guard, most of all.

He'd always been aware of his own unique intellect, the way you experience your body weight, as another person picks you up off the ground, and struggles, having to replace you on earth; exhausted. That was how having a twelve-cylinder head always felt to Alan. You could sense people around you sprinting to keep up. To maintain balance. To hold on.

And when Alan had combined his mind with creative fantasizing like some Technicolor logician's braid, there was no stopping him. He'd discovered that whatever he believed, he generally made happen. His imagination was like Federal Express. When he saw it on the brain screen it got there. Any weather, any distance. He'd always been able to concentrate. Obsess. Visualize. It was his gift. He'd been told a million times it would make him rich.

But writing had come late. And as rather a surprise.

In college, he'd submitted film reviews to the campus paper and stirred livid opinion. He courted it; created it. Knew what would piss the readers off. In a similar, yet reverse fashion, he'd bullshitted term papers at the last second through his ability to know what the profs wanted. What would affirm their tweedy myopia. It was the overall secret to his mind. He sensed need. Sensed how ideas, correctly dressed, could mollify and soothe. How truth could outrage. Sensed exactly the right subtext that would make people feel, exactly the right verbal pratfall that would make them laugh. Exactly the dissonant view that would make their heads burn.

Yet he'd never considered writing as a career; not even once.

When he and Laurie had made it that first night in Cabin C at that ditzy motel in Ithaca, during his sophomore year, he thought he knew exactly what he wanted. And it sure wasn't being a writer. Alan remembered the two of them making love with frantic explorations, drinking tepid cans of Coke from the machine and talking plans; dreams.

They were nineteen and it had all seemed somehow profound, like Columbus spotting land.

"I think teaching's the way I'm figuring to go," he could remember himself saying to her dumbly as she lay against him, face to his chest, snuggling into the protective cove of hair.

"You'd make a wonderful teacher," she'd whispered with sweet hesitation; in love. "But all those first-year girls would kill to get you, so I think it's a lousy idea."

And then, she'd laughed and tickled him and he could remember the damp warmth of the sheets and the incredible female odor of her. The dewy thickness which crept down his nostrils and settled in the base of his penis. Then, reviewing their hopes, she told him Kierkegaard had said "each of us is an exception."

Then, the snow began, covering up Ithaca.

He remembered getting out of the squeaking bed, naked, shivering. With feet numb on cold wooden floor, he walked to the window, parted the drapes, and stared out, breath staining glass.

The green neon sign that read PINE GROVE MOTEL had partially broken and now blinked its inaccuracy over the snow-crusted driveway: PINE ROVE MOTEL. Alan stared at that, then, farther below, Lake Cayuga, pewter-gloomy, somehow stunning. The pines all around the motel were burdened with snow and their boughs glistened like clumps of sequins. Ithaca was still asleep, cocooned under haunting blue dawn; a Christmas card.

Alan had turned to glance at Laurie, who said softly, "I love you. I'll always love you." She had thoughtlessly allowed the covers to fall and expose her college-girl body, its perfect contours and colors.

Alan smiled. Looked. Shivered more.

"Laurie, it says Roving Pines out there. That means the pines are . . . moving." The voice had been like Nicholson in *The Shining* when his neurons started bubbling. Or at least Alan remembered it that way. "Shhhh, I think I hear one moving. It's saying someone's name. A . . . woman's name . . ."

Laurie had widened almond eyes, playing along perfectly, gasping, tugging at the covers, gathering them beneath her chin, fearfully. Alan remembered stepping ominously closer, saying the pines wanted to eat Laurie; he could hear them saying so outside the window. She'd shuddered properly at the low-voiced premonitions of their dread hunger. And Alan had stalked closer, finally pouncing into bed and gnawing on her arm like some voracious tree. He'd gotten so into it he'd accidentally drawn blood.

Laurie screamed and Alan remembered a small blood-red goatee he'd rushed to the mirror to see. He apologized, kissing her arm to make it better, and they ended up making love. But it had always disturbed him how far he took the joke. How it had gotten quietly out of control.

He turned on the hot sand, sighing. Staring sideways at people walking, sticking out of the earth at a ninety-degree angle.

It was funny in life how you grew out of things. That place in Ithaca would just look like a bad Bates Motel in a slushed-out college town to him now. And Laurie would probably look like Jack Lord.

But a million, trillion years ago, he had felt like a prince sleeping beside a beautiful princess in a palace of ice; eternal, poetic.

But everything melts eventually, thought Alan, smelling coconut lotion somewhere nearby. And like Andy Singer had said, everything gets cancelled. And everything goes into syndication. That was simply the primal order. Alan figured God liked it that way or he would've put everybody on VHS.

"Alan, there's a call for you!"

Erica was carrying a drink in each hand, crunching over sand with a big smile.

Alan jumped up. "What were the numbers?" He looked half-crazed.

"They didn't say. But he wants you to call right away." She handed him a shivering Chi-Chi, kneeled in the sand; a willowy sphinx.

"Marty? Jordan?"

"Neither. Feiffer's office."

Alan's mouth opened a little. His voice rose, words slow, "No shit . . . ?"

Waves broke in the background and breezes skated the midget dunes stealing his towel. But Alan was a million miles away, already jogging toward the bar.

"Yeah, Alan White returning his call."

He was fingering a palmful of coins as the secretary vanished from the line for a moment. As he fidgeted, a nut-brown brunette with huge breasts and a tiny bikini leaned onto the bartop and ordered drinks. She was no more than five feet away from Alan, who stood at the giant-shell payphone, dusting Maui off his feet. She hummed and swayed, breasts moving under the macramé top. Then, she pulled her long hair from her face and looked over at him with amazing eyes.

"Hi," she smiled again and walked away, escorting twin Mai Tais. She looked back once and Alan watched her walk toward the blowtorch sun; a final shot from a bad "Magnum." Suddenly, Feiffer was on the line.

"Alan! How the hell's the tan coming?" He was loud, aggressive, and friendly. He had also destroyed or cinched the careers of at least six people Alan knew personally. Guys who ran networks could do that. They were like Nero with hundred-dollar haircuts.

Alan had heard from Jordan how Feiffer had sent one ex-wife into such a deep depression with his abusive personality, she'd committed herself after two suicide attempts and ultimately did succeed in wasting herself with a Gillette necklace. Feiffer had "kindly" footed the bill for the funeral. But the macabre scoop was he'd charged the ex-wife's new husband on the installment plan for the burial. The guy had been creamed by her death as it was and Feiffer finished him off by having his accountant call the man and cherry bomb his soul.

And it was no cheap funeral, guys. Fifty grand minus the folding chairs. Gold casket. Best plot in the place with a partial view of the Universal Stunt Tour on a clear day. Expensive twenty-piece orchestra playing a Gucci dirge. The gathering after was held at the Palm Restaurant and lobsters from Bangor were shrieking all afternoon.

Feiffer hadn't loved her; he loathed her whiny, finger-paint intellect, even though no other thinking woman would tolerate him. But he still couldn't stand the idea of another man touching her. Or having touched her.

But as usual he got his revenge.

The devastated new husband, who lovingly nursed Feiffer's ex through a full-frontal coke solo, had only married her two months before. They'd met at Betty Ford's Ping-Pong palace in the Springs and were trying to get her clean together. The guy had been her attendant and trying hard to make a career in medicine. The only thing holding him back was money to pay his tuition. He'd saved for years and was close to getting his start in med school. But for loving the ex-wife of Feiffer he was stuck and had to abandon all plans. And Feiffer, word had it, had hugged the guy at the service after she was in the ground. Hugged him and shared a manly tear.

That was the kind of guy Feiffer took pleasure in being. A toxic calculating prick.

He scared Alan and Alan tried not to show it.

"Well, hope you hate paradise 'cause I'm sending our jet over to kidnap you. We got ourselves a big, fat forty-seven share last night, my friend."

Alan was silent. It felt like a month passed. Then, clicking into automatic, he said it straight-faced: "That all?"

Feiffer rumbled a bear laugh.

"So . . . what's next?" Alan was in a state of shock. Jesus, fucking Christ! He'd passed his celestial law boards. Beat the intergalactic ticket in court. Awakened in the morning to find Kim Basinger next to him, moaning, using his body as a tongue depressor. All three oranges were lining up in the window spelling: *You Are Here.* He could see it all coming. Everything he'd ever wanted. Boats; Italian cars. Helping the hungry. Buying the hungry Italian cars.

He was shaking.

"What's next, is start thinking about a second season and warm up your laser printer. We're also discussing a possible feature release in foreign for the pilot." Feiffer went on run-silent, run-deep for a few seconds. "Be at my Newport Beach house at nine, day after tomorrow. That okay? No, better, let's meet at the Polo Lounge. Breakfast."

"Looking forward to it, Mr. Feiffer."

"Jack. Please. We're partners. Let's get to know each other better, huh?"

Alan said that sounded great, fearing it.

"Have a great flight. We're going to have one hell of a year."

They hung up and Alan noticed the girl with the hotel-room-key stare, strolling back again. She smiled at him and he did the same. But coming up behind her was a tall, Nordic, teste totem pole in cutoffs. The Viking swooped her waist with hairy arms and they scampered off, laughing, looking for Valhalla.

Alan went back to the beach and told Erica and she pounded on him with excitement as if trying to save a drowning man. Alan could only shake his head, unbelieving; stunned.

Drowning.

They celebrated by playing in monster waves; looking like drunk salmon trying to get home. Alan heard the Sheraton guy walking down the beach, carrying a remote phone, yelling his name.

He jogged up to the guy and took the remote phone like some primitive would've taken a coconut shell thousands of years ago to receive a call.

"Yeah?" He was hoping it was Jordan telling him he'd begun the numerical calculations to determine how many millions Alan would ultimately be worth. And how he was worthy of all this. Or his father calling from Palm Springs telling him how proud he was.

Maybe Hector, conceding Alan's talent from his headless ash pile. Or maybe even Laurie from Ithaca swearing she'd always loved him and knew he'd be famous.

But it was Corea.

It was hard to hear him. Alan was sure it was the tropic breezes flowing into the mouthpiece. Or the crashing surf. But it was neither.

"Alan . . . I just got word from your agent." The voice was a hoarse whisper.

Alan was amazed at how quickly news traveled in Hollywood. The speed of light would've gotten lapped if it tried to survive in L.A.

"Can you believe it?" answered Alan.

There was no answer.

Just the sound of three thousand miles sitting in his ear.

"I said, isn't it amazing?!" Alan was almost shouting.

The voice was slow, as if sick; weak.

"Alan . . . thank you for creating me."

"Hey, thank you for doing such a great job, man . . ." He didn't like the way Corea sounded. Was he drunk? Overwrought? Something was really wrong but Alan didn't know how to bring it up. "You okay?"

Again, silence. Nothing. Maybe the sound of breathing. Maybe just Alan's imagination.

". . . thank you for creating me. Thank you for creating me." And then he said, "You won't be sorry."

Alan felt his stomach tighten. Erica was waving to him from the meringue surf and Corea kept thanking him for creating him. Saying he wouldn't be sorry. Thanking him for creating him. Telling him he wouldn't be sorry. Thanking him for . . .

Alan suddenly saw Mimi in his mind, holding his hand, warning him. As he waved back to Erica and tried to look happy, he felt his smile losing life, going rigid.

Around him, hang gliders landed like the flying monkeys, in Wizard of Oz, coming to take Dorothy away and Corea's voice got more faint.

go-ahead

What Hollywood is all about is transformation. People in this town love the whole concept. In less sophisticated places in the world, transformation is called magic." Feiffer shrugged. "Way I see it, transformation is the more understandable version. Sound like bullshit?"

It was just after eight and the Polo Lounge was filling with agents and studio and network executives who met for breakfast at perfectly set tables. To pull strings, cut strings; wrap them around throats.

At lesser tables, rising producers took pitches from writers who'd driven Jap cars in from the valley, obsessing all the way over Coldwater. Every few tables, lives were bankrupting and hearts clogging as croissants withered and box office performances the previous weekend were examined like colon X-rays.

"We are simply and ultimately, aboriginals who use designer tools and swing on slicker vines."

"Very interesting, Jack." Alan felt a yawn tunneling out, still half asleep.

"I was a philosophy major."

"Uh-huh."

Feiffer was carefully sectioning his grapefruit; a calibrated violence. Alan kept thinking about how the man had ruined people's lives. Stripped them of dignity and meaning and called it a productive day. Yet here he sat, like Will fucking Durant, discoursing and scooping fruit. A sociopath, figured Alan, as Feiffer bit into a piece of toast, breaking its back, sweeping vertebral remains off the table, with a palm edge.

"Films are about transformation. Let me illustrate."

Alan tried to concentrate; shed the pajama head.

Feiffer drew on the tablecloth with a fingertip.

"An idea becomes a concept which in turn becomes a script which in turn becomes a film. A character's arc within a dramatic structure is nothing more than a description of the form of transformation. The curve of the change, if you will."

"So, it's the . . . form the magic took?" Alan was barely awake, mostly lost.

Feiffer's jaw worked, thinking that one over, his beard moving as thoughts and food were crushed in his powerful mouth.

"Yes."

"And in a way," Alan was getting into it, starting to wake up, "deals are the ushers who bring us in to behold the incantation. To witness the miracle?" Total bullshit.

Feiffer nodded. "To enable us to believe."

The two continued to eat and Alan began to wonder if Feiffer had been misconstrued; guillotined and mythologized. He seemed to have a need to talk. To extend. There was a seismic charm about him. Like Idi Amin with a liberal arts degree.

Feiffer took a fast call the waiter brought. Listened. Said yes, once. No, five times. Hung up. Had the phone removed like a slain animal. Resumed his thoughts.

"Of course, the business has gotten such a bad name." Feiffer sipped coffee.

"So much has changed since I started. Now it's all about these damn Siamese-twin profits. The studios get together with the big agencies and make one bomb after another. And the stars are their plutonium." He gestured, discreetly. "Look around this room: Tong Wars at every table. Programming emperors and agency mikados breaking bread. So desperate."

He nodded to various tables; the chic gloom of the dining room. Bleeding bodies lurked behind sunny smiles. Several of the majors had cooked their war chests on action blockbusters targeted for summer and found they had an hour and a half of dick, with a soundtrack that might spurt one top-ten cut.

Garbage movies, with ten-million-dollar box office, in full release, put everybody except the competition in a bad mood. It brought out the worst in people when major players in town were losing money. Nobody wanted to take chances when the box-office flu hit.

Feiffer smiled and Alan wondered what was really on his mind. This breakfast was starting to feel like a complex version of the dancing bears from Russia; all show and distraction. The man was too busy and too important to be sitting here giving book reports.

" 'Course things have become so punitive . . . so Sicilian. Your film or show does badly, you become one of the walking dead. Nothing happens to you anymore." He nodded at the roomful of voltage bullys. "No one calls except friends who call your machine, calculating exactly when you'll be out, to say hi . . . the conversational equivalent of leaving black roses on your grave."

Alan glanced up. Feiffer was looking right at him; into him.

"But they never actually call when you're in, for fear of making actual contact and resuming a relationship with a plague statistic." He smiled, emptily. "You want sentimentality, go to a Manilow concert. You smell flowers, look around for a coffin."

Alan finally got it.

Why Feiffer was sitting here. Why he'd brought his troubling inventory of deductions and inverted meanings. Why he wasn't talking about the show. Why he was so determined to make Alan feel the blood supply had been endangered and the horizon was crooked.

It was one more warning.

He knew that if the show didn't continue to do well, he would be shaken off the Etch-A-Sketch; a momentary life-form. And if the press and public crucified it, Alan would take the heat.

But it was actually worse than that.

"We do need to talk about one thing . . . just the network looking out for all of us. We're going ahead with this series, full order. But with one conditional thing. Minor technicality. If FCC doesn't appreciate what we're doing and takes this into any kind of litigation—which it won't, I can promise you—we can't indemnify you. It could become prohibitive. Any problem with that?"

Alan thought it over. They both agreed things would never come to that and if they did, Alan would be rich anyway and they laughed, pretending it was a darkly hip subject. Alan agreed to it and Feiffer said he'd have his legal people draw up papers and for Alan's people to take a look.

But without the agreement, Feiffer emphasized the show couldn't go forward with Alan as executive producer. Not given the controversial nature of what they were about to do. Alan nodded, sipping French roast.

"Good," said Feiffer. "We'll be fine. I wanted to bring it up with you myself, not let some lawyer scare you. They're all a tribe of fucking 'sue-warriors.' " He grinned and it made him look ominous. "Besides, FCC has better things to do than make an enemy of me."

He touched Alan's arm, trying to make it feel like they were friends. "Anyway, I always get ponderous and boring in the morning. We're here to talk about what a genius you are and how you're going to save the network."

No, we're not, thought Alan. That's not why we're here. We're here for you to deliver a death threat.

inspiration

It was four A.M. when Alan first heard the Mercenary's voice.

He'd been writing the fourth episode and dozed off after describing a sequence in which Barek was in Saigon, in bed with a twenty-year-old Cambodian dancer. As written, the camera would see her breasts and pubic hair and hear her screaming orgasm as they fucked. Her climaxing face and clawing nails would be quickly intercut with the bloodied, screaming face of the Laotian pimp she worked for as Barek beat him to death in a savage fist fight. Back and forth it would go, between orgasm and death. Agony and delirium.

It wasn't "McGyver."

"Alan. Wake-up!" It was Barek, frantically whispering.

Alan's eyes slowly opened and he could hear Malibu crashing, Bart snoring. He listened. Heard Barek, again. But not in the house. In his mind. Talking to him, as if from ten feet away.

"You *have* to stay awake. You have work to do. I know you think you're dreaming this. I know you think you made me up. But I *fucking* exist. I was in the Army in 'Nam. I had a cover in the CIA. Alan . . . I want this show to succeed."

His brain was bullshitting him and he ignored it, closing eyes, again.

Barek's voice shook him awake.

"Alan! *Don't* fall asleep! I've got ideas to help this script! You have to stay awake and listen to me! You have to stay awake and keep writing, *goddamnit!* Make more coffee! And do what I fucking tell you!"

Alan finally put on sweatpants and a T-shirt and stumbled to the kitchen. Began to grind beans. His eyes widened at deafening caffeine-munch. He yawned, slicked hair back with palms wetted under kitchen faucet. Smiled, amazed by the creative process. He'd had conversations before, in his dreams, with characters from various series he'd written for. Now and then, they'd spoken. Weird little chats with the subconscious that made the scripts feel like they were writing themselves weren't uncommon.

But this time, the main character of his dream was claiming to exist. Claiming to have the exact background he'd given it, in the pilot. And this time, he'd created the show himself. He wasn't just writing somebody else's creative vision.

Something he'd created had awakened him and was telling him exactly what it wanted him to write. It was telling him exactly how the Mercenary should blind an opponent with gouging knuckles; move for move, in vicious, colorized detail. And though he was half convinced he was asleep, dreaming the whole thing, when he awoke in the morning, the fourth script was done.

sympathetic
character

~~~~~~~~~~~~~~~~~~~~~ I loved Eddy. I know everyone here did.''

Alan looked down at notes; couldn't keep his mind straight without them. The pain would rush in, start to rise. Erica and Alan's father, Burt, were sitting together with Jordan, several network Scuds, and an immaculately dressed Andy Singer who'd cancelled a workout with his private trainer to make it.

When Jordan spotted Andy climbing out of the network limo, sad little face creped perfectly, buffed nails catching the gloomy sky, he told Alan that Andy was there to network. And to show Alan he cared, even though, Jordan assured him, he didn't.

Eddy seemed asleep.

Over in the buffed mahogany box Alan had bought, hands folded, skin fluffed by the mortuary. Alan sensed Eddy was listening to every word. Probably checking for grammatical imprecisions.

For Alan, it all felt disturbingly like his mother's funeral. He could remember it so well, though it was a lifetime ago. He could

~~~~~~

close his eyes and still see a sunny day shrouded by bowed heads; confused children. A ceremony of abandonment.

"He gave me my start as a writer. He took time to care."

He'd loved one of Eddy's old CBS action series, written a spec script while still at Cornell and mailed it to Eddy's production offices in Hollywood, instantly regretting the boldness. But to his stunned reaction, Eddy's assistant had passed it on and Eddy had detected an arresting voice somewhere in the amateur soup of plot and dialogue. He wrote back to Alan with a systematic autopsy of the work, told him he had some talent, and encouraged him to try again. It was all Alan needed.

He began to write constantly, sending one script after another to Eddy, out in California.

After two years and the completion of his twentieth spec, Eddy told him it was time to consider coming out to the citrus bedlam and giving it a try for real. He'd even offered to let Alan stay in his guest house in Bel Air until he got on his feet. Alan had been floored by the generosity and ended up working on one of Eddy's later ABC series "Rogues."

He came to adore Eddy and the bottomless top hat of his mind. He was a scarred and difficult man who immobilized others with napalm moods; jarring candor. But working with Eddy got people Emmys as much as colitis, and Alan always saw past the exacting armor. Maybe it was because Eddy was a bit like Alan's own father, Burt. Maybe it was because Eddy was like Alan himself. A version that said what it thought, rather than finding the right fabric to cover it.

". . . when I first met him, to tell you the truth, he scared the living hell out of me."

Sweet smiles. Hands taking hands.

"He was . . . intimidating. Tall, strong." Alan was looking at Eddy, speaking directly to him. The body was frail, like a dead child's.

". . . when he looked at you, he saw what was inside . . . who you were."

A poignant still.

"When I met him, I was new to writing and insecure. I don't think I was ready to be looked at."

"After a few thousand bad scripts, I . . . finally felt like I earned it. Eddy looking me in the eye . . . it's one of my proudest possessions."

A wind came up and the weeping crowd looked up at trembling leaves; soft castanets. As if Eddy whispered greeting. Everyone seemed to feel it.

Alan looked at swaying treetops. The wind was blowing harder; moaning. Squirrels scrambled up trunks and across limbs, scared. On the many folding chairs, black clothing fluttered; sad sails. Faces seemed unnerved by the incoming storm and bodies huddled closer. Drops of rain fell. Alan grinned a little, held palms up.

"Bet you anything this was his idea. He hated funerals."

A bit of laughter; human music. It sounded happy and alive, roving past inscribed stone; indexed death.

"You know, the truth is, I wouldn't have become a writer if I'd never met Eddy. Whatever talent I have, I have because he showed me what to do . . ."

He looked over at the body, as raindrops began to run down Eddy's face like tears. He seemed for a moment, truly alive; understanding all these friends and family had come to say goodbye. To wish him a safe journey. To let him know how much they loved him.

Alan looked at the sky, the leaking clouds.

"I love you, Ed . . . wherever you are, keep them in line till we get there."

Alan wiped tears, stepped down, and joined the line of bereaved who waited to walk by the damp coffin and bid farewell. Several spoke to him and said how they'd liked what he said. He didn't hear them say how thin they thought he looked. How exhausted. Someone said they'd heard he'd been nervous and overworked. Another said he was sick. No one really questioned it.

Andy Singer left directly after the eulogy.

"He was a genius . . ." was all Andy could manage, before floating away in the limo, to get to a lunch with Howie Mandel.

Eddy's widow was at the casket, talking to Eddy, and Alan waited. She and Alan had spent many days and nights together in the last year, in Eddy's room at Cedars, listening to priceless hours close weak eyes; never wake again.

Sometimes, after they'd both read to Eddy and he'd finally drifted off, she'd sweetly thank Alan again for taking care of everything. When there was no money, no more insurance. Only sorrow and doubt.

"It was a beautiful eulogy," she said to Alan, after kissing Eddy's cheek and being led to a waiting car. Alan loved her and worried what the months ahead would bring. She was so old, so dedicated to Eddy. So lost and childlike without him. Alan swore to himself he'd see to everything she needed.

He was next in line.

He leaned over the rain-spotted casket and stared numbly at the shiny skin and the reddish lips that tried to mimic blood; life. The hair was dyed, immaculately parted. He looked young; rewound twenty years by the ironing and glazes.

Rain fell and Alan wiped Eddy's face with a hankerchief. The skin felt hard and artificial and Alan soaked up the rain drops that gathered beneath Eddy's eyes.

"I love you . . . ," he whispered.

And as the others waited, Alan began to scream.

He grabbed strickenly onto the casket's open edge and it teetered, rocking Eddy. It fell under Alan's weight and Eddy's body dropped out, white suit soaking in mud. Alan went pale and as mortuary workers replaced the body in its casket, he kept swearing the corpse had spoken to him; that the eyes had opened and Eddy had looked right at him. Alan was helped away by his father, Erica and Jordan.

The mortuary explained rain had loosened the epoxy, causing the eyes to open. But no one could explain the voice Alan said he'd heard. Most just said he was so overcome by the loss, he'd imagined the whole thing.

Wishing and hoping. Missing his mentor.

That night, as Alan tried to sleep, listening to restless tide stirring like adrenal fluid, he could still hear Eddy's voice. The lifeless rasp, the little grin of dead teeth staring up at him from his satin bed. Amused and warning, breath full of preserving chemicals.

"You went too far," he had said. Then, he told Alan to make it stop. Exactly what the old man at the hospital had said when Alan had visited Eddy.

Word for word.

close-up

Alan leaned on Erica and wept.

His life flashed, like a precognitive REM warning; a keyhole glimpse of a lifeless form slumped somewhere in his thoughts. A sense nothing good could come from new days. Only tragedy, despair; as if hearing one's body bleeding deep within, where it's black and life seeps away without witness.

The limo did a plush crawl through Forest Lawn and Erica stroked his head.

"I know . . ." she whispered.

It was an unexpected bridging and he held her more tightly, at home in her arms, the heat of her skin.

"I haven't cried . . . since my mom."

Her soft hands touched his face, covered his eyes. She pulled him to her blouse, unbuttoned the front. Cradled his head against her breasts.

"Eddy loved you. He'll always love you," she whispered and Alan clung to her more, as the long car was swallowed in rain.

ten percent

Alan? Jordan. What're you doing?"

"I just had lunch delivered and I'm writing. What do you want, Jordan? In midthought here."

"Just take a second. Wanna run something by you. If it's not for you, no problem."

Alan made a go-ahead sound and chewed salad he'd had brought from Granita, up the road, across from the Malibu Colony. The sky looked like it was coming down with something. He needed a script to put into preproduction in two days and had nothing. The three freelancers who'd delivered needed heavy rewrites and Marty was going nuts. Lauren was trying to keep him out of her hair and Alan knew the only answer was to just stay home, away from all the phones and blast one out. It fixed everything.

"Look, the agency just signed one of those 'Pimp and Tearduct' couples who do a cable Bible show and—"

"Jordan, could you hurry this up."

Jordan started talking faster.

146

"Okay, well ... cut to the chase ... they're pulling in like a hundred million a year in blue-hair phone calls and just finished building a theme park based on Noah's ark, called Love Land."

"Uh-huh ... and?"

"Much bigger than Jim and Tammy but same basic coo-beg vibe. Theme park confiscates your life savings in exchange for salvation and some water rides."

"So ... what's the question?"

"HBO wants to develop a vehicle for them and they'd love to meet with you on your take."

"My take? Jordan, I don't have a take. If they want a vehicle, how 'bout just running them over with a fucking tank?" He was biting into a scampi that sat like a big, dead, pink comma on his plate.

"Totally agree. So, it's a pass?"

"Jordan ..."

"We could get you a very favorable back-end definition. My thought was, you could write something like this in your sleep."

"I don't have time to sleep."

"What page you on?"

"I don't know ... one?"

"Good trend. Talk later. Everything else is okay? I hear Corea is being impossible on the set."

Corea was blowjobbing on stardom and trying to fuck every woman who worked on the set, including guest stars. He was asking more and more for multiple takes on every shot to "refine his performance" and bitched about scripts, demanding rewrites. America loved him. Alan couldn't stand him. The show couldn't operate smoothly with ego problems. It was becoming a major headache.

"Fucker wants pussy and an Emmy ... what else is new?" Jordan upshifted. "Everything else is good?"

Before Alan could answer, Jordan suddenly sounded like he

was at gunpoint. "Alan, can we pick it up later, I got Arnold on four . . . I'll get back."

There was a dial tone. Alan stared at the phone. It was glaring at him. He took it off the hook, stared out at sky that looked like dead skin and started thinking about page two.

flashback

A voice; graveyard leaves.

"Alan . . . ?"

Faraway.

"Where are you . . . ?"

"QE II. Middle of the Atlantic. Fitting, don't you think?" No answer. "It's very wet outside this boat. Must be an ocean or something, do you suppose?" Words slurring. "Didn't think I'd find you home on New Year's. Don't you have anything to celebrate?"

"It runs in the family."

She began to describe the weather. The water. The sky. Nothing; a gallows of words, despair. "Interesting don't you think, sweetheart?"

"What's that, Mom . . . ?" He was keeping his voice down. Bouquets of fireworks rose in sky. Boarding school students laughed; Heineken zoo voices. His roommate snowballed the window, a soft grenade.

"Nothing. I lost my thought." A new entry code. "So . . . how's everything? Are you dating? How's school, how's your writing, grades, health, am I prying?"

He smiled. Bowed his head, unhappily. "I'm fine."

The ship-to-shore hissed; a closed garage filling with car exhaust.

"Must be late, Mom. You should get some sleep."

"Didn't I tell you? I've given it up. I don't like the waking-up part . . ."

". . . too many unexpected twists?"

She made a sound of happy agreement and he could see her staring into black sea. Her world in eclipse.

"Big boat?" Conversation.

"Titanic."

They both chuckled a bit and he fought an album of child's images. Closed eyes to forget, but couldn't. He watched himself going into his parents' room, when he was seven. Hopping up onto the bed with his mother. Listening to snow strike glass together. Watching Cary Grant movies on TV, loving his mannered perfection. Eating M&M's. Hours had raced; faded. Until the marriage went bad. Until hours got long and black, when days died, one after another.

"I met a very insipid man at dinner. Some kind of intellectual, according to him." A bleeding silence. "We strolled the deck and he explained the genesis of shuffleboard."

"Sounds riveting."

"He should have gone into riveting."

He could see her struggling cheer; the upturned discipline of it.

"Heard from your father?"

It was a trap. "Mom . . . did you take this trip alone?"

"What are you saying? Are you afraid I'm going to do myself in?" The amusement was ceremonial; propped-up. "Just because I'm feeling . . . a bit at sea." A swallow. "I think that was a good one. Was that a good one?" He told her it was and she told him to remember that distraught states were a part of the family DAN.

"DNA."

Her voice posed; a coy lean. "Of course, DNA. What was I thinking?"

"I don't know. What were you thinking?" He became serious. Trying to find her behind the chatty foliage. He hated when she drank. But she was so sick; it had to be irresistible.

"I was thinking that . . . I miss you. And that I love you." It was soft; needful.

His stomach tightened.

"Remember when we used to ice-skate together on New Year's Day, Mom? Central Park?" She said nothing. Was she remembering? He kept talking. Thought he heard ice scrape glass. "I used to love that. When I'd start to fall, you'd always make sure I didn't." He thought if he kept talking, he could stay ahead of the feeling. He wanted to cry; couldn't. "I can't think of anything to say, Mom . . . isn't that odd?"

Students were singing "Auld Lang Syne" outside and Alan remembered a Christmas in Maui when he had walked with his mother along a beach, arm in arm, singing it. Tipsy with possibilities; seeing hope everywhere. It all came back to him; New Year's Eves. Good ones. Ones that felt awful; wrong. Nights when bad things crept over a ridge, like death clouds and suddenly everyone was running, afraid of the downpour.

"Is that what's happening to me? I'm falling?"

"No." He saw her spinning backwards, mouth out-stretched, hands reaching; a Hitchcock effect.

"You won't let me will you? Won't let me fall overboard, get left behind? It's cold and black way out here."

The hollow dexterity was gone. She was just a place with no light or warmth. He wanted to die. He wanted to hold her.

"I'm sorry you aren't having a good time. I wish we were together. I love you, Mom . . ."

Their voices were touching, reaching over land and sea; a séance.

"... do you?"

He spent the next few minutes trying to convince her he did and when she began to almost believe it, the connection quietly, horribly cut off.

three months later

talk show

It has become a national phenomenon. The highest rated television series in the history of the medium. On average, eighty percent of the viewing audience tunes in to see it every week. We're talking, of course, about 'The Mercenary' and, let's face it, it's changed the way we think about primetime television. Huge movements are developing. Some pro. Others con."

The voice excited and seduced.

"Fans love the character and admire the way he violently stands up for what he believes. Critics say he's a psychotic sadist and by airing such 'reactionary garbage,' the network is contributing to the desensitizing of our culture. *Time* magazine, last week said, ' "The Mercenary" has further caused the manhole covers of repressed American anger to tremble and frustrated temper glands are overflowing. The show is a kind of reverse intellectual nutrient and is sending a bloody and disturbing message to America's youth.' "

Music cue.

Close-up on the announcer, an intense ectomorph. He stares the camera down, unflinching.

"Today on the 'Robb Overton Show,' we have the man who's brought this explosive controversy into our lives, Alan White, creator and executive producer of 'The Mercenary'! Also with us today is Professor Madeline Marx from the University of Southern California School of Graduate Psychology. Dr. Marx specializes in violence in our culture."

Applause. Camera sweeping audience.

"Joining in the discussion today is nationally syndicated critic Richard Frank of the *L.A. Times*, an outspoken critic of the one-hour show which he is trying to have banned and which he's called 'vicious poison.' Today, we'll be discussing 'The Mercenary,' violence, and whether the show is influencing our society to kill and hate, or if it is merely entertainment. We'll also be taking questions from the home viewers as well as from those live with us here today on location in beautiful Century City in Los Angeles. Stay with us. Robb's just around the corner!"

Alan glanced at the critic and the professor and knew he had it in the fucking bag.

Madeline Marx had an inky crewcut, and dressed like an angry man. She resembled Iggy Pop, minus the dermabrasion, and her tanning treatments obviously weren't taking right.

Richard Frank, meanwhile, struggled with a beard problem. Alan noticed Dick continuously sniffed at his peppery mustache as he sat and stewed in his superiority, and picked at icky eczema.

Alan figured Overton's audience would respond to some well-timed humor, a little philosophy to soothe their guilty viewing habits, and one or two show-biz anecdotes with some inside grime about the famous and revered.

The crewcut and the critic with the tic would regret showing up today. They were outclassed, outmoded. They'd look foolish, pompous, and stiff.

This would be fun.

Even the host would be easy. In the Green Room, as they'd all introduced themselves, Overton just smiled and generally exuded and Alan knew he would ask only what his staff had prepared. The man's teeth glowed as if he had a mouthful of light bulbs and his hair was so perfect it needed a car cover.

His plagiarized style was to wander the audience, a dim-witted Donahue clone, who always appeared semi-lost and did his best to artificially stir up the audience by talking softly, then suddenly yelling.

He was also able to cry on cue and often ended shows or made points by soaking up the phony tears with Kleenex and staring into the camera, cheeks ashimmer with calculated wetness.

But Alan had been told the guy used to do weather back in Baltimore and could barely figure out how to schedule oil changes for his Lexus.

The makeup androgyn came over to the stage and touched the three guests up, with heavy Pepto-Bismol crap that made you look like you were getting fitted for a box.

"Nervous?" Alan asked the bronzed professor, who was adjusting her windsor knot.

"No." She looked right through him.

Alan shifted in his chair and the director gave a cue. They were coming out of the commercial. The chubby announcer with the fearless stare grabbed the microphone and pitched his guts out, pointing centerstage with a porky finger.

"Ladies and gentlemen, Robb Overton!"

Robb trotted out and did a couple of minutes of dumb warm-up. His hair was a NASA craft, his nipples saggy. And the rumor was his romantic companion in life was a ten-year-old Cub Scout named Bobby.

Mostly what Alan noticed about him was that Robb clapped his hands together a lot to stimulate excitement and seemed to be giving birth with every thought.

"So Alan . . . how do you plead?" Robb was grinning and the audience laughed, chuckling good-naturedly.

"I guess . . . amused," said Alan.

Robb raised a brow.

"I'm a writer. I'm sort of like a court jester who traded his curved shoes in for a word processor. I'm not trying to tear down anything. Unless you count the work I'm having done on my kitchen."

"I'm afraid that answer is as glib as your morality."

It was the woman in the man's suit.

"In fact, you may be blueprinting bloodshed. Since your show has debuted, the incidence of armed assault has gone up three percent in this country."

"Only three?" answered Alan. "With the economy the way it is, that seems fairly encouraging. Does anybody want to talk about how we do the stunts?"

Richard Frank sniffed his beard. Robb sipped at coffee, nodding, listening carefully.

"Richard? How about a critics P.O.V.?"

Richard lowered his upper lip enough to speak.

"I think the show is an obscenity."

Alan sighed. Oh, blow it out your flabby dick, Dick . . .

"If we care about what's happening in this country, we should—"

"Cancel it?" interrupted Robb. Then, a new thought creased his vacuous face. "But isn't that—" he thought it over, "censorship?"

Robb was an eye chart, all right, thought Alan.

"Freedom of speech doesn't give me the right to cheapen life and incite violence. This show simply goes too far. I am, in fact, spearheading a group which is circulating a petition and trying to get this thing yanked off the tube. Make room for decent programming. I'm no prude. I'm a critic. But I'm also a parent and a person. Frankly, I'm deeply disturbed."

"Alan?"

"Well, he looks deeply disturbed," said Alan, making eye contract with a beautiful brunette in the front row who'd caught his eye. She was mouthing something dirty to him and her entire face looked like some kind of genital.

Professor Marx was vexed. "Our children pay attention to what we put on TV. We accept TV into our lives like an unassuming Trojan horse, coming into the home and disgorging lies."

Alan went on automatic. A cliché for a cliché.

"Parents can turn it off. They can unplug it. They can . . . sell the damn thing and buy a subscription to *Scientific American* and chain their kid to a desk if they want. Tell you what . . . if it is a piñata, don't let the kids whack it. Take their stick away. Exercise parental privilege." Alan teased her with a smile. "This is America, Professor. Try it sometime."

The professor moved uneasily in her crewcut and the audience laughed uncomfortably. Alan sensed he was losing their affection and tried to make a safer joke.

"Look, my show isn't compulsory viewing. Nobody gets detention if they miss it."

The audience was happy again.

Alan felt the tightness in the room ease and smiled. The girl in the front row seemed proud of him and subtly spread her legs, after lifting her tight skirt a little. He could see her panties and she waved with a long-nailed finger.

Richard Frank started up his pipe and Alan wondered if it made bubbles.

"Mr. White, where do you draw the line? Snuff films?"

"Well, I never liked snuff. It hurts your nostrils," said Alan. The audience was right with him, disliking Frank's arrogant, cement head.

"I think Richard is serious, Alan," said Robb, now up on his feet and drifting through the audience like a lost talk show host, wishing he had a desk like the big guys. "Where *do* you draw the line?"

Alan thought he ought to get a little serious. The snuff joke was really a conversation killer. But come on, what did this fucking critic want? A legitimate conversation or a snotty debate.

"Like I said, I'm a writer. Do I try to be creepy, kooky, mysterious, and spooky? Sure." Even Richard Frank was somewhat amused but he crammed his pipe in deeper to cork it. "I mean, I think . . ."

Everyone was watching Alan. The big camera pushed in for a close-up.

"I think that . . ."

Faces and expressions pressed in tighter. Robb looked terrified of dead air time.

"I think that . . . blood is pain in liquid form. I think maybe we're flesh robots and blood frightens us because it's a reminder we run on fuel. It reminds us that there's a community inside the body we can't control. Uprisings. Anarchy. Maybe cancer is even a sort of . . . cellular mutiny."

"What's your point?" asked Richard Frank.

Alan stared at him. Said nothing for a moment.

"That maybe . . . we are afraid of blood because it's a sign from inside that we're vincible. I mean, as long as we're talking seriously."

Robb was getting excited.

"Like a wet scream?" he added.

Alan shrugged. Go away, Robb.

"We're not talking about blood," said Madeline Marx, leaning forward, nose pores squeezing makeup. "We're talking about violence. We're talking about how exposure to violence infects the minds of those it touches."

Alan took a drink of water.

"Are we?" he asked. "I thought we were talking about what interests people. I can't be held accountable for that. I can only be accountable for myself and. . . ."

He stopped in midthought.

The audience was watching him. He couldn't make a joke. It didn't feel right. He was in his head. His thoughts. In a place that felt sharp and dangerous.

". . . and I don't know . . . maybe when I write, I'm in a kind of lightless place. Primitive people do a rain dance, don't they? Maybe when I write, I'm doing a light dance." He was speaking quietly; truthfully. "Maybe I'm just trying to get some light."

Richard Frank cleared his throat. Puffed his pipe.

"So, buy a lamp," he said.

The audience loved it and at that second, though Alan smiled, he hated him. Hated his smug face and his supercilious eye contact. Hated his stale thoughts and his ugly little gnawed fingers and the way he never created anything in his life that was original. How he simply walked through other people's art galleries with his fucking scissors.

It wasn't the joke. The joke was easy and Alan might have made it too if the setup were reversed.

What he despised, was the way Richard Frank sat there and made fucking, imperious pronouncements, sniffing for something to criticize like a bloodhound. Guys like Richard Frank were a dime a dozen and it offended Alan how this smug little fuck was trying to hurt his series.

"And has it occurred to you, that maybe you write this grotesque horror to get revenge? Pay back all those people who hurt you, betrayed you?" Madeline Marx was looking right at him.

"No," said Alan, masking his thoughts.

He thought for a moment. Returned to Richard Frank's incendiary claptrap. "Anyway, I don't think art can be considered instructive. If it is, then we better start looking at the religious art in all the museums of the world. The violence there is as brutal as anything I'm doing on my show. It's just my images move."

The professor stared at him.

"And your audience is made up, worldwide, of maybe a billion people. A billion people don't look at a painting."

Alan just looked at her, still felt loathing for Richard Frank. He decided to save the moment, instead of telling her she was a homely bore and needed to get laid decent for one hour in her life instead of spending her whole life bitching and looking like Robert Culp.

"Look," said Alan, glaring at Richard Frank, "there's a lot of ritualistic killing going on all over the country, right now due to gangs on drugs, and satanism and skinheads and lunkheads and who the hell knows what else. Things are a mess, everywhere you look. S and Ls are going under like they swallowed too many depth charges. Angst is everywhere. Did the show do it?"

He stared at the audience.

"Was it me who did it?"

And the director cued them into a commercial.

preemption

. . . Y eah?" Asleep. Two-thirteen A.M. Bart beside him, chasing dream cats.

"Alan?"

Alan falling back asleep.

"You don't know me. I saw you on that talk show today. You were funny."

". . . who are you? What do you want?" Listening to surf ice sand. Bart groan.

"My name is Seth. You seemed upset on the show. Is everything all right?"

"Seth?" Searching blank thought. Stopping at a dim scribble. "You wrote the book that psychic gave me. *Mind Potentials.*" Slurred exhaustion. "Bizarre shit . . ."

Seth laughed a little. Voice faraway. Where the hell was he calling from?

"Alan, if you ever need me . . ."

". . . what are you talking about?"

"I can't tell you yet. You'll know."

He told Alan to finish the book. That would be the perfect time for them to meet. Told him to have a good sleep. Then, he hung up.

perks

The Harley did a subwoofer prowl down Sunset. Corea had been stopped for no helmet but the cop let it go; took an autograph.

Nobodys in cars. Headlights flashbulbing his face. Voices yelling his name; following, quickly lost. Doomed leeches. He'd been in another argument with his acting coach tonight. Fuck it . . . didn't need classes. He <u>was</u> Barek. Always was; forever. Let the nobodys, in their glossed monotony, go nowhere; perfect the dead contents.

The coach was bullshit.

When Corea got pissed and pushed him down and kicked him, the coach didn't even seem believable. Just stared up with clichéd hurt, all his fucking vacu-form nobodys circling the fallen idol. Corea spit on him, told him how much he made, how the guy made nothing. How many people watched him, how nobody watched this fucking loser.

A town full of them.

He passed the motel he'd stayed in. It never happened. Nobodys stayed there. Scavengers; dead ends. Fucking sewage.

He roared up next to the Roxy, let his face change the world. Leather, in legs and nipples, turned; *Vogue* ghouls. He wanted to know who had drugs. He left with the redhead. Spent the night fucking, beating her up. When he woke, at noon, he took a piss, noticed the towels were bloodstained. Didn't remember why, didn't give a shit. Rinsed his face, saw she'd lipsticked her phone number on the mirror, circled in a heart.

Nobodys.

He stared at himself, in the mirror; his chapel. Posed his face, moved in close, stared into his eyes. Grinned. Made a call, had a fourteen-year-old fan sucking him half an hour later.

hero's fear

Heat and waves.

Doors open, Alan on his bed, half-asleep, in a sweater of humidity. Past midnight as he listens to sea gently wearing down the world. He feels swamp breezes as they blow in, bounce off walls and surfaces, bend around corners; wandering. Touching things. Blowing on them to see what they'll do.

Something loud falls and Alan sits up. Stares into a sleeping mind. Hears waves. Wind fingering chimes. His heart pounds. Something else falls. He hears footsteps, moving through the house. He stands, moves slowly to see what's happening.

He won't use the flashlight: it makes him a target. He stays low, in darkness. Stops before crossing in front of a living-room closet door. Listens. Waits. Is it in there? Hiding? Waiting with its huge butcher knife, to kill him. To jump out. Or grab his ankles, through banister bars, as he goes downstairs to check.

But there's nothing.

The house is calm. Warm winds blow and the blacks and whites of the lightless rooms are soft, charcoal sketches. He looks around, sighs, disgusted with himself. His fucking "imagination." He wishes he could get rid of it.

He can't function this way, not knowing if it's his imagination or his ability to see what others can't.

Voices at funerals. Screams of the dead; nightmare radio.

He needs to know.

He walks to the spot on the wooden floor where the couple had been killed and looks at it. He wants to feel it, disappear into it. He moves into the ragged circumference. Where the bodies had been nailed down in a helpless pentagram.

He closes his eyes, stands straight, trying to see the murder. He concentrates as hard as he can and waits. To sense something. But nothing comes. He thinks maybe he should create intimacy with the subject he seeks. He strips naked, throwing his clothes outside the horrific perimeter. Then, he closes his eyes, again.

His mind keeps trying to see something; anything. He shakes from the muscle tension and finally sags, furious at himself. He feels exhausted. Stupid. He allows his mind to drift. To twist slowly. His thoughts go blank, in a disturbing meditation. The surf pounds; a dirge.

He sees himself standing at the top of a high black cliff. Looking into a bottomless canyon, filled with something vast that moves and squirms. As he stares, all at once he realizes it is numberless human bodies, some dead, others writhing; a chasm of helpless, naked flesh.

He feels his arms move upward, stretch wide. He gently dives over the edge, keeping eyes open. As he is about to penetrate the surface of bodies, who reach up to pull him under, he hears it.

A humming blade.

Then, a woman's scream. Then, a man's. Alan opens his eyes. Realizes he's moved from inside the nail-hole perimeter. He watches, horrified, as a man and woman, nailed to the floor, naked, are being tortured. They seem to float in pools of blood and their heads toss from side to side, in agony.

Alan covers his eyes and screams for the image to go away. But it doesn't. It won't. It only fades, staying half-substance, like a movie projected on smoke. The image undulates. The mouths pour hideous noises.

"God, no!" Alan screams, as the woman is slashed again by the murderer, who crouches over the couple with his humming knife.

". . . no, please!" she shrieks, ". . . somebody please help us! Please help me! PLEASE!!"

Alan turns his head away, shaking, not wanting to look. He clears his mind, trying to make the ghastly after images disappear. But when he looks again, drawn by a grotesque gurgling sound, the murderer is cutting their larynxes. Their eyes bob and they breathe with terrible effort. Blood rapids down their throats and torsos.

"STOP IT!" Alan yells. He moves to the murderer, yells it again. But the man is freckled with blood and doesn't hear. Alan realizes it's because it's something that's already happened. Something expired; years old. There is nothing he can do. It is a chilling, time-space loop, doomed to repeat endlessly.

It will just keep replaying. It is stuck here. What happened will stay forever. A helpless couple nailed to the floor, being murdered, only Alan can see.

He becomes sick to his stomach, can't watch. Screams, again, as the couple's faces contort, eyes pleading.

"STOP IT!" his hands cover his ears. He is screaming, though he knows it is absurd; pointless. The tape-loop will stop when it is finished. Then, start anew.

But something is wrong.

The murderer looks up from his red-work and stares into Alan's eyes. He rises to a standing position. Smiles a torturer's mouth. He holds up the humming knife, covered with bits of flesh. The couple is screaming, but with cut larynxes make no sound. They don't notice Alan or the murderer who starts after him, knife held high.

Alan runs to the staircase, slipping on wood floor. As he turns to go down the stairs, he feels the humming blade slice his hand and looks up to see the murderer grinning.

Alan tries to open the front door, one flight down. It won't budge. Finally, it yanks wide and there is a brick wall blocking his escape. Blood weeps instead of wet mortar. He pounds against the rough brick, tears his hands. Runs down the stairs, into the bathroom. Slams the door, locks it. Waits. Sees himself in the mirror, terrified, skin white. His hand is *bleeding. He runs water on it. As he wraps it in a towel, the door is kicked down.*

The murderer holds up the humming blade. Alan's insides twist. He knows he's going insane; mind attacking him. There's no way he can be chased by a man executed years ago. He's become hysterical and run and cut his hand somehow. There is no one with him. The couple is dead, the murderer is dead. It's a dream.

Alan stands. Shakes. Tells the murderer to go away. Screams it. Over and over. The man, covered with the couple's blood, grins. He grabs Alan, by the hair, slits his throat and shoves his face into the toilet. Alan is held under the cool water, and begins to breathe in, through slashed throat, not wanting to live; trying to kill himself. Knowing he can't. Knowing it's a dark hallucination. A sick re-creation his subconscious tricks him with. He takes deep breaths. Pink water fills his lungs.

He blacks out.

Alan awakened, at nine-forty, the next morning.

He covered his eyes, managed to get to his knees. Could see the top half of his head in the mirror, as he rose. Eyes puffy and red, hair a mess.

He stumbled upstairs, found the banister covered with nicks, the living room sofa slashed apart. He went to the front door, opened it, finding a beautiful day. He stared at bees and flowers, slowly sat, cross-legged and began to cry; exhausted. Afraid.

That night, he had a quiet dinner by himself at McDonald's and bought a thick throwrug at a big mall. He brought the rug home and quickly tossed it down, using it to cover the spot where the slaughter had happened. To hold a pillow over its face.

Suffocate the memory, in the floor.

villain nears

Alan, he's doing it again." It was Lauren. She had Marty on hold. "And guess who'd love to talk to you? Bye-eeee . . ."

Alan took the call. Marty was hoarse from yelling. "He's killing us down here."

"What's he doing now?"

"Been in his dressing room all morning. Won't come out unless we change the whole script. Wants a new director, new co-star, new guest stars, new composer, new makeup . . . I'm barely kidding . . . do you want to hear this?"

Alan sighed. "I'll come over. Where are you guys?"

"San Pedro. We're set up in the hull of a freighter."

"You're still in San Pedro?!" Alan picked up the shooting schedule. Four scenes were boarded to be shot today. Five setups each. To get the coverage would fill the day until eight, even with a fast crew. And he had the fastest around.

"Marty, you guys should be at the bridge by now."

"Corea won't budge."

"Called his agent?"

"Agent is behind it, Alan. He wants to renegotiate. He's holding us up . . . I'm positive. I can feel it. He denies it. But it's bullshit."

They were both thinking the same thing. Alan finally said it.

"We can't re-cast. It'll kill us. People love this guy."

"I don't," said Marty, exhausted.

"Okay. I'll be down. Don't even bother talking to him. I'll handle it. Just cool out. See you in about half an hour. I'll get a helicopter."

Alan clicked off, buzzed Lauren.

"I want you to check into Corea's background for me. See if you can find anything that'll make it easier to deal with him."

"Like someone who knows him?"

"Yeah. Maybe. I don't know. Whatever. His Mom. Dad. Cult leader. We need some clue how to get along with him. Get him to act reasonable."

"I'll start with his wife."

"Start with his wife." He knew he sounded tense.

"Big problems?"

"Yeah. Listen, I need a helicopter."

Alan crumpled a Coke can. His whole morning was ruined. His production schedule was useless, a day lost.

Goddamn, *fucking* actors . . .

transition two

zzzxxxx . . . Li. .t
Breeth . . xxzzz
. . . strogrrr xxxxxxxxx
. . . mt. suun. snn. sun
alve . . .
. . . here
mt. mtmtmtmtmtmt
slp. slep-sleep. gt stroger
ʌʌʌʌʌʌʌʌʌ . . . e
m . . . e

feedback

The Long Beach Formula One Charity Race was one of those televised testicle-rodeos aired to raise money for children without heads. But it was really just another excuse for a bunch of celebs to drive fast and prove they weren't fags.

Teeth you'd seen on top-ten shows leaned over open hoods, in driving suits, staring at massive engines, sycophant crews at hand. They were unshaven and made banter conspicuously absent of wit, now that they were without scripted lines. Tight skirts were everywhere scoping famous dick; trolling.

Jordan talked Alan into going, saying the "Seinfeld" people were going to be there and wanted to "meet him." Alan didn't believe a word, but figured driving in a race would be a good excuse to get away from the show for a day; change longitude. Feiffer agreed to sponsor a car for the show, and Alan drove down from Malibu before dawn to do test laps for a nine A.M. flag.

At eight forty-five, he walked across the bustling track, a roped-off section of Long Beach road. Stealth photographers who whored to the *Enquirer* or *US* cruised with scammed passes and snapped Alan as he joked with the crowd that camped out all night to get a good spot. He grabbed a doughnut, walked to his car, and welcomed the "Entertainment Tonight" mannequins who swarmed his car, right after they'd interviewed Lorenzo Lamas, who'd glared and mumbled midway into another divorce.

As Alan climbed in, E.T. fired questions and laughed at his clever answers about how he wasn't nervous in the slightest. Engines were tuned, three-foot-wide tires tightened. Exhaust fumes wreathed everything, Woody Harrelson kidded around with Harry Hamlin and flashbulbs morgued their dimples.

No one noticed the woman.

She was in her early forties, dressed in a pink sweater and moved past busy crews. She seemed undistracted by the head-bleed engines and hectic crowds and didn't look at anyone. She carried a big cup of coffee and moved directly to Alan, though no one in his crew knew who she was. She looked into his eyes, without expression.

"Are you Alan White?"

He nodded, putting on leather gloves, smiling for Mary Hart.

"You created 'The Mercenary'?"

He nodded and the "Entertainment Tonight" cameras caught it all, moving from her face to his. It would be the perfect way to start their on-location piece. A kiss for the warrior, before sending him into fuel-injected battle. But as the camera zoomed in on her face, her features began to tremble; grow ugly.

"You *son of a bitch!*" she hissed, before throwing the hot coffee in his face, causing him to cry out in pain.

"What the hell are you doing?!" He was yelling, wriggling out of the car's kayak opening. A crew member got him a towel. Another grabbed her and she struggled.

"What's the problem, here?" asked Mary Hart.

The woman spit at Alan. Mouth stretching furiously. "He *wrote* it! What I just did . . . he *wrote* it! It was on his vulgar show and the boy next door did it to my little girl!" She was screaming. "She's in the hospital! *He wrote it!*"

Alan could feel blisters rising on his eyelids. Everything was out of focus.

"I'm going to sue you for her medical expenses you *bastard!*" She stared into Mary Hart's camera, half-insane, spit running down her chin. ". . . and I'm starting a letter-writing campaign to the sponsors who permit your *hateful* garbage to be aired!"

More network cameras were sniffing around; scoop ghouls. In seconds, everyone knew Alan was the guy who'd created "The Mercenary" and that the screaming lady's daughter had been hurt by something identical to what he'd written. They waited to see what would happen next. Alan felt like he was in a nightmare; scores of eyes watching, in beer hazes, wondering if it were true.

"You and your show are evil!" she screamed, pig eyes unblinking. "My church is going to *stop* you!"

"What's your name, ma'am?" asked a reporter from *People.*

But she just kept yelling for everyone to join her in her letter-writing campaign and for them all to help ban the show. She said she was a member of a fundamentalist church in Arizona and kept shrieking about Alan being godless. She managed to pull free of the guys holding her and ranted, out of control.

She held up a color photograph of a little girl with a burned face. Everyone wanted to see her daughter's flesh, the thick gauze that collected weeping infection.

"She's only six years old!" the woman screamed.

Alan tried to escape the glaring faces which leered, out of focus, all around him. They were disturbed by the graphic photo and some began to push him a little, drunk and stupid. His vision was smeared and he fell over something, trying to push through the choking crowd.

He was on the ground, bleeding, chin and palms cut. A Boschian jury stared down, eyes filled with question. Rising hatred. Over engine roar, Alan could hear voices yelling for Security, others for the track doctor. Cameras zoomed in on everything with stoic predation.

She twisted furiously, pulling away from people who tried to calm her. Another reporter pressed and she finally admitted she was from Tucson and her name was Linda Crain. She'd read Alan was going to be at this race and driven all night. Driven all night to make him hurt the way her daughter was hurting.

One of Alan's pit crew guys grabbed her again as she lunged for Alan and kicked him hard in the ribs. She pointed an accusing finger at him, pulled through the crowd.

"He hurts innocent children!" She was bright red. *"Alan White hurts innocent children with his show!"*

"Entertainment Tonight" broadcast the footage which included him holding his bruised ribs and her calling him a monster two days later.

station break

Pinks was one of those L.A. fester palaces built to resemble a huge hotdog. It slung in the sky, fiberglass buns and all, off Beverly; a phallocentric totem of breathtakingly bad taste.

Alan and Erica had just made out in her Honda Accord at a drive-in by LAX and sat on outdoor stools chomping chilidogs; urban wolves. The drive-in had featured a film-noir festival and 747s descending over actors faces.

"Colorization . . . end of fucking life. Those movies were perfect in black and white. Fucking Ted Turner. Why did he do that to all those films?" He pointed a chili-capped finger. "Who ever thought it was a good idea?"

"Just color, honey. Color won't kill you."

Chili sledded down his chin.

"Speaking of color," she said, "I had an orgasm, that's the key piece in this exchange, wouldn't you agree?"

She looked up at the erectile hugeness of the diner. "Is it just me, or are we eating under the shade of an immense genital?"

"Define immense."

"Over two stories."

"You haven't lived. Thought you said you'd been to Europe."
More chili in magma freefall.

A flirtatious whisper. "I like being with you."

She watched him for a reaction. No reply. Then, wordlessly, he
poured ketchup on his plate. Spelled out: DITTO in wet, red script.

She squealed in delight.

complication

The Oasis rose, fifteen stories, above the neurotic Nile of Wilshire Boulevard like a marble beanstalk. Its designer condos were filled with washed-up tales who'd saved their money, aside current darlings who wanted a class address and a roof-pool.

Some wanted anonymity. Some safety. They were all here; the distant and the dysfunctional, locked behind doormen and paranoia cameras. Performers. Real-estate smoothies. Actresses. Ex-wives of the powerful, who'd ruined their spouse's savings accounts and moved on. Gigolos and mistresses, living in gilded invisibility; perfectly maintained thoroughbreds, grooming in penthouse stalls, awaiting whatever sexual gallop expected of them.

The women were beautiful and call-girl perfect, with the edgy sensitivity of bonsai; needing just enough sun, water, and costly soil, or they would wilt and sulk. The men were sleek and bronze, living in chaise stupors until their owner got home, demanding attention.

As the night guard sat at his post in the lobby, beneath multi-security camera monitors, he didn't feel the incursion. The almost immeasurable BTU warmth; a frequency. Like what silently roars along boulevards of nerves as we sleep. The exact moment a match head does a tiny Hiroshima when scratching along its sandy runway. The movement in the lash that precedes a blink.

It went by the guard like a momentary sunburn; an unseen sensation of fever beneath his guard suit. His brow began to sweat and his stomach sledded. He opened his thermos, poured clam chowder, and tossed back two Excedrins; round, white head-warriors.

He checked back into Clive Barker's latest polonaise of suffering, looking up when the French couple from the fourteenth floor, who were in the jewelry business, exited the marbled elevator, taking their *Elle* faces out for a walk. They said hello; Truffaut dialogue.

Their matching white sweaters were amputated snowman torsos. Their shoes made costly clicks on the travertine lobby and they commented to one another that they'd felt an unsettling wave of heat enter the elevator when the doors opened. Like unscented exhaust.

But the lobby wasn't hot and the paradox intrigued them. The wave seemed a separate region, a satellite climate, roaming. Its equatorial presence eluded description yet created sensation. A wave. *Oui, un rouli,* agreed the wife, adjusting a pearcut earring. As they left the Oasis, they both felt ill, their insides cornered by some firing squad they couldn't name.

They had their 560 SEC brought up from the underground garage, tipped the valet. They began to pull out, from under an awning, to go to dinner. But as they opened the sunroof, they heard a faraway scream. They stopped and stared at one another, in confusion. It must be the people playing in the third-floor balcony pool, they said.

But it was too late.

A soft boulder had fallen fifteen stories and dropped onto the coupe, buckling the roof, turning it into a stepped-on can. A bloody face hung above the terrified couple, trapped in the crumpled sunroof opening, like some ghastly chandelier.

The man's limp features retained a frozen, macabre curiosity as he stared with bloodied eyes. Every bone in the upper half of his body had been turned to pointless dowel by the fall and his ulna had pressed through the flesh of his forearm, from the force of the drop. It protruded like a dripping beam, meant to support skin, now resembling a butcher's special.

Distant sirens began to choir and the night guard felt the heat and nausea pass over him again, as it sifted through the lobby. Then it left, moving beneath the glass door and away, past the gathered crowd. The people tried to help the well-dressed couple in the fancy car who were screaming and trapped, beautiful sweaters covered with Richard Frank's warm blood.

love interest

Alan was struck by how numbing a real police station was. He'd spent years trying to write scripts which filled the places with colorful, irreverent exchanges; unexpected moments. But the actuality was a dreary vending machine. Paperwork and tired faces. Phones ringing. Clothes from Sears. No one looked like an actor; everyone needed to lose weight, gain some, or buy a wig.

As he sat in the waiting area in Homicide, a woman with full lips and dark hair came out.

"Mr. White?" Her nametag said DET. CAMILLE JARRE. She was pretty; sensual. Her eyes were hazel, voice calm.

Alan took her hand and when they looked at each other, there were feelings of wanting to know more. A feeling that something deep, on their ocean floors, was moving; coming to life.

They went into an office and a tall husky man leaned against the wall, on the phone, gestured them in. He had a beard to hide an extra chin and didn't smile when he hung up.

"Detective Lichtman. Sit down, please."

Lichtman hitched up his pants a bit. He wore Frye boots with big heels and they looked out of place under creased, saggy slacks. A chunky, gold bracelet noosed his wrist and the buttons of his shirt strained. He wanted to talk about Richard Frank's tragic accident. But first he wanted to go back a few months and talk about what happened to Hector.

"Whatever you can remember, Mr. White. Probably no connection. Just want to be thorough."

Alan ran through it and Lichtman jotted notes. As he talked, Lichtman would look up now and then and glare. He talked more and Lichtman pressed big thumbs hard against a pen, bending it.

Camille reacted with that soothing voice. "It must have been terrible, Alan."

Not "Mr. White." "Alan." He preferred it. The personal approach felt good when you'd been called down to the big, badge hive. He looked over at Lichtman who wasn't smiling.

"He was directing the pilot for your show?" The arsenic way he said "show" . . . there was something gnawing on the guy.

"I had to finish up the work after he . . . killed himself."

"I see," said Lichtman. "Quite an ironic opportunity for you. His death."

The room fell silent. It was a fucked thing to say. Lichtman seemed to know it but wasn't interested in revising the comment. Camille caught Alan's eye and he saw she couldn't believe Lichtman was being like this.

"Suicide is a tragedy, Neil. Not an opportunity," she said.

"I didn't mean it that way," said Lichtman. "Anyway, let's talk about Richard Frank. Anything you can tell us would be helpful to our investigation."

Alan didn't like Lichtman. And it was obvious Lichtman felt the same. It had happened the minute Alan walked into the room. Maybe it just drove him crazy Alan's pants fit better than his. Or maybe he hated television. Maybe he had a faulty prostate and it made him leak nasty things. Or maybe he had a thing for Camille and saw something was happening between her and Alan.

Then again, maybe he was just a big, towering fuckhead who hated everybody who had only one chin. As Alan told them Richard Frank was a controversial guy a lot of people in television had it out for, he kept feeling that hatred from Detective Lichtman. The asphalt chunk the guy used for a personality just sat there taking notes, cold as ice.

"It's interesting his blinding came a couple weeks after one of your episodes had the same thing."

Alan just looked at him. "What are you talking about?"

"You tell me."

"You're the detective."

"You're the one who broadcast a vicious way to blind someone."

"That's absurd. He fell from a window."

"His eyes were destroyed. Maybe he jumped out of the window from the pain. He certainly couldn't see where he was going. He was blind. Or did I mention that?"

Alan's lips tightened. No one had told him. It wasn't in the papers. He was completely shocked.

"I'm not accusing you, Mr. White. I only said it was an interesting coincidence." He jotted more notes. "You're pretty sensitive for a guy who writes such tough stuff." He sipped coffee. "He reviewed your show awhile back, didn't he?" Then, a casual assault. "How'd he like it?"

Alan stared at him. "He didn't."

"Really . . ." Lichtman acted like he didn't know, nodding a little.

Fuck you, thought Alan. Fuck you and your dingy, shitty little office and your boring, shitty little job and your fucking clown pants. Fuck your ugly neck and your saggy face. And mostly, fuck you for not telling me, the minute I walked in, what really happened to Richard Frank. For ambushing me like that to get a reaction.

But he just grinned at Lichtman like it didn't bother him. Like he thought Lichtman was a trivial washer in a dull machine.

Lichtman smiled back. "Guess it's gonna be kinda hard for Mr.

Frank to do much reviewing in the future, don't you think? He won't be able to hurt any more shows."

Alan didn't answer, smiling at Camille, trying to act like he didn't care what Lichtman's problem was.

Even though he knew he had a point.

subtext three

Silence. A confession.

"There's something I didn't tell you. I didn't feel ready . . . I'm sorry . . ."

Hand on eyes.

". . . my mother committed suicide when I was fourteen. On the QE II, New Year's Eve. I was at boarding school in Virginia. We talked that night. I remember the call verbatim."

Aching "When she died it was worse than . . . after my other sister died. I'm ashamed I never mentioned her to you. She died when she was four. After being real sick. I used to wish my mother would die . . . because she was so depressed after my sister died. But I never said it to her. I was sullen . . . an angry little boy."

Terrible amusement.

"Oh, listen to this one: at my mother's funeral, one of my uncles said it's too bad I wasn't nicer to her. Like maybe I'd contributed to her using a pistol for a blow-dryer. Great, right?"

A finger raking hair off forehead, collecting it to one side.

"Just a minor little nuance in my development. Ate me up

inside. Horrible thing to say. Especially after my little sister had already died. I'm sure he was just one of those people who are unaware. The whole family was upside down. You know . . ."

Silence.

"Months went on and the house felt like lifeless soil, and I had this strange sense that . . . I felt I killed my mother. Like my repressed anger had escaped and found its way into her mind, while she laid in bed like some grieving cadaver. Crawling in through her ear. Murdering her."

A drink of water.

"I was ashamed my mother had killed herself. Everyone knew. I felt responsible. And I felt rejected. You know . . . Mommy killed herself . . . so, I wasn't valuable enough for her to stick around, that whole maze. I mean, I've read about it. I know parents who commit suicide almost never do it because of the children. I was just a kid but I came to fear anger. Mine. Anybody's. I'm so sorry I didn't tell you about my little sister. I hate talking about it. It makes me feel sick . . ."

Staring off. Reaching for Kleenex.

"I miss my mother, so much . . ."

ten percent two

~~~~~~~~~~~~~~~~~~~~~~~~ So,   Joey-the-fucking-hitman
makes an appointment through this producer we rep to meet some
development guppy at Lorimar, right? Hold on . . ."

Alan could hear him eating, getting mad at his food, squawk-
ing at his secretary. Covering the mouthpiece a little.

". . . is this angel hair? Who the fuck shaves these angels. This
isn't what I asked for . . ."

"Jordan . . . you there?"

"Alan . . . back. Anyway, the fucking hitman pitches his life
story to this tampon who's eating it up, sucking on the story. Studio
guy says—"

Alan interrupted. "Jordan . . . going into a meeting. How
about later?"

"Just take a sec. So, the studio guy says, 'Hey, Guido, I love
it. But I'll have to get back to you.' " Jordan oozed caustic glee.
"The guy doesn't get back to Guido and he shows up at his office
this morning only to find a wheelchair with a fucking note attached, okay? Says . . . 'Haven't heard from you. I thought you

~~~~~~~~

189

liked me.' " Jordan cackled. "So, now it's in development. Is that great?"

"Jordan . . . I have a meeting."

"Right. I'll make it fast. Two things. Number one: wanted you to hear it from me. Andy Singer is thinking about moving the time slot. Wants you Wednesday, ten."

"Why? So he can move his dross into our time slot? We can guinea-pig for him? Friday, ten is where the show works. He's an idiot. Fuck him."

"I know. If you'll think back, I was the one who first suggested Friday. Look, point is, it isn't about Friday. It's about Wednesday. He wants to hurt CBS. They own Wednesday."

"My show is not his personal chemical weapon. I'm gonna call him."

"No."

There was something in Jordan's voice. It wasn't fear but sounded similar. "Let the agency handle it. We represent him. We'll get him to back off."

Alan rubbed eyes; another all-nighter in the editing room working on the eleventh episode. A blizzard of red flakes fell in his head.

"Don't let him do this, Jordan. Or I'm going over to his office and personally ripping his two-inch dick off."

"One inch. Don't worry. Handled. Second thing: Tony Moore."

Moore was the hottest director of big-budget action pictures in the business. He was reputedly the skinniest man in Hollywood, had wanton self-assurance, and there was talk about him being born an actual hermaphrodite. Rumor was surgery had sewn up his socket and given him a plug.

"Wants to meet you. Major fan of the show. Has a big summer picture setup at Geffen."

"Interesting."

"Hasn't committed but he wants you to write it. His last three pictures have done over a hundred. This could get you into features exactly the right way. Very smart guy. Born with fucking 'Up's Syndrome'. . ."

"I hear he's skinny."

"What do you consider skinny?"

"Fifty pounds."

"Maybe he just has small bones."

"Maybe he just has small skin."

Jordan emitted throat noise; snide amusement. "I'll get back after we talk to Andy. Don't worry about the show, it's priority one. Don't forget, if you know you're gonna win, it isn't a game. When you leaving for New York?"

"Tonight. Be back in three days. Press junket."

"Call me when you get into the city."

The McIntellect brewed. A final concern:

"And by the way, you didn't hear that Guido story from me. Okay? I don't want this guy coming by and leaving a fucking horse head in my gym bag." His voice went up in cheery farewell. "Hey. Have fun in New York, pal. Chow mein." And he was gone.

Alan hung up, leaned back in his chair, hating Andy Singer. He tried to imagine how the self-revering little spaz would look in Tony Moore's mouth: legs dangling from Tony's dinky lips. Kicking helplessly, as the head and upper body disappeared down the skinny man's throat.

Oh, *yeah* . . .

script

EXT. VIETNAMESE POW CAMP—NIGHT

a suspended bamboo cage. Inside, a MAN crouches,
scarred by torture. Skin slick with heat; pain.
Face down, curtained by bloodied hair.

The socketed eyes peer out, filled with rage.

Dying fires smoke.

ANOTHER ANGLE—POW CAMP-MAN

he tries to sleep. Needs water. Mosquitos vam-
pire his skin. He moves, trapped by folded limbs;
cramped cage. A hideous aviary. We see the face
now: A.E. BAREK. Gaunt. Sick. Hating this place.

HIS P.O.V.—THE CAMP

Filthy. Carved from jungle. Rimmed by other cages;
fleshless faces within, waiting to die. Pigs hiss
over flame. Vietnamese GUARDS jabber. Hateful
glares; laughter.

We HEAR Barek's VOICE-OVER as CAMERA roams the purgatorial nowhere.

> BAREK (V.O.)
> (a rasp)
> . . . I won't be here for long. I'll
> get out. Kill all these motherfuckers
> . and get out. Go back to L.A. . . .

RESUME—BAREK

eyes closing. Thinking about another place. Another life. A GUARD approaches. Brings a metal cup;
water. Offers it. Pulls it away. Drinks half.
Smiles.

> GUARD
> (Vietnamese accent)
> . . . fuck you! Hey? Fuck *you*!

Barek glares. The guard laughs. Spits into the cup.
Offers it. Walks on.

CLOSE—BAREK

trying to ignore sounds of suffering all around
him. Sounds of torture; sickness. Death. A nightmare gulag. Birds high in trees, watch; scream.

> BAREK (V.O.)
> . . . I want out. I'll get out!

He suddenly grabs the wooden bars. Shakes them.
SCREAMS hatred.

> BAREK
> You hear me? I WANT THE FUCK OUT!

Play his toxic features and

SMASH-CUT TO:

break up

Alan leaned back in his seat, staring at New York. Skyline twinkled vacantly against black sky and Erica took his hand, afraid.

"How are you?" She was the one who hated takeoffs.

"Fine." Alan was an unmoving silhouette, still thinking about the phone call. The way Jordan had sounded so businesslike. The way he'd joked about some new development deal Eisner and Katzenberg were anxious to make with Alan to create the "ultimate" violent sitcom. Something about a gun and a funny guy.

Alan wasn't interested. Everybody told him working for Disney was a nightmare. Too much input. Some people hated the place so much they'd taken to calling it Mouse-schwitz.

Then, Jordan asked him if he'd heard.

"What're you talking about, Jordan?"

He told him Franky had been found in his office, O.D.'d. A post coke scatter. The paramedics faxed him to Cedars and he was in bad shape, not responding to anything.

"But he's still idling . . ." It was Jordan's comforting postscript.

Still, the Eisner news was more important. That's why it came first. Jordan always talked the important stuff first. Mister all-fucking-heart.

Erica studied Alan. "Hey . . . ?"

He looked out the little swim-mask window, unwilling to turn, staring at the glittering despair below. Erica tried to comfort him, sneaking him an extra pillow and one of those absurd, paper-thin baby blankets. Any reason to get close; to have a chance.

Alan looked at her but the look fenced her out and she felt it. Something was wrong; she was sure. It was more than Franky. More than the exhaustion of doing endless promotion in the city. It had started weeks before. Alan seemed different. He looked ill; didn't joke with her.

The flirting glances. The inside asides. Replaced by sullen quiet. When he looked at her, he didn't.

Passengers were noticing him and his fame drifted through the jet like a pheromone. The stewardess brought matchbook covers and coasters for him to sign; requests. Alan nodded; signed.

Then, he went back to his staring. Looking at nothing, trying to get some rest; to get away from the twenty-four-karat schism that had become his life.

"Have you thought about Christmas?"

Alan looked at her.

"Do you want to go away? Maybe Vail? Saint Johns?" He wasn't responding. "Maybe we just stay in L.A. Check into a sleazy motel. Bring Windex, stare up at ourselves?"

He wasn't smiling.

"Erica . . ."

She did a Marcel Marceau face of astonishment. "He *speaks*."

"I don't want to go anywhere. I don't want to make plans. Of any kind." He glanced at her. Then, away.

She flipped through the big summer *Mirabella* issue. Said nothing. "Are we breaking up?"

He didn't say no. She wanted to know why. He flashed back

into shadowed corners of his childhood, remembering how complex and scarring things had been. Oblique vistas of family dysfunction spread, then retreated. Things which felt like long-hidden secrets. Abuses. He suddenly felt angry at everyone; betrayers. Invaders.

He looked around at sleeping passengers, realized they all looked dead. He imagined himself, like A. E. Barek, in the pilot, swimming through the crashed jet, under the ocean, moving past drowned faces; corpses held by seat belts. He tried to escape the image; couldn't.

"I don't know," was all he said. "I thought we weren't going to pressure each other." He shut his eyes, trying not to see the sunken morgue in his mind. He struggled to speak. "We agreed in Hawaii." He saw Camille in his mind. The cryptic sexuality that drew him. The way Erica never had, never could.

Erica spoke softly; vulnerably.

"I want to have children with you, Alan. Start a family." A wounded secret. "I've been selfish my whole life . . . you know that. The marriages were . . . things." She took his hand. "You make me want to put us first. Not myself."

He looked at their twined fingers, wanted to get away. Close himself off. Save his energy. Protect himself and the show. Protect Barek. It was the only priority that mattered.

She took his hand, more tightly, in the dim cabin, gripping it. Knowing she was losing him. Unable to prevent it.

"Alan   I love you. I need you."

Alan just stared out the window, thinking about his latest "Mercenary" script. He pulled out his Toshiba laptop and started working on the new episode that would include a San Salvadorian nun who was crucified on the huge wooden cross of a rural church by leftist guerillas. Alan could hardly wait to write the scene.

Erica whispered, emotionally. "Goddamn you . . . how can you do this to us? I feel something. I finally *feel* something!"

He looked over at her, awash in laptop screen-glow, feeling

almost nothing as she began to weep. All he felt was something inside himself, expecting more of him. His energy, his focus. Maybe it was his own ambition.

But mostly, it was A. E. Barek.

Demanding more and more.

high concept

So, what we're thinking, is that maybe this thing can read a person's thoughts by say . . . subtle variations in heat from the, you know . . . the brain? And . . . the pulse, let's say. Not a lie detector, as such . . . think more like an actual thought reader. Okay? Able to perceive and assess cognition. Naturally, as time goes on, this thing becomes very dangerous to the company it's working in. Or maybe this thing gets recruited, let's say by law enforcement. It's even possible the judicial system begins to incorporate these things, okay?"

Alan nodded. Okay.

"But major problems are stirred up . . . we're talking a kind of Robocop, Orwellian, compromised privacy kind of world. We're talking the elimination of the individual. A paranoid culture. What was thought to be a good invention was in fact, a nightmare. A device so Fascistic and . . . and . . . and . . . inhumane, it encompasses a sense of absolute evil. Which we think could be a lot of fun as a picture."

Tony stopped his deep-voiced pitch to sip some chocolate

milk. His hands moved wildly, juggling nothing, then played with shoulder-length blond hair. His Texas accent bopped like a candy-apple pick up.

"Then, BOOM . . . *complications.* This thing goes chew-off-your-asshole nuts. So far, it's been great, been perfect, made the company lots of money, made lots of good decisions. It's the perfect executive and everybody thinks it's a human, and why wouldn't they, okay?"

Alan nodded. Okay.

"I mean, they would, the way we see it. Now imagine an innocent young junior exec brought into this company, knowing nothing and this robot can read every thought. Think Costner . . . Keaton for the young guy. We may be able to get Keifer Sutherland . . . just did another picture with him. He's very strong. We wanna make this our big summer picture, so we'll spend if we gotta spend."

He cleared his throat, narrowed bloodshot eyes.

"Anyway, this robot is like fucking HAL or something. It can read your mind by taking your—I don't know, I'm not a god-damned med student—but let's say it can read your skin temperature and when your pupils dilate if you're lying, it's right with you and it can analyze your breath while it's talking to you to see if you've been drinking, and it can analyze your voice to see if you're lying, and your urine to see what drugs you're using, so it can mess with you . . . on and on."

Another sip of chocolate milk. Now smoking, talking faster.

"So, this robot executive gets friendly with the new guy and they have lunch and all this shit, okay? But just when the guy isn't expecting it, BOOM, he gets fucked up the ass. This thing is out to get him. His marriage. His health . . ."

Snapping fingers. Nodding. Grinning.

"It fucks him over. Breaks him down. The new guy doesn't get it. Been doing everything right. But suddenly it's like . . . no promotion, no big future. Like, 'What'd I do wrong here, guys? I thought I was your fuckin' guy.' So, he tries to figure it out. Can't. Flips out.

Whatever. Marriage is wrecked. Health . . . thrashed. He's taken away, demolished. And the robot executive tries to move on to the next company. But a cop stops him. That's our Bruce Willis. Harrison Ford. Major battle. We think we're talking a hundred-million-dollar picture. So whattya think?"

Alan roughed out notes and looked up. Tony puffed, listening, long fingers drumming.

"Well, one question."

"Shoot."

"Why is the robot doing this?"

"We don't know."

"You don't know?"

"We don't know."

Tony's assistant looked at Alan through square Roger McGuinn glasses. His skin was pearly and translucent and he appeared to be no more than twelve.

"We thought you might have some ideas," said the assistant.

"Why is he doing it, Alan?" asked Tony, who was sitting on a staggering first-look deal at Columbia.

Now that Alan could see him up close, he figured Tony could weigh no more than 120 pounds, though over six feet. The guy was renown not only for stabbing people in the back but for removing the entire spine. He hired and fired writers at whim, was obsessed with fucking young actresses and though he had a tin ear, always personally rewrote scripts to get a shared credit. He had thirty films in development, and deals at every studio.

He took calls as they spoke. His other assistant, a mute girl who took notes, looked like a clinically depressed Eskimo. She wore clunky black Soviet shoes and fifty layers of clothes, none identifiable. Her name was Melissa because all girl assistants were named Melissa.

"Well . . . why is he doing it?" Alan had no clue.

Jordan had told him Tony's production company, *Heavy Weight,* had a fix on the project and to just go in for a meet. But these guys were missing four-fifths of the picture. He was going to kill Jordan for putting him in this position but started moving ideas around; trying to make something.

Tony stared, eating Almond Roca. He wore tight black jeans and had serious chapped lips; a Buchenwald Dwight Yoakam.

"I mean, do you like it or is it derivative crap?"

"No. I think it's interesting." Alan thought it was borderline.

"So, why is the robot doing it? What does the robot want?" Tony had to know.

Alan stared at him. "Well . . . you know . . . maybe it's what the guy who built the robot wants."

No one said anything. The boney satyr was listening. Glances were exchanged. Then, Tony stared at Alan.

"Interesting."

"Interesting," repeated the translucent assistant.

Alan built. "Yeah, so . . . I mean, let's say this guy who built it has a compelling reason . . ."

"Okay. Right . . ." Tony peered intently, deep voice shaking the room like one of those earthquake soundtracks.

"Maybe this is a company that hurt him. Took advantage of him. So, he builds this thing to get revenge."

"Or . . . is it possible . . . maybe he just hates all businesses and wants to exact revenge in general? He's a guy who got passed on, lost in the shuffle," said the creamy-faced fetus. "A kind of every-man's Willy Loman. He, in fact, is the robot, metaphorically. Just a thought."

Tony looked at Alan. Alan shrugged.

"Maybe. I mean, it's possible."

The fetus withdrew a bit. Hurt. Storing resentment that would be inflicted at a later time on someone he outranked. Like his mom.

"Go on," said Tony, crunching Almond Roca.

"Well, I'm talking off the top of my head here, Tony." Tony gestured he understood with frantic air shapes. "But maybe an interesting twist is that the robot isn't the bad guy at all. Maybe another guy in the company who knows he's going to get passed over for a promotion realizes he needs help and leases this thing for a year or so. In fact, maybe there's some strange business you can lease these robots from. Only maybe executives aren't the only thing available. Maybe there are assistants, too."

"Interesting," said Tony.

Alan nodded, going along with it. "So, you know, these assistants could just quietly come into a big company. You hire them . . . but your motives—"

Tony interrupted, holding up a callused palm.

"Who knows? You could be a self-serving, ambitious prick, right?" He was unscaling another pink vaccuum-sealed can of Almond Roca. *Vooosh.* "And any executive has the right to pick his own assistant . . ." Tony leaned forward, biting a piece of dry lip, making blood. "Keep going. I actually like this."

Alan kept going.

"And this assistant makes sure that everything you want, you get. She's programmed to get the competition in the office out of the way. She's deadly when she needs to be. Sweet the rest of the time. Everybody loves her. But she's a fucking robot. She's your bodyguard. She sees to it that you rise to the top and when you do . . . she 'quits' and gets leased to another person who wants what you want."

Tony was nodding. "And it's all done confidentially so no one knows anyone else who has one. No one can bust anyone else, right?"

Alan took a sip of Evian. "It's not an evil executive but maybe it works, Tony."

". . . *everybody needs a good assistant* . . ." Tony was seeing the poster.

"And you make it violent if you need it violent."

"Absolutely! Like what you're doing on 'The Mercenary,' which I fucking love, by the way." Tony had made a fortune with films that had vapid carnality and tons of gratuitous blood. Overseas his pictures were huge and though critics despised him, as they did Alan, he could get the biggest talents around to work with him.

One picture with Tony Moore, you were white hot. There was also the hermaphrodite rumor, which added bizarre appeal.

"You know, she like . . . tortures the asshole in the office that's vying for her boss's job. He goes flying out of a skyscraper window in Manhattan like it's a suicide . . . but uh-uh . . ." Tony was trancing out, seeing it in his mind.

". . . or maybe she expresses interest in going out with this guy who is trying to hurt her boss . . . but she takes him home and kills him," said the assistant. "Could get an amazing scene of her seducing and torturing him . . . to protect her boss and his promotion."

Tony was nodding. "That's good, that's good."

The albino child was happy again, capillaries flushing.

Melissa, the mute, tilted her dark face up and spoke. Her expression was stiff; semiterrified, desperate to contribute. She spoke quietly, like those battered wives on "Oprah."

"Tony, this may alter the tone, but . . . could the assistant be a man?"

Tony let the clutch out on his steamroller. "No."

Alan watched Melissa nod and descend back into her shoulder cave, chin tucked. Taking notes. He figured she'd resurface after a few weeks of therapy.

Casper-the-friendly-slide-of-plankton gave a smug little smile. He obviously thought she was nothing to worry about. But Alan had seen unexpected reversals too many times to count the Eskimo out, just yet. In five years, she could be running a studio and Casper would be stuck in some nowhere-fast production company, trapped in his boy's sample-size world of arrogant cruelty. And when he came to her to pitch a film project, she'd just politely pass over and over, and there would be balance in the universe, again.

Tony's secretary buzzed. He picked up. Listened, guzzled the rest of his chocolate milk. Hung up. Burped a little.

"Got the set calling, pal. Gotta take this. Alan . . . go ahead and do it. It's great. Bring me a story. I'm back from Brazil in two weeks. Fucking rainforest Indians are snagging a deal. I gotta go down and beat them up."

"So, you like it the way I said?"

"Yeah." Tony doodled. "Or whatever. Play with it. You know what to do. Maybe we do a whole other thing. Ditch the robot angle. Maybe do a really fucking evil like . . . female mercenary. Missiles for tits, whole bit."

He smiled, trying to seem like a guy who had fun with things. But Alan sensed he was a guy who hated himself and had no close friends. A guy who didn't know how to get close or be close. A guy who Alan could so easily imagine just staring at himself in the mirror and loathing the ugly, pointless reflection. Loathing it enough to just kill himself. And knowing deep down, no one would care except studio bookkeeping.

He was opening a can of Coke. "I don't know. You're getting me thinking here. Give me a call. We'll figure this out. There's a go picture in here somewhere. This is getting exciting." His noodle fingers waved bye-bye and he got on the phone, wedging it into his shoulder.

As Alan left Tony's office, within ten seconds Tony was screaming, telling someone at the other end he didn't care what they thought or what they wanted or what they felt. He said he was going to rip their head off and piss down their throat.

"Thanks for coming in. Call us," said the assistants, shrugging off Tony's annoyed mood, smiling like abused children as they walked Alan to the front door.

Alan said goodbye to the translucent boy and the terrified mute and drove home, deciding he didn't want the coveted Tony Moore summer picture.

violence

The police officers stood silent, staring up at the immense cross. Single droplets of blood, from her hands and feet, echoed on Cathedral floor beside the weeping priest.

Stained glass branded divine colors on their skin and they walked slowly, observed by paintings and statuary that surrounded them. The younger officer got a ladder from the priest who'd called, and climbed. He moved past her feet, which were pinned, one on top of the other, to the huge wooden cross by a commando knife. He decided to leave it in until he could detach her palms, held by similar knives. She was naked and blood ran from her pierced palms to her armpits, then down her ribs. Saints stared from ceilings and walls; a wake, in oil.

Two other officers steadied the ladder and looked up as he continued climbing. He was to her upper body now and they waited as he licked his lips and looked at her. Her head leaned to one side, left eye blackened, mouth leaking blood. Her face was klieged by the beams of holy light which softened the damage.

"Is she dead?" asked one, feeling the priest's eyes, in some unbalanced trance, on him.

The young officer on the ladder moved closer to her face, trying to hear breathing, feeling revulsion; pity. Her eyes were shut, body motionless. He reached a hand to her throat, to feel for a pulse, and as his skin touched hers, she screamed, eyes jumping open.

He was shocked and almost fell, losing his balance, tipping the ladder. As he held tightly to the huge cross, with one hand, and the cathedral filled with her horrible anguish, she tried to speak. He got close to her mouth and she strained to tell him something.

". . . just let us help you," he said, gently, as three officers and two paramedics who'd arrived began to lower her from the cross. Their nerves glistened and they tried not to look at her naked body, slick with blood.

She struggled, in protective hysteria, limbs flailing, unable to stop screaming. The officers' uniforms and hands were saturated with red, as they tried to calm her and the fresh blood made her skin slippery, like oil. As she wriggled, in howling pain, they lost firm grip and she fell to the floor, skull cracking. She screamed more loudly, writhing; a bloody brush, painting floor.

They finally got her into a waiting ambulance, toweled themselves of her blood. The priest began to mop the floor and brought a bucket of hot, soapy water to clean the cross and pews.

She died eight minutes later, two blocks from the hospital, hands and feet wrapped in gauze. As the siren sheared through traffic and one of the paramedics gave her last rites, they tried to understand what she'd been struggling to describe.

Even though her tongue had been cut out, she wanted them to know the man who'd done this to her was on TV every week.

guest appearance

So . . . is Buddha actually here, or is there an opening act first or . . . what's the deal?"

Shrine ducks paddled.

"Try to speak quietly."

"Nice ducks. Are they meditating, too?"

Soothing, dauntless tones. "They say the animals that come here don't fight." She gestured; squirrels, bugs. Smiled to make her point. Led him to a bench that overlooked the Self-Realization Center. They sat, listening to lake ripple. She closed blue eyes, breathed.

"This is where David and I were married."

Alan didn't want to know.

". . . the guru with the corporation? That David?"

"Thanks for meeting me here." A tiny smile bloomed, letting him know she could handle being teased. Her eyes were still closed. "I love it here."

"Yeah, it's great . . . makes me want to eat dates and shave my head."

It was an odd place; didn't quite belong. A small meditation park, right off Sunset near Pacific Coast Highway, with hushed devotees in carotene-orange bodies. Ashes of Muktawhatsit were in an urn and visitors sat, staring at them.

"So, these ashes . . . do they speak or do impressions, or are they just ashes?"

"I asked you to come so we could talk, Alan." Rising joy. ". . . something wonderful has happened."

"David's been declared insane?"

"I'm pregnant."

A little Richard Lewis shrug. Words parachuting; escaping, playfully. "Well, we know it wasn't me."

She didn't laugh. Just a well-centered glance; beatific nonreaction. Taking pity on his brittle humor. It was item one million on the dizzying list of what went wrong between them.

"I figured you'd hear on the grapevine . . ."

"I appreciate it." He threw a rock at a duck.

"Alan . . . don't do that. It's not hurting you."

"It would if it had a chance. Look at its eyes." It quacked, shook feathers in irritation. "It's rabid. We should shoot it. Do they rent guns here?"

"Are you upset? About David and me starting a family."

"No, you'll have all kinds of fun. He'll be a great dad. Mr. Down-to-earth. He still think the Bible's based on him?"

A no-red-meat, Nurse Ratchet calm, full of alpha superiority. "New Age is not a religion. We've talked about this, Alan. Why do you make fun of these things?"

"I have total respect for metaphysics. I just think David is a sociopathic bullshit artist, that's all."

"He sees the good in you."

A quartet of tall vegetarians, swathed in white, floated by, nodding. Their long toes crunched on lake path.

"Cynthia, he's a phony."

"This isn't the place to have an argument."

"We're having a passionate exchange. Remember passion, or does Dave have a seminar to control that one, too?"

"Can we talk about something else?" Neither made a move. "How's your agent?"

"Please." He was staring at the crystal around her neck. "What is that, kryptonite?"

"Is he doing a good job for you?"

"He's great. Wishes he'd invented polio so he could've signed Jonas Salk and taken a percentage of the vaccine. He still lies on spec."

"How's Eddy?"

"Died. Few months ago."

"Alan, I'm so sorry. But remember—" a happy tape began in her head, "there is no death."

"Yeah, well this time there was . . . he was definitely dead. Trust me."

"How's your show going?"

"Big."

"Anyone special you're seeing?"

"My shrink."

She breathed deep. A peaceful glow settled. Monarch butterflies sketched orange on sky.

"I love being pregnant. Having a little life inside me."

"With all due respect . . . that's always how much life you had inside you . . ."

"I'm calm. Not bored. I've always said that. Why are you so angry?"

"You and Dave . . . this how you talk?" He stood up, becoming annoyed, not knowing why. "Like little . . . tofu drones? Nothing bothers you? You're 'at one' with the fucking birds and these hostile, asshole ducks . . . and he records his little harp albums and gardens his billowy hair and—"

"Alan, *stop* it!"

"A reaction?" A nasty gleam. "Don't tell Dave. He'll take away your juicer privileges."

"You are so filled with resentment."

"I think your life is a joke."

"No. That's not it."

"Yeah. That's it."

"You're jealous."

"Of Dave? Yeah, you're right. I want white hair that hangs to my butt and my own little New Age seminar business that exploits dysfunctional fuckheads at a grand a throw. I want my own fucking mantra like Dave has. What's his again? 'We take VISA'?"

He stared at her stomach and remembered jerking off in the doctor's office in Encino, seven years ago, feeling absurd, ashamed.

"Just think . . . all those years of good sperm that got thrown away on flat stomachs and towels. The countless millions of lives, swept away like counter puddle," he'd told the nurse who handed him a beaker. She'd been amused despite a slightly offended smile.

When the doctor had called, saying he'd failed the test, Alan heard the continuing force of life as a makeshift infirmary, under the tent of his skin. The dying, the dead, strewn in a condemned ecology.

"Guess I'm a bell curve without a clang," he'd told the doctor and the guy'd said it could've been a lot of things. Career stress was right up there at the top, in his case. It did a pretty good arson-job on sperm, going in with bad-hour flammables, burning those little Alans to death.

Cynthia had watched him put down the phone, slowly moved to hug him. But he'd sensed her disappointment. It was in the slowness of her fingers as they squeezed him. In the way she'd said, "I love you . . . we'll work it out," and her voice was a dosage; an obligation.

Two years later, he'd wanted out and she'd married Dave. Potent, mystical Dave.

"Feel my stomach. Please, Alan? I'd like that."

He sighed, said no. Felt like an ass, finally agreed; spread fingers over the cotton rise. He smiled but it was for her and he sensed himself leaning slightly away. The idea of something growing inside her was parasitic and repelled him. He didn't understand why. Maybe all the toilet-plungers in Hollywood who clung to him, with their upbeat dependency, made him despise the idea of anything feeding on something else. Maybe he wanted to be a father; knew it was unlikely. Maybe he just thought Dave was a scumbag and had no right bringing anything vaguely human into the world.

She smiled with Zen closure. "We would've hurt each other too much."

"If we'd kept on?"

She nodded. "I love you. You know that?"

"I love you, too." He suddenly envied her the baby, and he suddenly wanted her to die. And he wanted Dave to suffer.

"Will you come and see the baby? Try to give David a chance?"

Alan hesitated, said yes. In his mind, he saw an infant's carriage with a dead baby inside. Its bullet-scored body, a hideous dalmation, its face exactly his.

He never spoke to her again.

ten percent three

"Did you hear?"

Silence.

"Jordan . . . right in the middle of rewriting . . ."

"I can't believe you didn't hear."

Alan was in the new multisuite production building the studio had given him once he'd made them so much money, they'd gone into toxic-shock and felt generous. His office was huge, with a built-in wall aquarium and a fireplace just like Franky's. Alan had always teased about the fireplace. But he'd always wanted one.

"Somebody broke into Andy Singer's house and beat the shit out of him." Jordan told him it had happened a couple of hours ago.

Alan fell silent. Last time Alan had talked to Andy, he and the megalomaniacal twerp had had a civil knockdown about the time-slot change, despite Jordan wanting the agency to handle it.

Alan hadn't been able to wait.

In their heated exchange, Andy'd said he wanted to make the other network's top shows run out their pants like Cream of Defeat and was sure "The Mercenary" could kill off anything; fun nerve gas. Alan didn't like the idea and told Andy he wouldn't agree to the move. The show worked where it was.

He'd hung up on Andy and from what Jordan was saying, Andy's week went straight downhill from there. The way rumors had it, some crazy had busted into Andy's two-million-dollar ego-shrine at the Summit, a Disney-perfect gate-guard community just off Mulholland, at around seven this morning.

Jordan said Andy had been terrorized. Tied up; beaten. The whole three-course gourmet service. When Armed Response finally dragged their asses up his driveway and kicked down the door, Andy was a Fig Newton. He'd suffered a nervous breakdown while tied up in the chair and was hastily and confidentially placed in a home for the seriously snow-burned.

"So, now what?" Alan felt bad for Andy, but not that bad.

"So, that's life. Send flowers. Make nice. Other fronts: I talked to Tony Moore. Loved the meeting. Loved you. Wants to make a movie. How'd you feel it went?"

Alan took a stack of messages from Lauren. All from people who wanted something. He fingered through, handed them back to her. Mouthed for her to take care of it. She nodded. Mouthed back, "Lunch?" He nodded. She added more wood to the super-fluous fireplace and left.

"I'd rather pass."

"No, you wouldn't."

"You asked me how I felt."

"Right. I didn't ask you to pass. Alan, I told him you wanted it."

"So, tell him I don't."

"Can't do that."

"Jordan . . . you and I didn't even talk it over. You can't commit me to stuff without asking me."

"You're absolutely right." That was the making-nice part. Alan could hear a manipulative thought coming. "Listen, it's a huge opportunity." That was Part One of the thought. "If I may make a suggestion, try it . . . we can always get you out of it later." Part Two.

"You packaged us."

"Who said that?" The answer came too quickly.

"Did you or didn't you?"

"Alan . . . we have a green-lighted picture here if you say yes. Katzenberg's been all over me this morning. What difference does it make?"

"You didn't consult me."

"Tony Moore can work with any writer in town."

"Let him."

"He wants you."

"Tell him it's a pass."

"I can't."

"Why?"

No answer.

"Disney wants to do it if you write it. I remove you, deal gets polio."

"So, the agency loses the packaging fee."

No answer.

"This could be a very big picture, Alan. What's a few attachments?"

"Jordan, point is, I don't wanna do it just because you make a huge fee off it. And the second point is, you lied to me."

Jordan sighed. "I get you a great opportunity and all you care about is a technicality? You have a t.v. perception, I get you a feature perception. You fucking kidding me?"

It wasn't a conversation.

As Jordan cajoled, pleaded, and apologized, Alan stared at a clown trigger doing a pudgy tour in his wall tank. It stared at him; a wet witness. Then, it swam by a smaller fish and unexpectedly took a big bite out of it. As the wounded fish squirmed, a quarter of its body bitten off, Alan decided not to send Andy flowers.

subtitles

Corea felt thick tape sealing his mouth. A blindfold covered his eyes, and his wrists and ankles were bound behind his back. He could hear someone walking through nearby brush.

He tried to remember. They had driven. He could recall shifting. Accelerating. Being forced to drive. Driving far. Being told to watch the road, not to look at the man's face. Could still feel bruised ribs where the man had jabbed him with the pistol barrel and made him answer endless questions. Made him talk loud. Soft.

Now he could see nothing. Could barely remember the man who'd approached him in the underground garage at his Marina condo.

The one who bore an eerie resemblance to him.

He'd forced Corea into his own Ferrari.

It was hot, now. He heard a fire being started. Was it day? Night? He had no idea. A wind came up and blew sand. He was thirsty. Had to take a leak.

The burning wood smelled good; like memories of campfires

when he'd done plays at summer camp. Comedies performed in front of the other kids, who circled the fire and laughed and clapped at the bad parts; the dumb acting.

Pain.

The tape was ripped from his mouth. The blindfold removed. He was blinded by the fire, eyes blinking, watering, overwhelmed by brightness. Smoke. Fear.

Then, he saw him. A dense-looking man dressed in filthy jungle fatigues, staring at him. The man watched him, curiously. Fascinated. Observing every detail of his behavior.

"What the fuck is this . . . ?" Corea asked, voice weak; scared.

The man looked at him.

". . . what the fuck is this?" the man repeated, trying to capture the same tone, the speed of phrasing. "What the fuck is this?" He said it several more times. Then, just kept staring, eyes primitive cameras, recording each move and facial expression.

"Who the hell are you?"

The man picked up a rock and threw it hard at Corea, hitting him on the forehead, making it bleed. ". . . who the hell are you?" the man repeated, a coarse mimic, imitating Corea's facial expression, as Corea winced in pain.

"You *motherfucker!*"

The man threw another rock. Made Corea's scalp line bleed. ". . . motherfucker," said the man, struggling with the word, tilting his own head, watching Corea's pain. Trying to duplicate it, making false noises of pain.

Corea was scared. Was this some crazed fan? Someone who loved the show? Wanted to be just like him?

"Look . . . I can get you whatever you want. You wanna come to the studio? See my dressing room? I can get you a jacket." He was looking into the man's uncomprehending eyes, getting more scared. "Great leather jacket . . . says 'The Mercenary' on the back. Only people on the show can get them."

The man walked closer, stared at Corea, studied him.

"Smile," said the man.

Corea was confused and the man poked him with a burning branch from the fire. *"Smile!"*

Corea managed a smile and the man watched him. Reached his dirty hands out and felt Corea's face as it struggled to smile through pain and fear. The man began to smile, doing it the same way, curling it a bit on one side.

"Who the hell are you?" said the man, duplicating Corea's voice. "Motherfucker . . ." Then, the man pulled out a knife.

Corea felt terror. The man grabbed Corea's shirt front, ripped it open, yanking hard. As Corea watched in horror, the man cut him, watched blood surface.

Corea began to scream and the man screamed the same way, watching and listening to exactly how Corea did it. Their screams echoed across the barren desertscape and animals returned their calls.

Corea stopped screaming, furious at being mocked, and the man cut him again to make him scream more. But Corea refused. The man kicked him in the balls and Corea fell to his knees, groaning, spitting blood.

The man memorized the move and did the same, groaning and falling to his knees. He stood and did it again, then forced Corea up and made him do it over and over. He kicked Corea in the balls harder and Corea stood motionless, eyes shutting, pain shooting. He made no noise, simply collapsing.

The man practiced it over and over, as Corea remained on the ground in agony. The man got down beside him and watched Corea's facial expressions as pain ground him up. He made the same expressions, the same noises.

Corea fell silent, hating this cruel parody. Refusing to make a sound.

"Cry," said the man.

Corea couldn't, eyes dry, body numb.

"Cry!" The man was yelling and began to poke him with the knife tip, making little eyelets that beaded blood. They were all over Corea's chest. His face. His stomach. Like a horrid pox. The man

was about to go lower and Corea forced himself to weep, crying out, screaming, face out of control.

The man was intrigued, moving close.

Wanting to see every detail, every spasm and twitch. He was beside Corea and poked him with the knife. Corea cried harder and the man began to do it the same way, an eerie impersonation of pain.

As the fire went out and the sun began to rise, the man reached fingertips out and touched Corea's tortured body. Licked the blood, tasting it. He smiled, sat cross-legged, and watched the sun climb from the ground.

arc

Alan was at the newstand on Laurel Canyon when Patrick Benson walked up to say hello.

"Alan?"

Alan turned from the article he was scanning in *Esquire;* the piece about him. He was mid-way through a half-serious quote from himself about how wealth and power were, "a rabid mastiff that walks you."

". . . Patrick?"

Alan knew he looked terrible. Hoped Patrick wouldn't mention it.

"So, how've you been? Other than owning network television?" Patrick had grown a beard. Gotten chubby.

Alan smiled, looked down at the sidewalk. Glanced over to make sure no one was bothering his new Aston Martin. He didn't want to be talking to Patrick. Patrick's special about children whose mothers had died of AIDS was decimated by a "best-of" action sequences from "The Mercenary" and the somewhat obscene paradox seemed to haunt the moment.

"Just busy with the show. You know . . ."

They had worked together as story editors on one of the most wooden-headed action shows ever, "Rough Waters," which featured two cops who rode around in a boat, exchanging cretinous thoughts while working on their tans.

It had been painful.

The executive producer had been a paranoid drunk with Al Haig hair and Rancho Mirage skin who abused the staff in creative meetings, insisting the dialogue have a "fun" sound. During particularly late and ugly sessions, he actually resorted to cracks like, "people with your talent don't deserve to write," before snorkeling back into his scotch and bile, glaring lifelessly.

Alan had managed to ride out the hundred-proof iron-maiden, finding the guy a pathetic cartoon. But Patrick had always been stung by it, sensitive in ways that made people care about him; worry about him.

"You ever see my special?"

Alan said he had but it wasn't true. Patrick nodded and it was hard for Alan to tell if he felt betrayed and lied to. Alan asked him what he was up to; how come they never saw each other anymore.

"I'm quitting the business. I just don't want to do this anymore. All the things I think are important, nobody wants to do. My agents don't put me into anything socially relevant. The networks all want that seventy five share Matterhorn. I never could come up with hits like you do, Alan. You have a gift."

Was it admiration or contempt?

Alan thought maybe it was his own imagination. Patrick was never a nasty or indirect kind of guy. He was nice to everyone. Maybe it was why he was losing.

"Oh, it's just a fucking fluke, you know that, Patrick. 'The Mercenary' is not exactly out to help dying kids. It's just a roller coaster. You always shot for stuff that had something to say." He heated-up a grin. ". . . especially when we were doing 'Rough Waters' . . ."

Patrick smiled.

Alan was being nice and he appreciated it. But Alan meant it, somewhere, though he mostly pitied Patrick. Looking into Patrick's open eyes and seeing someone who still had the right idea. Even if no one wanted to buy it.

"Marcia and I and the kids are moving up to Portland. I'm going back to writing plays, if you can believe that."

Alan always envied Patrick having a family; love and forgiveness to come home to every night.

"Playwrite. What are you kidding?" Alan was teasing him. "You're not depressed enough. You have to lose all reason to go on."

Patrick had no response.

"Anyway, you can't live in Portland. People who live in Portland are lumber."

Patrick laughed, teeth squeezed together tightly and Alan noticed a couple of women gathering around his Aston, looking at all the people at the stand, wondering who owned this magnificent machine. He felt slightly self-conscious; didn't want Patrick to see the whole thing.

"Anyway, there's things I always wanted to write that are important to me and . . . I'll never make it here." He peered through an insecure smile and Alan realized how much he missed people like Patrick. He didn't know anybody like him anymore. Everybody was too successful to be open; too much to gain, too much to lose. That was the deal. The gig.

The dirty trick.

"Anyway. I better get going. We're still packing up the house and everything. You ever get up to Portland?"

They both smiled. Yeah, sure, he did.

"Hey, Alan . . . fucking amazing stuff you're doing on 'The Mercenary.' You pushed the envelope."

Alan nodded. Didn't know what to say.

"It's just ratings, Patrick."

Patrick nodded, said nothing.

"Hey, say hi to the family, will you?"

"Sure. Marcia asks about you."

"Well, for chrissake invent something that makes me look good."

They hugged a little and Patrick drove away, looking back in his rearview to see Alan being approached by the two girls.

ugly twist

Alan heard Tinkerbell trapped, screaming for help, and turned down the music. The car phone was ringing. He put it on hands-free, answered.

"Yeah?" The heat outside was trying to break in and he kicked up the A.C., turning the Aston into a Margarita.

It was Corea's wife; a rained-out voice. "I called you in your car so no one could hear." A frightened whisper. "I'm . . . if anyone knows I'm telling you this . . ."

Alan asked what was wrong. Waited for a red light. She cried. Her signal was fading.

"He's been raping me. He's been . . . hurting me."

"Rape?" He tried to understand. ". . . you're married. What's going on between you?"

Her emotions were slurring. "It's the show. The character. It's like . . ."

Alan was ski-jumping down La Cienega; downshifting. The

engine sounded like the MGM lion. Her thoughts were breaking up, words a dotted line.

". . . yes?" He wanted to hang up; to leave his day behind with the push of a button. It was all starting to get to him. Every shape and random crease.

". . . he's like someone else."

Alan listened.

"Will you talk to him?"

He felt too weak to put himself through it. Still didn't know what was wrong but felt awful.

"What do you want me to say. This is more like something a marriage counselor should—"

"Please . . . he'll listen to you. He always says you understand him."

"Look . . . he's kidding you. We don't get along . . ."

"I'm afraid he's going to hurt someone. I'm afraid he's really going to . . . hurt someone. I've never seen him so angry. It's like he's—"

Alan stabbed his horn. Some hustler was flipping him off. Alan didn't know what to say to her. "What does he say when you ask him what happened?"

Her signal was balled-up plastic wrap.

". . . he says . . . that he llccoonntodpspsps."

Alan lifted smoked lenses, stared at the phone. "Hello? Are you there? Hello?" Dead air. *"Fuck!"*

The city felt Alan's little car crawling on it and didn't move; waiting to scratch him off.

". . . hello?" She was back.

". . . I lost you. Could you say it again?"

"He's home. I can't talk." She was barely audible.

"What were you going to say?"

Her mind pressed down on a knife blade.

"He said . . . everything was going to be different now. He said . . ."

Alan could hear a door slamming. An angry male voice. He could hear her scream as she was hit and thrown down, breaking something made of glass. As Corea started to rip off her clothes and rape her, grunting like an animal, the signal broke up.

subtext four

Is it possible I've always been violent but it's hidden out in my mind?"

No answer. Eyes red. Skin hanging loose.

". . . it was always there in my work. Producers and actors who
read my stuff were always impressed with my ability to . . . I don't
know . . . mimic sociopathic creeps. With the show . . . I've gotten
brilliant at it. Is that weird? Come on, it's weird, I know you think it
is. I came from a nice family in Connecticut. People in Connecticut
don't get angry. They circulate petitions."

Eyes sweep; owlish. Brittle nails chewed.

"If I had to be absolutely honest about why my writing works,
it's because I have a gift for capturing the sound of these derelicted
pricks. It's why my show works. Maybe I shouldn't knock it. Maybe
it's even why writers write. It's our subconscious gang graffiti. I feel
cold. Is it cold in here?"

A cold sweat. Forty-five minutes flatlined.

"Way I look at it, as long as my writing entertains people and I get a fifty share, what the fuck. I mean, I'm getting rich, right?"

Moving to the door. Features trembling on sick flesh.

". . . what's happening to me?"

partial reveal

No one ever stopped there.

It scared people. Like news footage of TWA crashes. Or photos of dying children. It could've been a slaughterhouse. Or a crematorium. An asylum for hideous states of flesh and mind.

It was seventy-five miles from L.A. But when you saw it, it didn't remind you of anywhere you'd ever been. And it made you feel scared inside.

The neon sign above the door flashed a sore color. It was called *Skinners* and twenty or so H.D. Panheads, Knuckleheads, and chopped Sportsters sat outside; rabid, chain-driven creatures. Black, tear-drop tanks and mutilation artwork shone like underworld manes. Grinning skulls. Screaming faces.

Inside, nobody heard the Aston Martin that pulled up and parked. Two minutes later, Alan entered, pried smoke apart, walked to the bartender. A sign behind the man read: FUCK YOU TWICE.

Pool balls clicked like snapping bones and septic faces tracked; eyes in a horror painting.

Alan said he was looking for a guy named Corea.

The bartender shrugged, smiled just like the artwork on the gas tanks. Eyes watched. Grunting laughter and hungry voices moved across the floor toward Alan, twining around his feet and legs.

The bartender pointed to a table, near the back.

Alan moved across the room as faces stared, chins resting on vertical cue sticks. Huge bodies moved in front of him; intimidating obstacles.

". . . excuse me," said Alan, making a cautious path through the tough men who smelled of sex; violence.

Then, he saw him.

Seated at the back table, face flecked with reddish freckles. Some whore was under the table, on her knees.

Alan stood over the table. Corea looked up at him. The flecks on his face looked like dried blood. The whore's head moved up and down, faster and faster and Corea had no expression, waiting; an eerie cipher. When she'd finished, wiping full lips, she stood on black stockings and heels, went to the bar for a chaser.

Corea kicked a chair out for Alan.

As Alan stood there, a short-skirted waitress brought up a plate with an enchilada, a piece of steak, and fries. It was hot and she held the plate with a thick cloth. Corea leaned back while she put it down.

"Very hot," she said.

He reached up into her panties and slid a finger in, moving it deep inside her, up and back. "Very hot," he repeated, in hollow repetition. She whispered something in his ear, moved off.

Alan watched Corea moving the plate with those fingers that looked bloodstained, undisturbed by the hot ceramic surface. Alan squinted. How could he do it? The heat would burn anyone's skin.

"How the fuck are you, *Al?* Hungry? Like good twat?" He held up a glistening finger. Alan didn't move.

"We have to talk." Alan was trying to attract no attention. Spoke softly.

Corea tilted part of his upper lip, showing brown teeth. But they didn't look grease-penciled like the ones makeup applied every morning. They seemed like the teeth of a primitive. Alan watched as Corea started to eat the steak, so undercooked it was wet; as if freshly cut from an animal. Trickles of blood creeked his chin.

Is he kidding, Alan wondered? Is he trying to get more leverage on the show? Otherwise, why the absurd act? Why this place? This belly of the beast, head-fuck job? The theatrical extremity. Corea was pulling down four hundred and fifty grand an episode. They could've had lunch at Mortons. This was a fucking game.

Alan figured some agent must've gotten to Corea; told him how to position himself to renegotiate for even bigger weekly. Maybe points. If it wasn't that, Corea was believing his own press. Believing he was the character. Melding; seeping.

Franky once told Alan about an actor he'd worked with who played a drool-pan in a sitcom called "Shaved Nuts" who'd gradually started acting crazier and crazier, off the set. The press loved it, running endless articles about the guy throwing inexplicable tantrums in sedate settings. Trying to swallow an entire microphone on the March of Dimes telethon. Or just displaying his dick, in general, anywhere he could unzip and flop.

He'd been found, one night, playing Donkey Kong, nude, in some 7-Eleven, eating Good and Plenty. During his arrest, he bit one cop's ear off and they had to pump his stomach to get it out. The whole stunt made the cover of the *National Enquirer,* "Shaved Nuts" ratings popped hole number two in the ozone, and the guy's contract was renewed for twice his weekly. Franky said he thought it was a total act until the show was cancelled and the guy swigged some Drano that permanently hit the spot.

"You never really know," Franky had told Alan. "With fucking actors, the good ones . . . it all looks the same. Be careful."

Corea was scarfing more bloody beef. "I tell you how tight my wife's pussy is? Should try it some time, Al."

Alan pushed upward on his forehead. "So . . . what the hell is going on, Corea? A lot of people are talking about you."

"People are scared of me."

"Why?"

He looked into Alan's eyes and it felt crawly to Alan; the way Corea didn't blink, didn't waver. Something about him was genuinely upsetting. Much more than that first meeting way back when he'd sneaked into the studio and Alan's office.

It was partly the rapacious stare.

But it was more. Something about Corea, in this bruised lighting, seemed unfinished. Crude. Overall, he seemed more dense. There was a dimmed civilization to his reaction time. A Neanderthal fixation about incidental objects. The way he held his fork and tore at the meat with it. The way he moved his face. His body. The muscles seemed almost too close to the surface, like some evolutionary link between a powerful creature and a man.

As he ate, and Alan watched his hands, he noticed Corea had virtually no lines on his palms. Was it always like that? Had he missed it every other time they'd been together? Were some people like that?

"I want to ask you a couple questions, Corea."

Corea kept chewing. Stared tar-pit eyes.

Alan asked him about his childhood and family. His schooling. The places he grew up. Friends. Jobs. Romances.

He kept chewing, saying nothing.

"I had my secretary do some checking around. You never served in Viet Nam. You were never in prison . . . like you told everyone on the set you were."

No answer.

Alan kept going. "Wanna know why I've found nothing but inconsistencies? You wanna know who you are?"

Corea wasn't interested. Alan leaned in closer.

"How about you're a guy who never did smack. How about you're a fucking theater major from Chicago who did off–Broadway Albee and detergent commercials to pay for headshots and decent coaching."

"You borrowed money from your mother, Gail, who works for Toshiba as a secretary. You have two brothers, you did fair to bad in high school. Your father died of heart disease. You two never got along. You didn't go to his funeral. You've had your tonsils out. Shall I go on?"

Silence.

"You're married. You play a little guitar and do a passable Spanish accent. You can horseback ride, fence, and have a brown belt in aikido. That's what your old résumé said, anyway."

Corea said nothing. Blood ran stakes from mouth corners. His muscles siezed up; shuddered like a horse shaking off flies.

"I wanna talk about the show." The voice flat; distant.

"Look. Drop the fucking act. I take my hat off to you. You're a clever guy. You obviously heard about us casting 'The Mercenary.' So you figure, hey, I'll just come in and convince these producers I'm a tough, heartless, 'fuck-you' kind of guy, right? Am I warm?"

"I wanna talk about the show."

"My secretary even called your old acting coach in Chicago. He said all you ever thought about was success and career. He said you always did whatever you had to to get the part. He said you even got a tattoo to remind yourself. *DO IT*? Ring a bell?"

He reached over and pushed Corea's T-shirt sleeve up. There was a tattoo. But it read DOIT. There was no gap between the letters. Alan blinked; taken aback. Looked into Corea's dead smile.

"Who you fooling Corea? What do you want? Huh? You want a goddamn motor home that's twenty-five feet longer? Fine. You want to break shooting at six? You got it. Or maybe you want to direct an episode. You stop beating your wife and raping her if I arrange that for you?"

Corea stopped eating, picking dirty fingernails on the table. "I want the scripts to be more. I want more."

"More? What do you mean, more?"

Alan noticed bikers watching them.

A six-foot-five freak with acid pupils was walking closer, curious; stupid. Pig flesh gathered around the sweaty neck of another who watched, sitting on top of a cigarette machine, laughing.

"More . . . me," Corea said. "More . . . de–tail."

Alan noticed Corea hadn't had anything to drink since he'd sat down. And the way the plate hadn't burned his fingers. The tattoo misspelled. The vacant ferocity all over him. It was a great act. The attitudinal DNA was all there. The arrogant, antisocial pose. A great act.

But Alan wasn't sure exactly how he was doing it.

"You mean the character needs more definition? It takes time. The character is finding itself. I'll work with you but you gotta lay off your wife. What if you really hurt her? You'll go to jail, man. There won't be any goddamn show."

"Taking too long," said Corea. "I need more . . . *now.*"

Ego mired in lower-case intellect. They all wanted to be stars. And the ones who already were, were terrified it would end. Alan sighed, knew exactly what to do. He and Marty would talk with the other writers, find a way to add a few memorable quirks to the character and a good scene here and there, so Corea could strut his megalomania. Make a call, help Corea get a series development deal. It would placate him.

Every baby needed a rattle.

"We'll punch up the scripts."

"No! I need more identity!" Corea was yelling and Alan froze, the brutish aggression stunning him. Slushy pronunciation made the words sound almost retarded. "I NEED . . . *MORE!*"

Alan watched Corea's mouth working, as if the words crawling out couldn't breathe in there. As if talking confused him; was something hard and new.

The biker was standing over them; speedballing. Insane. Staring at Corea.

"Hey, *fuck*head?" The biker moved a veiny arm, tipped over Alan's untouched beer. It pooled like piss on thrashed tile. The acid pupils knocked Corea's bloody plate aside, breaking it on the floor.

". . . I know you." His tattooed neck tightened, angrily. "You're that tough prick on TV, right? The fucking Mer-cen-ary? I bet you ain't so fucking tough without all your fucking stunt men, asshole."

Corea didn't respond.

Alan's breathing slowed; fear rising.

"Leave us alone," said Alan, trying to stop things. Trying to do something. "We don't want trouble."

The biker glowered, ugly; squalid. Reached down to grab Alan's hand and bend fingers back, break them.

"Get used to it . . ."

Before the biker could make another move, Corea instantly broke a glass across the man's face, causing him to scream, face a slashed map. Corea grabbed the biker's wrist, forced the bleeding pig to the floor.

He grabbed the man's huge right leg, at the ankle. Started to twist. The man tried to turn his body as the leg was turned harder. He screamed as his hip joint began to loosen, then separate, the ball forced from the socket.

"What are you doing?!" Alan was screaming.

As the bar looked on, fascinated, Corea grinned, grabbed harder. As the biker struggled, Corea kicked him repeatedly in the face with a steel-tipped combat boot. The sound of the biker's jaw dislocating blocked his scream of pain, and his head slumped to one side, eye dangling.

Corea spread his own legs to steady himself and began to twist the leg harder until meat and muscle began to tear, as the screaming biker's leg was nearly shorn off the body.

Corea smiled, just like A. E. Barek. Alan watched in horror as two more mammoths attacked. Corea instantly broke a pool cue over a table and jammed the raw end of the cue through one's eye, driving it in.

He snapped the other man's arm with a broken-off chair leg and the attacker slumped, head dolling, vomiting slowly.

As the others backed away, terrified of Corea, Alan felt his mind collapsing. The whole fight, move for move, was an exact duplicate of one he'd planned for an upcoming episode of the show. But no one had any idea what he had in mind. No one had read it.

They couldn't have.

He hadn't written it yet.

conflict

Four A.M.

Waves drove full speed into the coastline and Alan slumped in a sofa, staring at his Mitsubishi. A tiny man, on a yacht, surrounded by women in bikinis was screaming about how to get rich. Alan switched to a cable station. *Lethal Weapon 2.*

Okay.

Mel would take care of everything. Fucking Mel with his Slinky face; nervous-breakdown smile.

Alan was almost crying, trying not to.

"Erica . . . ?"

She hadn't said anything in at least a minute.

"Alan . . . I have to go to work tomorrow. I'm exhausted."

"I know . . ."

Another minute.

"Did I tell you my mom saw you in *Esquire?*"

He sighed. It meant nothing to him. "Erica . . . listen. All I'm asking is for you to go away with me for a few days. We need to talk. Maybe . . . I don't care. Anywhere you want. Anywhere you say."

~~~~~~~~

She told him she couldn't.

"You can't do this with this guy. It's absurd. You don't know him or anything. You met a month ago. It's a rebound."

"We went to law school together. I knew him. We dated. We always had feelings." She stretched. "Alan, I have to go to sleep. I have court tomorrow."

Danny Glover was sitting on the toilet with the bomb under it. Officers were clustering around, putting a thick bomb-squad vest on him. Mel was licking lips, fighting redline worry. Alan played with the color until Danny looked green.

"I don't want you to marry this guy. He's from one of those dull little places back East. He's boring. I hate him. Everybody does. They took a poll and everyone hates him. Did I tell you that? Whole country. Even tolerant people responded in the negative." He could feel her smiling. Half a minute passed. "Can I come over?"

Silence.

He could hear her covers and sheets rustling. Imagined her naked body, warm and soft, a gentle nautilus. Imagined how she used to hold him tightly and breathe with sweet urgency and when they'd finished, make lullaby noises.

"We've set a date."

"Cancel it. I can't . . . I don't like not having you around."

"You were the one who lost interest. Alan, why are you doing this now?"

Alan's eyes filled. "I don't know. I feel alone."

She softened her voice, to be kind.

"Robb and I want the same things. What you and I had was . . . wonderful. But I want a family. I wanted one with you."

Alan sat up straighter as Danny and Mel and the toilet were blown out the window.

"Okay. I'll do that."

She laughed a little. "I don't need to win a point of negotiation . . ."

"You sound like a lawyer."

"I am a lawyer . . . that's why I'm so tired and have to go to sleep. Alan . . . I don't want you to do something before you're ready. I just want to get on with my life. I . . . have feelings for Robb and I want to build something."

Alan's stomach split down the middle.

"Erica . . . I'm unhappy without you. I can't think straight. My writing is bad. I don't sleep. Everything is fucked . . ."

"What about the show? All the success? It's everything you wanted. It was your fantasy."

"I'm starting to hate it."

She sounded concerned. The old concern. The voice that soothed and protected and wanted to know everything.

"Why, baby? What's happened?"

He couldn't tell her all the things about it that were terrible and frightening. The waves were shaking the house and Alan closed his eyes, imagining the couple that was murdered. For a moment, he thought he saw them on the deck, necks slashed, barberpoled by kelp. He thought he saw their glassy eyes staring and their hands, eaten by sea, pounding on the sliding doors.

His body spasmed.

"Erica?"

"Alan? What is it?"

". . . nothing. I don't know. I must be exhausted or something. I feel so weak all the time . . ."

He felt sick. Scared. Needed to get off. Was afraid to. Sounds of sea level prowled outside the glass and wood. His head felt like it was bleeding.

"Will you think about it?"

She said nothing. Told him there was nothing to think about. He couldn't accept it. Didn't believe it.

He felt he was in a casket. Couldn't breathe.

"Is there anything I can do?"

She told him he'd had his chance. She would've given anything to be with him. To marry him, have his children. But that was then. She didn't trust him anymore. Everything had its time. And everything changed.

He hung up, killed the TV, and sat in darkness.

Waiting for something to change.

suspects

Malibu pier needed a John David-
son telethon.

It was bent and old and when tides threw fits, bits of it would
fall away, unable to fight back. It grew from the waves and as you
walked on it, you could hear it moan; as if your weight added to its
pain. As if it wanted you off.

Alan and Camille strolled along the wooden boardwalk of the
pier; doomed pirates, walking a plank. To either side, Shar-Pei faces
with buckets and bending rods sat on benches, sending worms on
suicide missions. Lovers whispered by like Ludlum double agents,
and a plump tour boat slid through Malibu blue with camcord
spudheads who pointed at everything.

Alan wore jeans and a tank top and Camille commented on
how pale he seemed. Did he have the flu? He said he was just
depressed about all the death and pain surrounding his life. Linda
Crain. Richard Frank. Eddy. Franky almost dying from the over-
dose. The terror in the screening room; Hector's suicide. It was
overwhelming.

"Plus I've never been the athletic type, I guess," he added, examining his white forearms which did seem somehow scrawnier than he'd remembered. As if someone had sewn a boy's arms to his torso. It had always embarrassed him that he wasn't more physically powerful; muscular. He'd been born a "before" photo.

She reacted with X-raying restraint, tightroped between a smile and that other thing she had done from the beginning that drove him crazy. That alluring way she'd blink and consider and tilt her head slightly. Where Erica would laugh easily, Camille would watch and await the exact moment when she could get in because you weren't looking.

Cops.

They were tax-paid Kafka characters; functional paranoids who feared betrayal and lived in worlds of worthless truth, blood-shed lies. They were the Horror Soldiers. The Psychiatric Attendants of shattered cities. After a while they all got the look. The thing in the eyes.

Alan knew Camille wanted to go over the latest roster of suspects her investigation was checking out. They'd already talked twice this week by phone after she had suspect photos faxed to his office. But she was in the neighborhood and needed to show him new names and faces; see if anything connected. He'd suggested they get some air and asked why she'd come alone; why Detective Lichtman hadn't joined her.

"He's not crazy about you or your show."

"And I thought he just didn't like me."

"He served in Laos. Lost friends. Thinks the show exploits real pain. He's very sensitive. Thinks you're getting rich for a bad reason."

They bought coffee and pretzels large enough to feed the antenna crowd from *THEM*, kept walking. Looked out at the postcard-perfect bay, recently found to contain enough industrial contaminants to end life.

"So, they send you to handle the cynical, profiteering producer?"

"Yeah, I'm your crime Sherpa. Let's just say your boss and my boss are friends . . ." She shrugged. "Chief of police and Feiffer? They both have places in Newport Beach . . . go to the same parties. Life down there is a spring break movie with Bentleys."

Alan nodded. "So. What does it mean?"

"Means my people like to keep your people happy. LAPD has certain officers and detectives who work entertainment crimes. Lichtman, me. Few others. We're supposed to have a softer touch with creative-slash-artistic types."

"Like working with the handicapped."

"That way, when you guys do a movie or a series about cops, you remember us being nice guys and give us a break. You know, write flattering versions of cops. Make us into human beings."

"P.R. . . ."

"Everybody goes to the movies. That's why Lichtman asked off. He couldn't handle your show. He also thinks it's giving people ideas . . ."

". . . popular theory."

Camille licked mustard from those Bardot lips and pulled out black-and-white photographs from a leather valise. Handed Alan the top photo.

"Anyway, I get to keep you all to myself while the other detectives look into the dull stuff."

Alan was looking at the guy, stamped onto the black-and-white square, who looked like a thinner Uncle Fester. She pointed.

"Barry Canning. They call him 'OverLoad.' "

"Creepy eyes."

"He's nice. Reasonable. Periodically, he just can't handle pressure. Two years ago, he went into a drive-in on a Saturday night, walked from car to car, and blew away twenty-six people because they were honking at the good scenes in *Crocodile Dundee Two*. It just seemed to kind of . . . piss him off."

"I've always hated it when people talk in movies."

"He managed a clock store in a mall the rest of the time."

Alan thought it over. "I say he did it. Clock store tie-in is a dead giveaway. Cover for some weird, pituitary thing. Object displacement. He's winding his little Timexes, setting his little alarms, but what's he really thinking? He's thinking, 'I hate everybody.' "

"Except Crocodile Dundee. He loves Crocodile Dundee."

"I don't recognize him."

"He escaped from a federal prison in east Texas, eight months back. All this could be him. It's his style. Brutal."

"Or it could just look good on paper."

"That's why I need your help, Alan. You know how this stuff works as well as I do. You write it everyday."

". . . seems to be the problem, doesn't it? That's what they're all saying . . ."

"Not everybody. Most people love your show."

"They say it's giving people ideas . . . just like Lichtman thinks. All these crimes are just copycats."

"You feel responsible? You can't. No one can prove a connection." She smiled. "I'm a cop. Even I can't."

He didn't answer. But Camille saw it in the way he moved his eyes. He was beginning to more than simply wonder. He tried not to fixate on the trauma "The Mercenary" beamed to its astronomical audience, but knew he'd done more than create a monster hit. He'd provided a perfectly detailed, one-hour, weekly seminar on suffering.

"Maybe the critics were right. Maybe I'm not a creative genius like all the network spirogyra swear in their fucking . . . profit trance." He looked away.

"So, you're a what? Evangelist of pain? Come on, Alan, your guilt is boring. It doesn't work like that. You're being simplistic. Nice TV shows don't make people nicer. Funny shows don't make them funnier. You're being narcissistic . . ."

"The whole fucking thing is my idea. I'm not sure anymore. What if there is a connection? What if the higher the ratings, the more my scripts and episodes are in the atmosphere detonating reaction? In some quiet brain, on some quiet street, somewhere." He looked into her eyes. "If so, on some level, I'm guilty."

She stared at him. His gaunt, troubled face.

"Look . . . why don't we try and find the guy doing this? That's the most constructive thing we can do. Here . . . take a look: we're also wondering about this guy."

She handed Alan a photo of a guy who looked like a malefic Dick Clark. His skin had a strange, wrinkle-free, stay-pressed look. It shone, looked imported.

"Doctor Adam Steinberg. Plastic surgeon. Re-did his wife. Re-did himself. Earns big bucks, sanding and shaping. Went to prison for tightening a woman's eyelids a little too far. All she can see is her forehead."

"Looks like he's been Turtle-Waxed."

"Should see Mrs. Steinberg. Did a hundred grand of lasar carpentry on her. I've interviewed her. Right out of the Barbie Dream Kitchen. Apparently he'd been her doctor and after her face-lift, he married her."

"Love by Mattel."

"So, on the honeymoon, they decide her nose is too big and her ears are a little LBJ."

He smiled, liking her objective humor with the horrors of humanity; the survival mechanism that sought the ludicrous in the grotesque. It had a reassuring effect on him.

"So, as a wedding gift, he trimmed her head. She got hooked, went the whole way. Higher brows, cheeks shaped, pert mouth, sleek chin, flatter tummy, smooth hips, slimmer thighs, smaller knees . . ."

". . . knees? She had big knees?"

"She said they were so big, people thought she was wearing knee pads."

"Big knees. That's weird." His stomach felt empty but he couldn't eat any more of the pretzel and tossed it to a pelican that looked like Jay Leno.

"So, she tells me she's totally restored like a beautiful, old Victorian. But Dr. Adam goes a little 'enthusiastic' and starts jigsawing people who don't really look so bad to begin with and the AMA is getting a little embarrassed. He gets sued and before you can say 'my tits are infected,' he's in for six years."

Alan looked at that taut, plasticized face and then up at Camille, who was licking salt off the pretzel's mulatto elbow. She looked very appealing and he told her so.

"Are you flirting with me? I thought this was professional."

"Well, I meant as a professional you look appealing."

"You want to know who else we have?" She liked that he was interested but didn't comment.

"No. This whole thing is giving me a stomachache. I have to get into the studio; we have a read-through. Why do you think Steinberg did it?"

"He's good with a knife. Whoever pinned up Linda Crain and blinded Richard Frank knew what they were doing. Cut-work was top-notch. It might've been him. Too early to be sure. We're just starting. And we have almost nothing to go on. No prints on the bodies. Anywhere around them."

Alan blanked out, feeling guilty, anew.

He could clearly see himself sitting at his word processor, writing the fourth "Mercenary" script, several months back. Describing the sounds and smells of a murder. How superb Barek was with a knife. Trying to imagine the slaughter in extreme close-up. Trying with horrid adjectives and helpless terror to be in that pink satinized suite, in Vegas, with the honeymooning couple who were Colombian drug dealers as Barek killed them; sought revenge.

They'd killed Barek's best friend; hung him upside down in a basement, by the ankles, naked, and removed the skin, over a period of hours. Trying to extract information about a competitor's hidden jungle labs where cocoa paste was moving up the profit chain like diamond toothpaste. They'd skinned him alive because Barek's friend was a cop who'd been trying to bust the couple. As Alan had written the episode, he'd tried to envison the couple's Bogotá skin slashed into nightmare fabric by Barek.

Tried to envision their meticulously sliced remains, dead in the heart-shaped tub, steeping in Type-O tea. Alan remembered feeling ill, he'd captured it so perfectly. It had made his shirt soak with sweat. But there had been a sense of justice in what Barek had to do. No matter how brutal the character became, he was always just. Alan always insisted Barek's violence be almost biblically fair. It redeemed everything. Created a moral updraft.

Some said it merely excused sadism.

But for Alan, at the moment of writing the scene, he remembered finding it hard to distinguish the scene as false or true experience. It had felt that real to him; he'd made it real in his mind. It may as well have existed. Existence and experience, more often than not, for him, were merging.

"Who else you have?" He leaned on the pier railing; weak.

"Few repeat felons. But none of them really have the chops for this level of . . ." She could see him waiting for her description; knew the wrong words would plunge him into deeper guilt. "I just think we should keep looking."

Alan looked up from a mob of gulls, debating atop sleepy currents. She stood, leaned against the pier railing, with him, swallowed the last of her coffee. Alan couldn't decode what her silence expressed. The wind blew her hair, momentarily veiling her features with its delicate storm.

Fog began to mourn at the horizon and Alan decided to say nothing more. He was starting to like Camille in a way he'd never felt about Erica. Liking her too much to start slyly excavating. To start making familiar, teasing allusions designed to draw her out. She would come out with her hands up when she was ready. It was enough she'd come here today to talk.

He knew she could've insisted it be done in some official place that had deafening phones, bad coffee burning; cardiac faces crashing into bad news. He knew she could've done it the "formal" way. But she didn't.

She'd suggested Malibu, saying she was returning from an investigation on the navy base at Port Hueneme, midway to Santa Barbara. Malibu was on her way.

"Besides, I wanted to see you," she said when she called at eight-twenty this morning and suggested they meet at the pier for a talk. She'd said it was official.

She also said she'd been thinking about him.

She'd read the novel portion he'd sent her and found its layers and concerns different from his usual conversation; the edgy banter and testing humor. The entertaining avoidances; amusing contortions of thought that moated off real feelings; revealing truths. Passions forbidden by charming armament.

But he knew his personality had always buried the fuse; hidden the explosion. It was his gift. It was his curse. And though this strangely charming woman, who was a detective and looked at dead bodies and could shoot people, was nothing like anyone he'd ever dated, he wanted her to come closer.

He wanted to peel back his skin and let her see bones and emotions; fears that moved through him like vicious gangs. But he didn't know how to open up to her. To admit the expanding sense of terror without sounding like a rambling fucking idiot. A Hollywood flake with big success and repugnant immaturity, interchangeable with fifty other self-contaminated "names."

He'd given her the novel portion as an emotional offering; a kind of child's drawing of what it felt like to be him. Like the finger semaphore cards mutes hand out in public places to connect with those who can speak. He wanted to be understood for more than his furious show and his guilt. He didn't just want her there because people had died. He didn't want tragedy to be the connection.

He wanted a loving, tender mother, again. A mother he never got for long. One who would hold him and tell him everything would be all right. Tell him with soothing tones and warm touches. Protect him in harboring arms. Sing softly until he slept.

Camille kept staring and watching. Smiling at strange times, her interest in him, beyond the ghastly investigation, evident. Deeper thoughts impossible to gauge.

"You're sure you don't have the flu?"

When he got into his Aston Martin and tilted down the mirror, he noticed it, too. Something was wrong with him. And it was getting worse.

advice

~~~~~~~~~~~~~~~~~~~~~~~~ Alan needed to see a doctor who'd keep everything confidential. The press would jump all over his life if they knew something was wrong with him, and he wanted a pro. Someone who didn't sell tips to tabloids.

He called Jordan, got shot through the Agenda Temple and Jordan's assistant, Traci, told Alan about the guy they all used: a former Harvard Medical School professor who'd moved to L.A. because of allergies.

Alan met Dr. Stuart Wessler at eleven sharp at UCLA Medical and as the doctor ran warm, inquisitive fingers over Alan's shoulders and torso, he wanted to talk "Mercenary."

". . . it's daring, Alan. Iconoclastic."

The big word sounded like ectoplasm, stretching its way out of Dr. Stu, who had a Hippocratic-gigolo look; like one of those daytime soap-opera erection-types and a Corvette, gene-spliced into an upbeat dildo.

"Taking chances. That's where it's at." Dr. Stu was now at the

~~~~~~~~~~

sink, lathering furry fingers with decanter soap, looking over his shoulder; a smocked pinup. "Especially for creative people."

"Yeah," said Alan, too tired to think; doing a shoddy retread on the same thought, ". . . risks." He yawned. A decent night's sleep would feel like a heart transplant.

"So, let's see what's going on in there . . ."

Dr. Stu pulled chrome devices from his drawer and was now leaning in close, staring into Alan's nose; Carl Sagan exploring Martian tunnels.

"Tell you, I sure love show business people though," he said, in response to nothing. "I grew up around it. My father managed a movie theater in Panorama City. I get all kinds of interesting cases in here."

He wanted to drop names. It was all over his barely mowed monkey face. Alan revved a wan, half-curious smile. Let it slowly idle.

"Yeah . . . I consulted on a flu case for one of the Bee Gees. I forget which one."

Alan tried to contribute, though Dr. Stu had the skinny searchlight up his left nostril, hunting for bad guys.

"Well, they're brothers," Alan suggested.

Dr. Stu nodded, meaningfully; two men sharing truth.

"The Gibbs. They're the best. I also did work for one of those Italian movie stars. You'd know who I'm talking about. Whole family acts. Major substance abuse problem. Wife problems. Mistress problems. Kid problems. Tax problems . . ."

The examples just kept coming.

He was starting to drive Alan crazy.

"Yeah . . . wouldn't want to be this guy for ten minutes . . . but he's a genius. Is it fair?" He looked at Alan, thought it over. "Don't ask me. I'm no philosopher."

His conversation was a cranial mallet.

"Alan, be honest with you. I leave philosophy to the gossip columnists." He winked, went on, lost in nasal canyons, eyeball lakes.

Dr. Stu was inches away and Alan began to notice his curly hair was a wig. His mustache freefell under designed nostrils and his collagen lips docked under the suspicious vents.

A fiberglass man.

Alan figured it added to Dr. Stu's popularity. The doctor who sort of looked like a doll. It was a nightmare. He told Alan he was soon expanding his practice into plastic surgery and in the next couple of months had to take his certification for liposuction.

". . . been cramming for the 'suck quiz.' Have to be careful. Once you have them in the vaccuum bag, can't get them out."

Dr. Stu droned on like childhood polio, parked the tongue depressor in Alan's mouth, and told him to say, "Ahhh." Alan's gag-reflex was thrown ten feet back, then rushed forward.

Dr. Stu smiled. "Nice."

Alan cleared his molested throat. Dr. Stu wrote something on his clipboard, then began to ball-peen knees. As he gently hammered, he told Alan he'd also worked as a part-time actor, whenever a patient in the business needed him. He said he'd done background atmosphere on a "21 Jump Street" as a strung-out cockroach and had a two-liner as Clifford, Barbi Benton's ex, in a Movie of the Week about infidelity and breasts.

On the set of "Jump Street," Dr. Stu said he'd gotten a personal moment with Johnny Depp and that he was "real." Dr. Stu also said Johnny had very nice skin.

". . . smokes too much," added Dr. Stu, inflicting Everett Koop omniscience. "Keeps it up, he'll sound like a Harley." He thumped on Alan's flour chest, listening for telling echoes. "Good. Sounds nice in there."

As he checked Alan's fingernail moons for size, Dr. Stu brought up a film treatment he'd written, two summers back, that was optioned by Warners. He said it went into turnaround when the producer, who was attached, died. The guy had smoked five packs a day for thirty years and shovelled a million acres of Marlboro Country on his lungs.

"Medical thriller," said Dr. Stu. "Too bad. Would've made a great film. Sort of like *Hunt for Red October* but it all takes place in a medical clinic." He considered. "Johnny coulda done it, though. I probably should've shown it to him."

Alan shrugged. "Maybe just shown it to his skin."

Dr. Stu looked at him, not really hearing. "Anyway, you gotta really be careful with smoking."

"How we doing?" Alan asked, knowing he had to get back to the studio for a scoring session.

"Almost done." He tapped Alan's sternum, lightly. "Yeah, real nicotine nursery. Be careful what you pour in. Might not like what starts growing." He nodded, seriously, pleased with the botanical simile.

"Uh-huh . . ." Alan was beginning to wonder if Dr. Stu was like the pleasant guy in *The Stepfather;* ready to pop, amid the inanity.

Dr. Stu paused, removed the plastic stethoscope fingers sticking in his ears. Patted Alan's back. "Well, everything looks okay. We'll wait for the tests, but so far . . . you're doing fine."

"Really?"

"Surprised?"

"It's just . . . a few people have told me I don't look so good."

"You're underweight for your age and frame. Makes you look a bit drawn. Easy to fix."

Alan gestured without detail. "Truth is, I really don't feel very good." He was confused. ". . . I don't exactly feel bad either. Just weak." He realized it sounded hypochondriacal. "Probably just overwork. Nerves. Am I whining?"

Dr. Stu grinned. "Listen, most of my patients are burning both ends. I tell them, you lose sleep, you try to catch up with yourself, you can't. Can't rip off your own body. It knows." Alan was listening, wanting to believe it. "All that REM stuff keeps stacking up. You don't dream it out, it'll drive you nuts. What kind of sleep you getting?"

"Sleep? How do you spell it?" He tried to make it sound funny. It missed.

"That's not enough. Eating right?"

"Imported coffee."

"Alan, I treat a lot of people in the industry. It's my practice. I know the hours and demands. But be good to yourself. You get one you."

It sounded like a ballad.

"I'm really okay?"

"I'm not going to lie to you. You're very worn down. But you're basically okay." He smiled, warmly; a hairy den mother. "I'd like to see you in two weeks. We'll get you on a higher protein diet. Supplements. Maybe a shot or two of B-12. And Alan ... they're called pajamas: introduce yourself, huh?" He chuckled like Marcus Welby always did; the call-me-in-the-morning Gandhi.

Alan was starting to feel Dr. Stu's calm voice sink in, soothe his chapped brain. He shook Dr. Stu's hand; the new, best pal he never wanted to be without.

When the test results came back, three days later, Dr. Stu called and a set of cutlery scattered in Alan's stomach. He was in the editing room, at the studio, working on the new episode. Dr. Stu told him the test results were highly unusual; that he'd never seen anything like it before, except in cases of extreme starvation. Metabolism so utterly strip-mined. Vital minerals reduced significantly.

"I've gone over your last physical. Eight months ago, you were fine. Now—" he paused, unnerved, "it's like somebody broke into your body and stole half of everything."

Alan clutched the phone. Felt nothing, stricken. Imagined his innards being burgled while he slept; awakening to find an empty house beneath his skin. He responded; a vacant irony.

"I wonder if they left fingerprints ..."

Dr. Stu told Alan he didn't know what was happening, but that he wanted to step up the supplements and get him in for more tests. He told Alan to try and not worry, it was some explainable depletion they'd turn around. As long as Alan was basically feeling all right, Dr. Stu advised against immediate hospitalization.

"We'll take it one step at a time ..."

Alan listened, saying nothing, looking down at himself. Wondering if the burglars would return; break in to his body for more. He imagined faceless prowlers inside his skin, with flashlights, ransacking tissue. Ripping blood cells off walls. Bagging priceless fluids. Rifling organs for mineral content that could be fenced later.

Shredding. Searching.

Taking him apart, piece by piece.

horror

The yacht rocked in still sea.

Infinite fish silently steeplechased beneath currents and inside bloody fingertips had left a mischievous trail on teak.

Sea Major was moored half a mile off Redondo Beach, twenty miles south of Malibu, and the man was at rest in his own red liquids, eyes dead Waterford.

He was tied to the bed, and had been stabbed over fifty times. There was so much blood on the sheets, the effect was a cardiac operation the surgeon had walked out on to have a smoke. A bucket of champagne was at the bedside, opened and undisturbed.

Romantic music played on the stereo and a woman was frantically dialing the cellular phone, shaking so badly she dropped it several times, whimpering in terror.

Her face had been attacked; cut apart into an unrecognizable Picasso. Multiple gashes went to bone. Her nose had been crudely slashed off and it left her face nearly flat. She couldn't breathe right and inhaled blood; choking on it.

Blood guttered into her mouth and eyes, and she grabbed for a paper napkin from the wedding reception they'd had that afternoon, on the yacht. It soaked up blood that oozed from her ruined face and tore in her hands, soaking wet. In seconds, the gold-lettered ROBB AND ERICA was unreadable.

reverse angle

Alan's limo hushed down PCH at six A.M. He was in back having coffee and croissants, reading the *Hollywood Reporter.*

Andy Singer was on the map again.

After the terrible ordeal of being beaten and terrorized, he'd disappeared. After two months or so of lethargic speculation by all, word around was he'd met a guy in the cortex spa, in Palm Springs, named Rick who'd poisoned his entire family, including cats, and that the two had hit it off.

People swore they took walks, played Trivial Pursuit, swapped desserts at mealtime. The grapevine was abuzz. Andy had a new buddy and he was crazier than Andy.

But that wasn't the good part.

The good part was that, owing to Andy's questionable judgment, after the assault, Alan's time slot never got changed and "The Mercenary" just kept rising on million mile legs, picking up more affiliates, even running twice a night in most markets.

Thanks for leaving your window unlocked, Andy.

Alan sipped coffee and glanced out at the ocean. A beautiful day; the kind of happy morning the Ventures probably decided to dry off and buy a tape recorder.

He got back to the article which was going on about what a fucking genius Andy was and how the whole universe mourned the terrible tragedy which befell him. Then, they dropped the bombshell.

Andy, the Cambodian spin-fuck chair, was quoted as saying he'd had much time to think about his life while on "leave"—a polite way of saying he'd blown his amp and was currently in fulltime residence at Shatter World—and that he missed television. With such "brilliant triumphs" as "Cleo" and more currently "The Mercenary" on his list of accomplishments, he was ready to get back into the swing.

And the little Cheshire Führer had an idea.

He talked for a couple of paragraphs about his new friend Rick and what a funny guy he was and how the two had spent countless hours together just talking and kidding around in the programmer's room, while Andy awaited the proper time to re-enter the world. Rick, of course, never could. Only genuine lunatics were released.

The *Reporter* article went on to say Andy's new series concept was called simply "The Roomie." Andy was further quoted as saying it was about an insane, bipolar roommate with a terrible but "hysterically funny" temper and that he'd already set it up at CBS with a firm order for thirteen, on the air.

Alan poured himself another cup of coffee and shut his eyes. He heard about Erica twenty minutes later when he called his office for messages.

TV Guide

Talk about *bad* luck.

"What can I say?" says Executive Producer and Creator Alan White. "We've been assailed by horrible things. It's been a nightmare."

Talk about *weird* luck.

"We're also the number one show in the world," adds White. "It almost feels like some awful kharma. Hopefully these bad things are over. We've lost a lot of wonderful people."

You've seen it by now. Everyone has. It's the hottest series on network television and it's a sizzling outrage. Managing to stun with its mixture of nudity, shuddering violence, dizzying action, and a strange messianic morality, "The Mercenary" is acetylene hot. It seethes attitude and danger and so far five people who are somehow connected to it have died.

It's not that people haven't died on other shows, or other movies. Hollywood is rife with productions that went tragically awry and ended up with unwitting body counts. Stunt men die like seasonal plants in a business that strives to design ever more spectacular action sequences. Older actors have died in midscene of natural causes. Younger ones have died with something in their body you can't get with a prescription.

Excesses and danger seem to go hand in hand with the dream biz. But never, in memory, has a single production been so battered by tragedy.

April 17. Renowned "bad boy" English film director Hector Blackman commits suicide in a screening room which is showing footage of "The Mercenary" pilot Blackman has directed. In that same room, Second-Unit Director Bo Bixby and network liaisons Scot Bloom and Greg Gunnar are shot by Blackman. Bloom dies after two hours of trauma surgery.

November 12. Nationally syndicated television critic Richard Frank falls to his death from a Los Angeles high rise. Frank was the most vocal critic of the show and the circumstances of his death, in which he was inexplicably blinded, are still under investigation.

February 24. Linda Crain, the leader of a fundamentalist church, who wrote angry letters to the advertisers and companies which promoted products on "The Mercenary," disappears, is found tortured, and dies en route to a hospital. The brutal, bizarre circumstances of the murder remain confidential, pending further investigation.

April 2. Network executive Andrew Singer, the man responsible for giving the green light to the controversial series, is severely beaten in his home by an intruder. He was recently released from a psychiatric hospital with possible brain damage, which he denies.

June 16. Erica Ritter, longtime friend of Alan White, is attacked and disfigured during her honeymoon. Her husband of two days is murdered.

What does it all mean? Theories abound.

"Anybody can have a bad year. Or a great one. Or, in this business, both at the same time," says one prominent entertainment attorney who asks to remain unnamed. But other television insiders are saying it means certain shows just shouldn't stay on the air.

Still, a show this massively popular won't go down without a fight. It's simply far too profitable for far too many people. The bottom line, as they say in corporate Hollywood, is that a show is big business. And a show this successful seems to have a mind of its own.

hero's collapse

~~~~~~~~~~~~~~~~~~~ It's okay. Alan ..." a perfumed whisper.

He stared away and her hands moved gently on his back; a Ouija touch. The room was dark, coppered by candlelight. He felt things breaking inside, embarrassment pushing against his skin. He sat on her bed, gathered a sheet around himself; a shroud.

"... it's not you," he said. "It's all this ... blood. Death. Thinking of Erica. How helpless she was ..."

Camille rubbed his shoulders and her strength relaxed him. She asked him if he wanted to try again and when he nodded, she held him down like a man would. He responded, without intellectual review, liking her control; the assertion of her movements.

He felt protected. Taken away.

"You be me," she whispered, as she held his wrists more tightly, pressing him against the mattress.

As she made love to him, guiding him and directing his body, he tried to imagine how she looked doing this to her girlfriend, Lena. How their soft curves fit together; a perfect wrongness. How their lips and painted nails tenderly traced each other. How she would tell Lena she loved her; that she was in love with her. That they would always be together. That no one would come between them.

"Maybe I should go . . ." he thought, but didn't say, instead allowing her mouth to search his neck and ears, telling him the things she wanted to do to him.

He'd been drawn to the sensual ambiguity at first; the forbidden Oz of her bisexuality. The safety of knowing she was in love with someone else. But as his body weakened, health losing shape and color, he couldn't stand the confusion of roles. Couldn't respond; perform.

He didn't know if it was her, himself, or a numbing combination of both. But as he looked up at her beautiful face and lost himself in her warm breasts, her long, dark hair curtained him like a delicate cage. She whispered tender demands and he drifted into the nurturing urgency, trying not to.

She thrust down and he felt damp pubic hair sliding on his penis, back and forth. She leaned down and kissed him, tongue slow; hypnotic.

Her palms were warm on his and he closed eyes, trapped in a secret bay, imagining Lena as him. Hearing her sweet moans; her aquiescing struggle. Held down, as he was.

". . . I wanna fuck you," said Camille, in some ravaging spell, mouth tight with need.

But he was suddenly a spectator; in a thought, rather than a place. Nothing happened, no matter what she did and though his breathing raced, his reaction was vacant. His muscles felt cut-out, afloat in a bottle of formaldehyde; dead specimens.

She looked down at his pale face, placed her cheek against his, whispered that it was all right. Everything in this room was safe. He was safe. He felt her sweet perspiration on him and pulled her closer, knowing he was losing her. Knowing he'd never had her. He suddenly thought she looked like his dead mother and smiled, then felt sick.

She blew out the candle and he plunged further into blackness, suddenly filled with terror. He clung to her, unable to form words, unable to tell her how nothing in his world seemed like his anymore. As if he'd been put in someone else's circumstances and told nothing. As if his parents had pulled over to the side of the road, in some ominous little town, put him out and driven away forever. As if everything in his world had vanished and abandoned him.

He trembled in Camille's strong arms; a frightened hand clutching a crucifix.

subtext five

Terrified. Bones showing.

"I'm leaving the show . . . things are happening. I can't concentrate on my writing."

Voice shaking.

"Erica . . . her new husband was killed. She was maimed."

A sick feeling.

"Am I going crazy? Am I the one doing this or is it someone at the network? Maybe someone on staff at the show? There are things going on. Corea is changing. *TV Guide* did this big article about how jinxed the show is . . ."

Hands knotted.

"Am I killing people myself? I mean . . ."

Not knowing what he meant.

". . . things have happened . . . information only I know about in scripts I've written . . ."

Eyes shut.

"Something is happening . . ."

Weeping.

"Something is happening . . ."

awards

Alan picked at his veal piccata; a thirty-dollar scab.

The beautifully set circular table chattered and laughed and every now and then Jordan would reach under the starched cloth to feel his date's panties. She was an actress named Joey, Jordan had just packaged into "Off the Curve," an ABC pilot, for midseason replacement, about a woman who had a genius I.Q. and ran a school for gifted girls with large breasts. Joey's breasts seemed to suffer from clinical gigantism and Alan sensed she'd bring a lot to the show.

As she chewed her veal, her cleavage did a distracting Panama Canal from neck to dress and she giggled at everything Jordan said.

Alan had decided to come without a date.

Erica was talking to him again but still recovering from her husband's murder and her own savaged body. He'd visited her at her condo in Venice, two weeks after the attack and been shocked. She was doing legal work by fax from her living room, but couldn't return to the office for fear of infection. Seventy percent of her body had been stitched back together and she'd nearly bled to death.

Full recovery would take months. Then would come the countless plastic surgeries to reshape, restore. To make a face from torn skin.

He'd cried when she answered the door and he saw the damage. On one side of her face, the laceration went straight across the long, perfect smile he used to love touching. Another seam was a swollen meridian which ran across one cheek, over the nose, onto the other cheek.

"I miss you," she had told him, as angles of sun crept through shutters and warmed her monster's face. There was springy thread all over her features and when she smiled, it pulled open healing skin.

"What exactly does People's Choice Awards mean?" It was Jordan's Sominex test rat, trying to make conversation.

Jordan stared at her a moment as the others at the table waited for his answer. He looked at Alan.

"It means . . . that . . ." he felt eyes like faces in bleachers. "It means that . . . the people choose it."

"You mean . . . like as their favorite?" She'd gotten it and Jordan seemed relieved. He smiled, anxious to switch subjects.

"Right," he said.

"I see." She was feeling more a part of the evening and nodded, waiting for the insight to permanently cling to the tiny bulletin board in her head. The others at the table, which was toward the front of the Hollywood Palladium, nodded politely, starting on dessert.

There were two others at Alan's table who were involved with "The Mercenary." Simon Buss had been nominated for his role as General Garris and the show's cinematographer, Jimmy Orsatti, was also nominated for his work on the pilot. Alan was up as creator and executive producer/writer for best one-hour action drama series. Neither he nor the late Hector had been nominated for directing.

Corea hadn't been nominated and it had infuriated him. He chose not to come and when Alan tried to coerce him for publicity reasons, Corea had told him to fuck himself and gone off on some dark, cathartic odyssey.

He'd disappeared, left no message. Not even with his ex-wife, who was now suing him for half his entire fortune. She'd agreed to keep mention of the marital rapes from the press in exchange for a fast settlement and the house in Lahaina.

Corea was now living at the studio, in his $250,000 motor home, although several stagehands swore they'd found him sleeping on "The Mercenary" set, as if it were home. As if it were all he needed; just his bed in the dingy little hotel room, at Blacks Hotel, where the character lived. No matter where he was, Alan was sure it would be Monday before he'd hear from him. When Corea went, he went over the horizon.

"Hey, man, how you doing?" Jordan was whispering into Alan's ear; a tanned Yoda. He lassoed a protective arm around Alan's shoulder. "Okay?"

Alan said he was okay and Jordan told him the People's Choice nomination was a sure sign the show would sweep the Emmy's. Nothing else on the air could touch the adrenal Hiroshima of "The Mercenary"; its hypnotic menace. Its sheer artistic risk factor.

"Hey, pal, if Bart Simpson blew Cosby and swallowed, we'd still have it in the bag."

Alan was staring off into space, feeling sick; weak.

Even with all the stuff Dr. Stu had given him to pump his energy, he had no appetite and couldn't finish his food. He caught his curved reflection in the perfectly polished water pitcher. Even with the makeup they'd put on all the nominees at the fifty or so tables filling the auditorium, they couldn't mask his hospice complexion.

He nodded at Jordan. Thought of Camille.

He'd called her and asked if she wanted to come. But she'd said she had to work that night. The slaughter at the fast food chicken place near Wilshire was a mess and she was going to be busy sponging up blood and Original Recipe and interviewing survivors for a full report.

The shooter had been a USC Film School major who'd been depressed over not getting an agent with his new ten-minute film, *Schmooze,* a clumsy satire about ambition. He'd been sent countless letters of disinterest from the top agencies who'd seen the effort on cassette and thought it sucked. In reaction, he'd weed-whacked fifteen people before pressing the AK-47 to his heart and hitting his OFF switch.

Camille said Alan could call after he got home but not after midnight because Lena worked early and needed sleep. Much as he and Camille chemically sparked, she was in love with somebody else who, as luck would have it, was a woman. Maybe it was a good time to back away from relationships anyway. His faltering body was beginning to frighten and humiliate him. He couldn't make love. Could barely keep up with Camille.

But he missed her. Missed Erica. Missed Eddy. His mother. His little sister. John Lennon. Himself.

The table was cleared, the lights came down, and Alan endured the canned show. The hosts were a beloved sitcom mom, who was rumored to have beaten her children, and a young frenetic comic with annoying lips. The hours dredged by with formaldehyde banter, witless punch lines. When Alan's name was finally called, he felt stunned by the previous two hours of festive horse tranquilizer, straightened his bow tie, stood on shaky legs.

All he remembered seeing was Jordan's eerie smile and a grinning, tuxedo corridor as he trotted up to grab the award. There were murmurs of shock at how bad he looked. But he took the camera head-on and nodded for effect, staring at the award in his frail hand.

". . . well, I guess this just goes to show you that good taste will always out," he deadpanned and the place cracked up. He smiled but anyone who looked closely could see a man bleeding to death.

He thanked everyone he could think of. His mom, his dad, Eddy, Andy, Jordan. Corea, who he said deserved this as much as he did, though it felt strange to admit it was possible.

Then, he stared out at the hot lights, the swamp of power beyond. He gripped the podium tightly, lips dry, legs shaking. The place went silent, hundreds of expectant smiles in glittery gowns and designer wire-rims, waiting. The director saw Alan's dislocated trance and had the band poised to go instantly into "The Mercenary's" percussive theme and get Alan off stage.

He wanted to tell them all how terrified he was of what had happened to his life. How he wished he could stay in this big, safe room for the rest of his life with all these people who thought he was so great, where he couldn't be hurt. Where his ravaged life could become no worse.

But he didn't say anything; too weak. He just kept staring, feeling lights pressing in, eyes crawling all over him. As they all watched, wishing they could be him, Alan collapsed, like he'd been shot.

crisis point

~~~~~~~~~~~~~~~~~~~~~~~~~~~~~ *Voices.*

Faraway. Things in his arms, his nose. His eyes wouldn't open. He tried to imagine the room. Filled with floral arrangements. A TV bracketed high, watching over him. A roommate with a sheet pulled over the face.

Sirens.

Fresh wounds; incoming. Maybe a gang shooting. A baby abandoned, hungry for food, touch. A light plane crash. He saw flesh, frightened eyes. Heard moans of anguish.

He wanted to open eyes, see the place they'd brought him to. He remembered the awards, the big round tables, the room filled with desperate smiles. Jordan eating. The music and the television cameras . . . the sequin prattle on stage . . . then, nothing.

Just sirens and whispers. Eyelids that pressed the back of his head hard against the pillow. Eyelids that locked him into a dark theater, in his skull. A place without EXITs, made of mildewed cinderblock, filled with a rotting stench. The torn screen showed movies with appalling close-ups. Ravaged victims. Black-and-white

~~~~~~~~~

traffic-school footage of hideous things on roads. Then, it would quickly change to color. Dwell on deformity and helplessness, in perfect chroma-keys.

He tried to get out of the theater, running up the aisle into a bricked doorway. The projectionist's windows, gunned out bright light and Alan looked up, screaming for help. A face came to one of the yellow squares and stared down at him and grinned, shoulders shaking with sick laughter. Alan couldn't see the face, then as it turned slightly to see him better, the light hit it and he realized it was his own, staring down at him, hatefully. It gradually turned up the tortured soundtrack, as Alan begged for a way out.

The screen filled with bloated corpses, crippled bodies. Children with missing arms and legs, shrieking for their mothers in languages that didn't exist. Barek moving through dense jungle, turning toward the camera and staring at Alan. Smiling, releasing a mouth of blood which drenched his shirt and chin.

The projectionist turned up the volume until Alan felt he was crouching, hands over ears, screaming. The projectionist watched him, an exact duplicate of himself and the grin fell. Now there was loathing and anger. The theater shook from the deafening soundtrack of pain and Alan began to claw at the cinderblock, trying to get out. The vibration was grabbing the walls and they began to wobble. Alan looked up, seeing the ceiling and walls collapsing in on him.

Then, silence. Blackness. Nothing.

realization

"Alan . . . ?"

Alan's eyes were closed. Drugs.

"Were you sleeping?" The man wore blue jeans, deer moccasins. His white hair was long, uncombed. He was almost seventy, resembled an ancient Paul McCartney. The Sergeant Pepper mustache drooped neatly, and he looked ready to pound Blue Meanies.

Alan's eyes lifted. The man came around the wheelchair. Kneeled. Took Alan's shaking hand. The warm skin felt like a desert. The smile full of vitamins; minerals.

". . . I'm Seth Lawrence. Your secretary Lauren called . . . told me you needed to talk. I called you one night. Do you remember?"

Alan let the sun creep up his legs, into his robe. His head felt heavy. "The book. You wrote it. . . ." He was whispering. "A woman told me we'd meet." Alan tried to remember her name. ". . . a psychic."

Seth slowly pushed the wheelchair around the UCLA Hospital grounds, said Mimi had died last year. A car accident. Alan told him so many had died.

~~~~~~~~~

"... murdered."

Seth asked it casually. "Who's killing them?" A test.

"Something that wants to get me. What I care about. Because of ... the show." His voice trailed. "... it made something happen."

Seth stopped the wheelchair near a kinetic sculpture and the two watched water crawl on steel. Alan tried to remember; see Corea, in his mind. He remembered a bar full of smoke. Someone screaming. A monster's smile.

"The man I hired to play the character ... he's changed ... it isn't him."

"... who is it?"

Alan had no answer. He could see him now; the man in the bar. Dense body, hideous grin. "Lines. Didn't have lines on his ... palms."

Seth nodded, saying nothing; interpreting. Minutes passed. Alan stared into space, wordlessly. Seth stretched, smiled brightly.

"Wanna hear a story?"

Alan sipped on the water bottle in his lap. "What kind of story?"

"*Adventure.*" He stretched more, organized thoughts. Talked fast. "Okay ... went like this, last summer I'm in Recife, Brazil, with some friends, doing research on a new book I was writing, about psychic surgery ... you know, when they cut you open with their hands, no tools or anesthesia." Alan knew. "Right, well, on the way to the surgeon's apartment, we all wanted to see something different, so the taxi driver took us to this place, in the ghetto. Kind of an outside dancing area for the poor. Military goons, in machine-gun nests, watching. Making sure no one went crazy. Fingering their guns ... just hoping, you know?" He closed one eye, aiming, mimicked pulling a trigger. "POW!"

Alan reacted to the loud sound and Seth cracked up, apologized. "Anyway, we had some time to kill, so we paid a couple bucks to get in ... ended up dancing with the peasants. This big rainstorm came ... all of us got soaked to the bone. I can still hear the rain on the mud, bare feet dancing."

He waited for Alan to visualize it. Alan's eyes began to close. Seth watched him carefully.

"We played primitive instruments, pounded empty cans with sticks. Real 'Emerald Forest.' Drank local poison called cashasta. Hundred proof. Talking mule piss."

He winked, shut his own eyes, recalling detail. The closed eyes trembled. He could hear the beat; the numbing chorus of brown-skinned voices. His voice fell.

"Coupla peasants flipped . . . you know, from the cashasta, the beat. Started screaming." His face froze. "This one peasant . . . he freaked . . . tried to rape this woman. We heard CLACKING. Machine guns. Looked up, saw the guards laughing, guns bouncing against their shoulders. He was shot at least twenty times. Big mess . . . he's on top of her, she's screaming, soaked with his blood. Major scene. The body gets taken away, dragged through the mud." Seth opened eyes, rolled a cigarette. "Everyone kept dancing."

"I don't like this story."

"Wait till you hear the good part. So, everyone kept dancing, right? Totally oblivious. Finally, it's appointment time and I go a few blocks away to the surgeon's apartment. He sits me on a chair, removes a benign tumor with his hands; no anesthesia. No pain. The perfect can-opener."

Smoke in, out. Seth pointed with his cigarette.

". . . hour later, I went back to the dance and there's this flash of lightning, right? Suddenly, I see the guy who got shot, dancing in the rain, grinning ear to ear, eyes dead. Clothes bloody. Bullet holes all over his face. You could see brain tissue, bone. Horrible." Seth sat on fountain edge. "But there he was. Try explaining that one, Jack."

Alan shrugged.

"Who knows what he was, at that point. I mean, he was dead. But he was alive." A point. "Go enough places, you see things that seem crazy."

"What happened to your tumor?" Flat; unimpressed.

"Still had it when I got back to L.A. Guess I got ripped-off." Alan folded hands. Saw how loose his skin fit over bones.

Remembered, again, he was dying. "Look, this doesn't really help me."

"Things that seem insane are possible, Alan." He dipped a hand in water. "Your secretary told me what's been happening. The things you told her. This lunatic you've seen. Know what I think? I think you're right." A look from Alan. "Maybe this thing you say you spoke with at the bar isn't the actor. No lines on his hands. Pretty weird."

". . . then, who is it?" Alan could only think it so far.

"You're a writer, think like a writer. If you wanted to tell a story about a man who encounters what he thinks is a monster . . . who would the monster be? The perfect one? Get thematic."

Alan was in a story conference now. Riffing; sawing, pounding invisible nails for imaginary supports. He stared off, tried to get into the motives of the characters. No longer his problem, now just an interesting fiction. An algebraic stimulation.

"Simple. A monster the man needs."

"For what?"

Alan thought. Weighed options.

"Choose something." Seth kept pushing.

"Maybe he's angry."

"Generic. Everybody's angry."

Alan paused. "Maybe the man doesn't know how to let it out."

"Cliché. Who does?"

A glare. "The guy I met in the bar does."

They looked at each other.

"We done with this game?" Alan was impatient.

"It's not a game. So, why are you in the middle of this whole thing? What's your role in this 'story'?"

Alan gestured; a random thought. "Who the fuck knows. Maybe this thing has become like my hit man, killing all the fucking creeps in Hollywood I can't stand?" It was a classy guess at best; he wasn't trying to hide it.

Seth listened, thought. Shrugged. Kept himself out of it. Alan shook his head, displeased. Contemptuous.

"It's simplistic. Derivative. Nobody would watch. People would change the channel." Then, he thought about how many there were. The ones who'd wounded him.

The *Creeps.*

The hurt they'd brought. How he stored quarts of it in canisters of gloom and unforgiving resentment like radioactive material. All that pain. All those lies. All the cruelty. The fucking *Creeps* were everywhere.

"You're right," said Seth, "it is too simplistic." He killed his cigarette under a boot; a glowing victim. "I think you're nuts."

"No, you don't . . ."

Seth smiled. "You know what I think is interesting? This 'monster' looks almost exactly like the star of a show you created." Seth said nothing more. Waited for Alan to respond. Alan came up with nothing, lost; mind exhausted. Then, something.

"You saying the character and that thing are the same thing?"

"Getting warm."

"You know and aren't telling me?"

"What do you think?"

"I think I'm sick of riddles. Why did you come?"

"You asked."

"Look, you can't leave me in the dark, like this. I'm sick and I'm scared. People are dying. I feel like I'm dying. If you know something, you have to tell me."

"I'm telling you everything that can be said right now. If there was anything else, we'd both know it. But if you want a suggestion . . . suppose you wrote the character differently? Make him nicer?"

Alan got angry, couldn't believe they were exchanging fucking lunacy about zombies, and evil Creatures, and changing the primal order of a fucking television character who was a slightly elevated scribble.

He sighed; a trapped noise. "Look, what the fuck are we talking about?"

"You're the one who's talking. I'm just smoking a cigarette."

"Who the hell are you, anyway? Why should I listen to you."

"So far, you're not. I used to be a psychoanalyst. Wanted to know more about the mind . . . traveled the world, trying to inventory all the natural hallucinogens that grow wild. See how they might cure mental illness. Lived with primitive people. Saw magic." He weathervaned a finger. "From there, got to here."

Alan backed off, cooled down.

"I want to know if there really is something inside me. You know how to do hypnosis or . . ."

"Too complicated. Annoy both of us. Better idea . . . we give you a pen, you close your eyes, start writing. Whatever comes out helps us to see inside you. Shrinks use it to help patients contact the inner child. We use your opposite dominant hand. Tends to bypass the conscious mind. Have to. Thoughts have incredible power. *Never forget that.* It's the key to everything."

The two moved to a bench and sat. Seth pulled out a pad. Alan held pen above paper for ten minutes but nothing happened. He began to perspire slightly and there was a fractional slippage of ink on paper.

All at once, his hand began to move, skating angrily, as if gouging something into tree bark; gripping the pen, like the hilt of a knife. He pressed it so hard, against the paper, it broke, exposing words he'd written; ragged, angular scrawl. They stared up from the paper; gloating bullies:

YOU DIE

moral support

Alan and his father walked on the beach, near the house, and as Alan talked more about quitting "The Mercenary," Burt was stunned by how sick Alan looked. How scared he was. It was the first Burt had seen of him close-up in almost a year, and he was shocked by Alan's appearance; the wasted flesh. He'd seen him on the "People's Choice" nightmare, but makeup had partially hidden the ruin.

"Is your marrow supposed to hurt, Pop? I think I need to make a marrow escape ..." He tried to sound like he wasn't terrified. Tried not to shatter into a million pieces.

Though Burt asked about his health and obvious weight loss, Alan didn't tell him everything; it was too complicated and he wasn't sure what to say. About the collapse at the Awards. The UCLA stopover; encroaching madness. What he and Seth had talked about. He was afraid of making it worse. He knew his father could see the avoidance.

Burt told him he could always tell him the truth. It was the only way to flee internal tortures. Alan felt him struggling to open a

subject and Burt confessed he and Wanda had been having trou-
bles. There had been recent arguing. Sexual tensions. They'd been
to see a therapist and the truth had emerged about her rape.

". . . rape?" Alan's face died.

Burt said she'd barely been able to talk about it, but the
therapist encouraged trying and she finally told them both in
agonized fragments.

She'd been attacked on a beach in Florida, during high
school; six guys took her to places, on that wet, night sand, she'd
never returned from. Places Burt said he could still see in her
little-girl face. If he looked for a second longer than normal, a
private slide show crept out: men with pants at ankles, rocking,
laughing. Slapping her. Stretching her on the sand; a bruised X.
Beer bottles thrown against cement pier pilings. Lifeguard truck
beams, roving sand, just missing the spot where the savage party
writhed.

Burt looked off, said it had been when the original siezure
struck. The men had been revolted and kicked at her naked, torn
flesh, shouting at her to stop. Screamed at her, spit on her. Walked
away, leaving her to die, in sperm and blood.

Burt said every detail was there in her eyes. Then, a second
later, it wasn't. She'd gotten so good at living with it, she could nail
terrible doors shut; make it go away.

". . . things don't go away," said Alan, feeling awful for her. It
was like discovering the ghastly ways circus animals are trained to
seem happy. He felt condemned.

> WE ALL HAVE TERRIBLE SECRETS. NO ONE CAN
> KNOW US. WE ARE ALONE.

It was a T-shirt that gained popularity back in college. Over
time, Alan's had faded, became a rag. He used it to polish cowboy
boots, but the thought, the full-frontal despair never went away. He
remembered the shirt, realized he'd treated Wanda like a one-
celled smile. He knew he had to sit and talk with her. Sit and tell her
all the pain he understood now; the anguish.

As they strolled sand, Burt said he understood Alan wanted out of the show and suggested the two work together on a film in France, he'd just been offered. He didn't say how awful he thought Alan actually looked; didn't want to alarm him.

"A comedy, thank God . . ." he added, as foam soaped their feet.

He said Alan could produce, and he would direct. It was also in bad need of a rewrite and Alan was the perfect guy. Burt's famous directing would "roar again," and give Oliver Stone "the hot-angst popper," and all those "fucking two-hundred-million-dollar brats" a run for their massive bank accounts.

Alan skipped a rock. Coughed and felt dizzy. Burt steadied him and the two sat on the warm sand, watching a group of porky scuba guys bobbing in a boat. Then, Alan grew quiet and said yes, he would do it. He admitted, he needed the picture in France.

Burt smiled, putting his arm around him. Told him he needed to change perspective; stop thinking about "The Mercenary." "Hell," said Burt, doing his best to cheer Alan up, "maybe we'll even win an Oscar. If not, food's better in France. We can get fat. You could use a little meat on you."

Alan knew his father could see how sick he was and leaned on him a little. Burt gave him a hug and felt Alan's thinness. How cold his skin was. How he seemed to be shaking though it wasn't cold out.

They watched the sun flatten on blue and for the first time, since Alan was a kid, Burt told him he loved him. It felt wonderful.

And to Alan it felt like what you tell a dying man.

ten percent four

~~~~~~~~~~~~~~~~~~~~~~~~~ Jordan. A personal visit? I'm stunned."

"What *exactly* do you think you're doing?" He was raising his voice.

Alan leaned back in his desk chair. Jordan moved to desk's edge.

"I've been on the phone all the way over with Jack Feiffer. The man is insane."

"You just heard?"

"Who gave you the right to start changing 'The Mercenary'?"

"I created it. Remember? It came out of my head."

"The network owns it now. And the agency packaged it. That means we get a fee. Shall I explain that?" Jordan stared, a sheet of ice. "Why are you fucking with a good thing?"

"For me, it's a bad thing."

". . . for you it's a bad thing. It looks like it. You look like shit. Thought they were going to do something for you in the hospital. Alan, Feiffer told me the new script has Barek helping a destroyed

~~~~~~~~

enemy village rebuild itself. That he's got a scene where he plays with enemy children!"

"... they're just children, Jordan." Alan looked up, pleasantly.

"... another where he goes for a walk with a gorgeous young villager and there's no sex. No nudity."

"They hold hands."

"No. *Wrong*. They don't 'hold hands.' "

"What do they do?"

"They roll in the grass and he tears her clothes off and they *fuck* and she *loves* it and she screams and claws his back on camera and we see her nipples get hard and everybody is happy. Feiffer, the affiliates, fucking world audience, the studio, me ... *everybody!*"

Alan popped a Trident.

"What you wrote is not the show! It's not what people are tuning-in for. What are you doing, 'Highway to Heaven'? Where's the violence? The naked girls?"

"The character is changing."

Jordan laughed low; ugly.

"No. What's going to change is you running the show. Feiffer wants to bring in somebody else immediately if you don't get this thing on track."

"*No!*"

Jordan stared, waiting.

"Not yet. I'll get out of the way. But not yet."

"You leave the show, agency loses major money on you."

"Sorry."

Jordan tried to be reasonable.

"Alan ... why are you trashing your own show?"

"I'm trying to make it better."

A cutting stare. "... you're killing it."

The phrase wasn't lost on Alan who said nothing. "I'm trying to make the character nicer, Jordan. Make him less filled with hate."

Jordan was tired of talking.

"Alan ... let me try and break this to you, while you're still lucid: hate is the whole point! *Hate* is what people love. Take the *hate* out, you got *nothing!*"

Alan stared at him. "Jordan, listen to yourself."

Jordan stared, with his charcoal soul. "What did you expect?"

". . . I don't know. Everything?"

Jordan said nothing.

"You're my agent. You're supposed to be concerned about me. Not just my money."

"We can't work together anymore, Alan. Our priorities differ. I suggest you find other representation."

Jordan remained silent. Then, he walked to the door. Turned. "By the way . . . Tony Moore is doing a picture about an insane android assistant who kills for her boss. Ripped off your idea. Hired a twenty-year-old kid out of film school to write it. Just heard today. If I were you, I'd sue."

Alan nodded. Said nothing. Realized it was Jordan's sentimental postscript.

revenge

The room was fifteen-by-fifteen and included a Jacuzzi, sauna, shower, and small bed. When Burt and Wanda had first come to the place, they thought for sure it was a gay hangout. Right there on Bob Hope Boulevard, festooned by slim young men with twenty five inch waists.

Burt was having his spa-room rebuilt, at the house, while he and Wanda and Alan were in France, and everything was in pieces. They'd be leaving in two days and Burt missed the heat and jets. This turned out to be the perfect place to unwind. Little jacuz, little sauna, little lovemaking in between showers. After a while, you felt light-headed; every muscle had hopped a tiny little 747, headed to Honolulu.

"How's it feel, babe?" Burt was naked, sixty-three-year-old flesh a tanned tarp. He was hanging his slacks on a hook.

Wanda stripped, stepped cautiously into hot, swirling water. "Greeeaaaaattttt . . ." The word was a hundred feet long.

He smiled, admiring her smooth stomach, trim arms. He slipped into the steaming cauldron; a head-hunter's bisque.

Leaned up against the wall of the hot tub, feeling jets bomb his spine.

Steam baled thicker and Wanda dimmed the red lights. She turned up the royal blue light in the spa and the two colors met; purple haze, all in their eyes.

Wanda wrapped herself around him and the two drifted, heads tilted back on limp necks. When they opened eyes, minutes later, they saw him standing there, grinning.

Before they could do anything, Burt had been lifted and slammed against the glazed tile. He collapsed; unconscious, forehead bleeding. Wanda began to scream and was struck across the jaw.

Burt was lifted into the sauna and as he bled on cedar slats, the door was slammed shut, the dial turned to 10. Wanda moved in dazed horror, on the damp floor, until heaved back onto the small bed, legs pried apart. She screamed again and was slapped until pale; silent. Her wrists were held tight and he entered her, violently.

"You like to fuck?" he was biting her nipples, making them bleed. "You like to fuck?"

She could smell him. The filth and sweat coating his hard muscles. She begged him to stop and he grabbed her chin with thick fingers. Forced her to stare at him, lifting an executioner's smile.

Her eyes filled with terror.

There was something wrong with him. As she kicked and writhed, making him harder, inside her, she tried not to look at his face. Tried not to look at how parts of it were missing; not cut away as if surviving facial surgery. More like they'd never been there.

As she struggled to escape, he lunged for her shoulder and bit it. She screamed. He bit again. She screamed louder and he pulled her hair tight. Whispered hard.

"You like to fuck?" he smeared the blood from her bleeding nipples on his face; war paint.

She couldn't answer and he bit her again, ripping neck flesh with primitive teeth. She was bleeding bad, chewed skin a sickening necklace that tomatoed the bed. He sucked at her swollen nipples and shoved a dirty finger up her anus, making her scream. She could feel it rubbing against his penis, on the opposite wall, inside her.

He was plunging; stabbing himself into her. Then, out. Then, re-entering the wound, traveling deep toward her uterus. She was crying and managed to free her hands, reaching up to claw his eyes. She glanced up, for a moment, to see his unshaven face, staring at itself in the wall mirror.

She began to scream.

Parts of his face were filling in.

Bits of the cheek and nose joined the rest of the face, as if putty made of tissue and blood. He was beginning to come and rocked wildly. She spit at him, shaking her head from side to side.

He pulled out and hit her, over and over, until she didn't move. He lifted her by the blood-matted hair and threw her down again. Smashed her face with his boot, until it was a gumbo.

He sat on the cool floor and watched his penis shuddering but ejecting nothing; ghost sperm.

He examined his incomplete face, in the mirror, and became angry, tearing the mirror from the wall; smashing it. He watched her slumped body bleed and twitch, and waited for the epileptic seizure. Then, he zipped up his camouflage pants and left.

It would teach Alan a lesson.

reversal

The first thing Alan noticed was blood.

It brush-stroked the entry wall and continued upstairs, over the Lichtenstein Jordan and the other defoliants at the agency had given Alan. He reached up to touch it: still wet.

He smelled something burning and stepped cautiously upstairs to the dark living room. Rain car-washed the house and waves stormed on shore; saltwater artillery. He stopped, at the top of the stairs, froze.

The Creature stood beside the fireplace. Inside something burned, gushing smoke upward.

Alan didn't move. "What are you doing here . . . ?"

The Creature poked at the fireplace, turning its back. Its body was getting less bulky, more defined. Face less bestial.

". . . my house," said the Creature.

Blue clawmarks tore clouds. Trees bent outside, as if leaning to get sick.

The Creature turned, stared. ". . . how's Daddy?"

Alan went numb. The Creature watched his expression, fascinated by the pain that crept across Alan's gaunt face.

". . . what do you mean?"

It said nothing.

". . . she has a tight pussy. Daddy's wife."

The Creature was amused. Alan felt panic rising. Wanted to call his father. Instantly fought the impulse, not wanting to anger the half-man grinning at him.

"You tried to kill me," it said. "But I stopped you. I own you. You only think about me." Its voice was deep; stupid. "Daddy doesn't need you now."

Alan closed his eyes, felt like throwing up. He opened them and the Creature was standing in front of him, looking into his face. It's breath was cold. Odorless.

"I need more. You're dying. Give me more."

Alan knew what it wanted. It had become horribly obvious.

It would take everything from him it could get. Then, when it had what it needed, leave him so emptied, he'd dissipate into nothing. Or it would kill him in some cruel way that mocked Alan's own worst fears. It could intuit his mind; instinctively find the way to torture him that would most traumatize. Alan knew it would even enjoy it.

The Creature began to anger. It grabbed him, reining his hair, exposing his neck. "You don't hurt me. You don't quit. You don't leave town. You see what I do. I'll kill everybody . . ."

Alan said nothing, knowing he had to destroy the Creature to save his own life. The lives of future victims; people Alan despised. His enemies. The hated. The ones who must be punished; the dark shopping list he carried in his subconscious. The one the Creature would take care of, one name at a time.

He pushed away from the Creature, who walked out onto the deck. Alan moved to the fireplace, drawn by the troubling odor. It was filled with ash dunes and he took a poker, sifting. The poker slid through smoothly, finally stopped. Alan kneeled, grabbed iron log tongs.

The Creature stood on the deck, arms spread, staring up at rain that fell like soft shrapnel. It knew it would win. It was getting stronger. Nothing would stop it. It grinned at the falling sky, baring filthy, animal teeth as Alan began to scream inside.

"MOTHERFUCKER!" He was staring hatefully at the Creature.

The Creature stood under lightning, watching as Alan wept. It hated that Alan cared that much about anything other than it. Even a fucking dog.

Hated it so much, it kicked a boot through the floor-to-ceiling window and walked through glass dunes, to Alan, who cradled Bart's crushed skull. It grabbed his shirtfront and bared teeth.

"ME!" it screamed. "ME! ME! ME! ME! ME! ME! ME! ME! ME! ME! ME! ME! ME! ME! ME! *ME!!!"*

hidden motives

Seth . . . what do I do? . . . it's killing everything."

"*Shit.* It didn't work."

Silence. Alan's decimated voice weeping into the phone. ". . . god, this was never what I wanted. I wanted success. I didn't want death. I didn't want people tortured. This thing isn't me!" A terrible guilt.

As Alan wept, he could see Seth, in his mind, rolling a cigarette. Holding the phone. Looking out at his ten acres of Ojai countryside. Watching animals gather, stare. Watching clouds drift; death ships.

"Somewhere inside you, you did want it. Somewhere it is you."

Alan's chin stubble rubbed mouthpiece as he struggled to piece his mind together. He was almost whispering, face wet with tears.

". . . you know, it's sick . . . for the last year or so, every time I sat out on my deck, I saw the ocean as blood," he said. "Sky and land as flesh. It's this fixation . . . I don't know . . ."

He said nothing more, thoughts thinning. Seth asked him to go on. Alan wiped his cheeks.

"It's like . . . I've been creating life from inside myself . . . from a hidden world, under my skin." Alan sounded disgusted with himself. "I've become a metaphor. " He laughed, pathetically. "I'm fucking losing it, man. "

"Maybe you're figuring it out. "

"Yeah, right . . . " He sounded crazy; laughing, crying. "You mean, like I'm really the Walrus. "

"I mean . . . the world is a body and life is an idea. Everything in between is the lesson. "

"Goddamnit, it killed my dog, Seth! It almost killed my father! Raped my stepmother! What the hell are you talking about?!" Fears slit deeper. ". . . all this death is my fault. "

No reply.

"Look . . . if this thing is me . . . what *exactly* does the show have to do with it?"

"I have no idea. Except maybe the character you created . . . A. E. Barek. Mean motherfucker. Angry. Violent. Your own inner anger is exactly those things. Let's say your insides start to come out through the work . . . "

". . . in scripts?"

". . . at first. Then, who knows . . . maybe, it starts to literally form. You write more and more, adding more detail, it becomes more real. Your id is the blueprint for Barek and the whole series, Maybe A. E. is the blueprint for this thing you met. "

"So all this death . . . means what? It's protecting itself. Wants more attention from me?"

"Yep. "

"How long have you known this?" Alan instantly sounded caustic, without gratitude.

"Long as you have. "

"What the fuck is that supposed to mean? You knew and you let all that pain happen and didn't try to tell me?"

"I've been trying to tell you from the second we met. But I can only tell you what you can tell yourself. "

"No! You were *vague*. Just like now! You stay on the perimeter. You make it a puzzle. This is real! People are being hurt! My dog was killed. What the fuck is the matter with you?!"

"Alan, what we talk about, what we understand . . . it's all up to you. Doesn't matter what I know. Matters what you believe. "

Alan fell silent. He hated Seth.

"Alan, you gotta get it together. You have to stop this thing. You think you're the first guy this ever happened to? You're not. "

Alan kept hearing Bart in his mind. Saw his struggling form, hammered against the entry wall, yelping helplessly. Saw his father beaten unconscious. Wanda, bleeding between the legs, thrust back into another rape trauma.

"And you have to do it alone. "

"Then, I'll go somewhere where this prick will never find me. "

"It's *you*. Where you gonna go?"

"Then, I'm dead. My own creation is more powerful than I am. "

"You've let it get too big. Part of you is stronger than another part . . . but part of you is smarter. "

". . . so, what do I do? Challenge it to a goddamn debate?"

"Kill the character. "

Alan was gripping his forehead. Becoming furious. "*How*, Seth? I tried to write Barek as a nicer character and I told you, that thing raped my step-mother . . . " He coughed; empty pain. ". . . tried to kill my father to force me to stay on the show. Killed my dog. It's insane!"

"It wants to live. It's protecting its life. That's all it was ever doing. " A touch of irony. "You'd do the same thing. " Anchored calm. "If this was a script, know what the conflict would be?"

Bitterness. ". . . man versus Neilsen ratings?"

"How about two people who both want control of the same life. "

". . . how does it end?"

"Cancellation. "

As Alan listened, Seth began to describe the murder. How Alan should do it; in exact, minute detail. Alan memorized it all, finally asked Seth if he would help; he was too weak to fight alone.

"Nothing I can do. I've done my work. " A last suggestion. "Alan . . . keep a good thought. "

Seth hung up.

Alan tried to get some rest, as Seth had suggested; he would need strength to fight and kill the Creature. But he couldn't close his eyes and after half an hour, called Seth back. An old woman answered. When Alan asked for Seth, there was dead silence.

"Is this a joke?" she said.

Alan didn't understand; told her he'd just spoken with Seth. She began to anger and Alan couldn't understand what she was saying, words muffled. She finally blurted out hurt words. "Seth is dead!" She fell silent. "Why are you doing this to me?"

Alan didn't move. Spoke slowly. "But I spoke with him . . . I met him. He visited me . . . to help me. "

"He had a heart attack!"

"When did he have a heart attack? What time?"

"Time?" she repeated irritably. "I can't remember that far back. It's been fifteen years . . . " She hung up and Alan stared at the phone.

His blood ran cold. He instantly realized he'd created the man he'd spoken with, just as he'd created the Creature. He'd needed Seth so badly, he'd taken everything he knew about him, from the book he'd read, and brought him into material form.

He now understood why the first meeting with Seth had been so vague, so infuriating. At that point, Alan's own understanding of what Seth had written about was equally vague. From that talk had come only instincts; mostly Alan's. Once he began to truly understand what Seth had been writing about, once the truth solidified, the conversations changed. Seth sounded more specific; exact. It was Alan's mind accepting; comprehending.

Everything was a circle. Seth had said thoughts were everything. So had Eddy. Alan finally understood.

It was time.

finale

Alan was stopped at the studio
gate at two-thirteen in the morning.

The Aston rumbled and the guard peered closer, grasping
his clipboard. Alan was in some unbalanced trance; lost in exhaustion, saying he was there to do rewrite work on his series. He tried
not to look directly at the guard who froze a statue face, looking
curiously.

Alan knew the man could see the eerie snow that fell inside
him and smiled thinly, saying he was just coming down with something.

The sky dripped water, though it was almost eighty-five out; a
muggy storm steaming L.A. alive. The Aston was waved through
and howled through the dead lot, headlights caroming off dream
city.

It passed Hitchcock's former office and did a hairpin where
the Universal Tour Trams stopped to empty tourists into the funny
makeup show. To either side, soundstages rose up like canyon walls.
Huge promo art was painted on the side of each, advertising the

latest movies and series the studio had going. Enormous actors' faces grinned, bloated and frightening.

Alan's production building was a quarter mile ahead; the suite of decorated offices financed by the incredible success of "The Mercenary"; a mosque built on decimal point madness. His body felt starved; empty.

He skidded in front of the WHITE ENTERTAINMENT building and killed the headlights as drizzle fell, razor thin. He sat in silence, feeling bleak and clammy. He tilted the mirror down, looked at his milky face. Bedlam pain swirled in his mind. Should he turn back? He knew he didn't even have the energy or strength to defend himself.

It's why he'd brought the gun.

He pulled it from his inside jacket pocket and decided he had to go through with this. Everything else had failed; been pointless. It was painfully obvious to him, now. Trying to change the show. Get it cancelled. All useless.

It was time to fight; blood with blood.

Alan knew the Creature had the overwhelming amount of the vitality they both shared and he was at a terrifying disadvantage. Freud had talked about it; the distribution of essential energy. What the id and superego shared. What they should both be drawing from equally. In Alan's world, all that was gone. Inside out. He felt the Möbius imbalance hollowing him out.

He got out of the car, moved heavily through humid rain, toward the three-story soundstage door. His shoes were drenched by puddles and driving rain stabbed his skin. He pulled open the heavy door and entered, leaning for a moment in the entrance, head spinning.

Inside, air hung stale; icy. The silent soundstage was dark, looming. Every standing set used on "The Mercenary" stood, waiting for lights and cameras and reasons. It was all there.

Everything Alan had created.

Barek's dingy apartment. General Garris's office. The hellhole cell Barek flashed back to; his POW days of torture and captivity.

The room where he was strapped naked to a steel chair and electrically shocked, feet in buckets of water. The nightmare chamber that forged his stoic obsessions.

Beside it, oblivious to the proximity, was the bedroom Barek had had as a boy, growing up in Sacramento. Its baseball pennants and hot-rod posters watched over the room with haunting innocence. Directly beside the room were the cutaways of Barek's helicopter and cargo plane, gray process screen behind them, waiting to receive images of sky.

It was all there; the character's whole life, in idealized, symbolic fragments.

The makeup tables and mirrors sat motionless, ready to bring warpaint. Wardrobe racks hung with bloodied clothing; a murderer's closet. Crates of gutted weapons, squatted uselessly, ready to create artificial death, fueled by blanks and dubbed sound. It was a vast crypt of illusion and lie. The places Barek had been; come from.

The place the Creature now lived. Where the police had picked him up, after Alan called. Taken the Creature to jail. Away from here, from where it could stop Alan from doing what he had to.

Alan hit a light switch and banks of overhead lights went on; heating elements in a huge oven. He touched the gun reflexively and moved through the sets, still half-looking for the Creature. For some sign it was there, in its fictive home. Even though he knew it was locked up in a cage by now.

As he walked, the folding chairs with all the names of the production crew stood, legs crossed. The one that read A. E. BAREK, with its script pouch hanging to the side, was the fanciest, done in tooled leather; a gift from Alan.

He moved through the sets, feeling sick, helpless; kicking over furniture and yanking aside drapes. He was growing weaker. He knew it was only a matter of time before he wasted to nothing and the Creature siphoned everything. If he let it, it would take every piece of his life. Thoughts. Emotions. Memories. Like some thieving, metaphysical appetite, he could feel it eating his cells; the things he was.

On the floor, beside the bed in Barek's apartment, Alan found several porno magazines and an empty package of steak from Vons with the blood licked off. He moved to the other sets. Nothing.

On a table was a stack of Xeroxed scripts.

Scripts.

Alan's unconscious world seeking form. His feelings and insides shoving aside everything to become substance. The terrible fantasies and horrific, amoral realities. Pieces of the inevitable whole. He was afraid to look, afraid of what it all meant. Filled with revulsion for himself. For what he'd created; what he'd released. What he'd been unable to detect within.

He began to open cans of flammable gel used to stage contained fires and poured the thick liquid everywhere, walking with the open cans, as if chalking a playing field for some grisly sport. Fumes gathered and the gel darkened floors, walls, and furniture. Alan walked to the stacked scripts, began to ball up pages, and lit them with a lighter. He threw the crumpled plots and speeches, and watched them burst into flame as they connected with the gel.

The apartment drapes began to burn, spreading to the thinly built facade walls and doors that shriveled black as flames swallowed; moved on.

Alan watched unnerved, as the sets erupted. Suddenly, there was a deafening noise as a car crashed through the soundstage wall, shredding the mattresslike insulation. Lemon beams raced at him and he dove from its path.

He was on the ground, not moving. Clutching his gun for protection. The engine blew pillows of exhaust, then died. There was no sound. Only rain, striking puddles and metal outside and the sound of sets burning. Alan belly-crawled to the driver's door, stood slowly. He sleeved rain from the windshield and jerked back.

Inside, dyed by pulsing dash lights, two cops slumped, throats cut, eyes plucked out; a sadist's surgery. One uniform shirt had been ripped away in the back and a message carved into one officer's skin; crude and deep.

A. E. Rules

As Alan stared, a jungle knife speared his shoulder and a deep hunter's scream filled the soundstage. He looked up and the Creature was dropping from a catwalk, two stories up. It landed on him, with bared teeth, as fire rampaged from set to set.

As they struggled, Alan aimed and fired at the Creature. But he missed, only grazing its cheek. It wiped the diagonal line of blood on its face, kept coming at him. Panicked, Alan fired over and over, blinded by fire and fear, emptying the gun without hitting the Creature. He managed to pull the guard's bloody knife from his own back pocket and jammed it into the Creature's ribs. The Creature screamed, stiffened.

Alan felt the pain in his own torso; a ghostly repetition. He dug the fat blade in deeper and again felt the agony in his own body. The Creature rolled to one side, in anguish, and Alan ran, hearing the Creature's heavy, booted steps chasing.

As it passed the burning bedroom it dimly recalled having slept in as a boy, it stopped and looked on in traumatized horror. Pain racked its features and the Creature bellowed loss and torment, trying to stop the fire; unable to touch it. Recalling a childhood which never existed and had no detail, gouged by emotion it couldn't fathom. Standing in a room it never experienced. Never knew.

Alan ran from the huge building that glowed orange death as the door opened. His side ached and the sensation of a piercing blade making him look down again to check but see nothing. He clutched the tender midsection, dragged through deep ponds of rain, and began to realize it was more complicated than he'd considered. More fundamental.

The sets weren't the key.

They were only a component. A layer. Only what the Creature instinctively reasoned was home. With fire, Alan had rendered it homeless; ravaged its history for now. But it wasn't the key. He ran through the storm and suddenly understood what he must do.

Burning the sets was only superficial. The original film negatives would be where essence hid; where genetic codes rooted primary definitions. The negatives weren't simply an animate photo album. They were the record of a maturing fetus.

The sky was lowering and as he groaned, he suddenly felt in Viet Nam, rain clouds dense with contaminants, ground seized by blinding mist. He ran toward his production building and couldn't see more than a few feet ahead; smothered in nothing.

His breathing went down into body corridors filled with injured flesh and he could almost hear the weightless footsteps of guerilla snipers, hiding near. He imagined trip wires, everywhere he stepped, that would release sharpened pungi sticks, on contact, crucifying his flesh.

He could see no sky and easily imagined treetops that weren't there; grinning Vietnamese death angels, ready to soundlessly drop; slit him open.

Rain fell harder and thunder shook the ground. He felt his cheek, sensing pain. He touched it and saw it was bleeding, exactly where he'd grazed the Creature. He moaned in horror and stopped, eyes darting. Were those the sounds of villagers? Southeast Asian birds? Bare legs moving through rice paddies, knives held in small hands? He crouched down, swallowing. Afraid. Drenched by rain.

Was he losing his mind? He stood, slowly, head bursting with images he'd written for the show. Faces of slaughtered villagers lunged at his mind. Explosions. Bodies, hanging upside down, skinned like animals. Screaming children, ravaged by napalm, running into his brain, right through his forehead.

He saw the murders, too.

Defenseless victims holding hands up to protect faces as glimmering blades cut them apart. Skin, instantly sunken by bullets that left red-black wells. Stacks of bodies, rising higher, soaring into a bleeding spire of distorted faces, clawing arms, voices crying out in deafening misery.

He clamped hands over ears, and without warning the Creature emerged from mist, face half-melted by fire. It lifted a ghastly smile and elbowed him in the chin. Alan fell to the wet ground, groaning, bleeding from mouth and nose.

The Creature approached, slowly, leaned down, and touched Alan's bleeding features, then licked the blood off its fingertips, savoring his taste; gory mother's milk. It wanted more of him, and Alan immediately lunged out and slashed at the Creature's leg tendons with the knife. The Creature cried out, reaching down to the cut muscles that split to reveal unfinished tissue; no blood.

Alan began to run but felt the sensation in his own leg muscles and screamed in pain. The connection between the two was getting stronger; cross-pollinating with almost no delay.

He knew he couldn't go back toward his production building; the Creature could be hiding. It could hear him. Get him before he had a chance to kill it. Overpower him. Cut him open and dump his insides. Alan realized if he felt its pain, and it felt his, it could be thinking what he was. It would know he was heading toward the production office to destroy it. It could anticipate him. Trick him.

Ambush his thoughts.

He would have to hide out and circle back. Struggle to keep his mind a total blank. Give the Creature nothing to work with other than a monochromatic void. Alan knew if he could get to the narrow drainage pipe that traveled beneath the main road and emptied near his building, he could squeeze himself through and sneak into the main vault where he kept the negatives.

He moved ahead, trying to fight the pain in his legs, and found himself at one end of a narrow wooden bridge. He started across.

climax

It was the stunt bridge.

Trams would drive across, theatrically stall, and the bridge would collapse, threatening to drop freaked tourists into a death-lake below. Everybody got a hard-on for their photo album.

Alan knew the drainage pipe was across the way and the bridge the fastest route to its ridged mouth. He began to cross, wincing as the wood creaked and fog hedged; silver neon. Crickets and mosquitoes shrieked and the lake bamboo released air bubbles at shore's edge as water lapped, filing it down.

He moved across the bridge, weak.

Though he feared the Creature was under the damp boards, ready to get him, he was allowed to cross undisturbed. He could hear ducks huddling on the artificial shoreline, rain tapping softly. But the Creature was nowhere close. Or if it was, it did nothing to stop him.

Alan knew it was as strong as he was weak. As he dissipated and thinned within, robbed by its demands, it became more real. More complete. He tried to guide it to leave him alone, repeating again and again the same thought; a single, insistent mantra.

"Nothing," he repeated, saying the word quietly, hoping its sound might make it more real. Hoping the Creature's instinctive radar couldn't track him.

He stopped.

Sirens. Kniving sky; rain.

He could wait. They would find him. Protect him. Get him out of this nightmare. But the Creature would find some new, more devastating way to punish him. To pay him back for burning its home. For trying to kill it. Who would it hurt or kill this time? Who mattered to Alan?

He clutched the knife more tightly and stepped slowly, watching his shoes move, looking in all directions for some sign of the Creature. Fog ran its eraser over everything and he could swear a squad of Vietnamese were hiding under the bridge, clinging to the underside, ready to attack. Ready to reach up, drag him into the water, and force his head under the surface.

Fuck.

The Creature was doing it. Filling his mind with images. He was convinced it was learning to think; to imagine. As he lost parts of his own mind, it moved in; took over. *It was doing this to him!* Suggesting ideas; torturing his mind.

Or was it . . . ?

It couldn't think. It was a killing animal. That's all he'd ever written it to be. That was its whole complaint. It wanted to be more than just a flesh machine with mere survival in its primitive program. Alan knew that its current only ran in one direction; he'd seen to it. He'd even made it have elements of compassion in the one script he'd written that the network hated. It had added a small measure of humanity but that wasn't the same as being able to think.

All it knew how to do was survive; it was its disadvantage and its advantage. It lacked so much; things Alan had never given it. Ultimately, it was only brute force; dominating impulse. Though it could physically overwhelm him, he could outthink it. Everything it knew, he'd thought of. Everything it wanted, he'd told it to want.

It would only kill him if he let it.

He stopped, halfway across, hearing a noise.

Something was under the bridge.

He stood there, eyes moving frantically and screamed as a blade was shoved from underneath, between boards, and went all the way through his right foot. He stared down at the gleaming metal rising out of his shoe, trying to lift his foot off the blade. He reached down to grab his leg, to help pull.

He turned, strickenly, hearing the Creature coming toward him, from the other side of the bridge. Saw it grinning. As it stepped closer, Alan lifted harder, straining to free his foot from the blade. It was excruciating and the foot slid up, slowly, releasing blood.

Alan began to limp away and turned to see the Creature hobbling on its own right leg, coming after him. Fog masked the distance between them and he could see the pipe ahead, its rusted lips forming a narrow, three-foot opening. He picked up rocks, tossed them in another direction, heard the Creature momentarily follow their sound.

"Nothing, nothing, nothing . . ."

He fell to his knees and climbed in, shimmying through the wet metal that ran uphill toward his office. It was narrow and smelled bad and he pulled his body with skinny, unmuscled arms, digging the toes of his shoes into the pipe's ripples, using them like rungs.

Rain and mud thrashed through the pipe and Alan turned his head to avoid the filthy current, fast-moving rocks cutting his hands. He kept climbing, moving up through the roaring throat. His hands slipped on the mossy walls, bloody; raw.

He couldn't remember exactly how long the pipe was and there was no end in sight. His foot was still aching and bloody from the knife wound and the muddy water made it worse. He heard something up ahead. Something shrieking; struggling. Scratching at the cold metal. As he tried to see, a cat twisted closer, trapped in the current. It was half-drowned, fur slick, and clawed at him in terror.

He tried to pull it off and it went insane, baring teeth, struggling for life. It tore up his face with sharp claws and Alan finally shoved it away. He heard it disappear, crying out like a frightened kitten, washed away.

As he kept moving, he heard another sound. Sirens pulling into the studio; red banshees. They would go to the soundstage and spray water on the glowing death. They wouldn't understand what it meant. Insurance companies would settle and the studio would rebuild the sets. They would be ready to commence shooting within days. But Alan knew the show was dead. He was going to kill it.

If it didn't work, he began to think of another plan: he could trap the Creature. Pen it up somewhere, where no one would ever come. Let it starve to death while he stood outside the bars and watched with his good qualities; watching the bad ones wither, beg for life.

He suddenly screamed, dragged backwards.

Something was grabbing his ankles and he looked back to see the Creature, pulling harder, dragging Alan backwards; downhill. Alan's chin was gouged open by the rough, galvanized metal and he struggled to hold on.

He tried to inch himself away, breathing hard, unable to get enough air in this metal vein. But the Creature was too strong. He tried to make it stop, tried to think thoughts that would make it let go.

"Nothing!" he screamed, kicking madly, voice hoarse.

But he knew it was too late. The Creature was too far along; too developed. He could no longer control anything about it. He was trapped. It would pull him out and murder him. A new executive producer would be put on the series and it would continue its cancerous popularity. The Creature would get stronger and stronger. Kill. Rape. It would become more and more monstrous as it became more real.

It wanted to be a complete man. Part of the human community. That's why it wanted more detail. But he knew it would continue to ravage and destroy; it would never be in balance, once Alan was dead. He was the only thing that could provide emotional texture; conscience. Without him, it was doomed to be nothing more than a monster.

But it didn't know that. He'd never created it to know anything, except violence and an obsessive need to win. Just like in the pilot when he'd had Barek kill the guy in the bar in Saigon who was hassling him.

The one who broke Barek's jaw, thought Alan. A jaw that remained permanently vulnerable; fragile. It had all been rooted incontrovertibly in the pilot.

Alan instantly kicked backwards, hard as he could, forcing the Creature to stop his foot. He kicked again with the other foot, managing to kick the Creature's forehead. Then, again and again, until he'd finally connected with the mouth and jaw and the Creature screamed, filling the drainage pipe with echoing pain. Alan kicked again and the jaw was damaged worse, dislocating, causing the Creature to let go, clutching the lower part of its face.

Alan shimmied upwards through the pipe, ignoring the extreme pain in his foot and palms, torn by the pipe's surface. Rainwater plunged faster, as he neared the pipe's source, and his gasping mouth opened wide for air. The grainy water raced to the curve of his throat and slithered in, filling his stomach with thick, cold mud. He choked and threw it up, looked back to see if the Creature was following. He was alone and could hear a mix of sirens and the Creature crying out, halfway down the dark pipe.

Alan was to the pipe's opening and climbed out. He managed to stand on shaking legs and looked at his foot. It had soaked his cut shoe with blood, though the water had rinsed most out. He limped toward his production building and heard the fire company rumbling up to the soundstage. Heard faraway voices. Axes crashing. Pressurized water slaughtering flame.

His imagination being extinguished.

He moved to his building, entered the security code. The door unlocked and he limped through the lobby, past the reception desk with his steel logo behind it, on the wall. He fell as he moved past the desk, got back up, and staggered weakly down the long hall to his office.

In his office, he went to the fireplace, turned the gas key, pressed the auto-start button. He squinted at the blinding ignition and moved to the wall vault, trembling; and working the combination. The metal door opened soundlessly.

The master negatives were stacked neatly, twenty-two cans in all; the first season. He gathered an armful and walked to the fireplace, leaving a bloody path on the white Berber. He stood at the mantel, opened the cans, began to toss them into the blaze.

The Creature stood in the doorway, looking at him.

"... please ... don't ..." Its jaw was wrong, distorting its features.

Alan threw two episodes in and the Creature howled, grabbing at its body as flames hissed and film smoked. It dove at Alan and fell to the carpet, looking up at him with pleading eyes. Its hands were starting to fade, fingers nearly gone. As Alan threw more film into the fire, the Creature's limbs began to shudder, its mouth working helplessly.

It tried to speak but couldn't and Alan scrabbled back to the vault, grabbing more cans. He opened them with shaking fingers and threw them into the flames.

The Creature was making inhuman sounds, its solid mass now opaque as Alan threw in more film and fire destroyed polished surface. The Creature yelled, in agony, as its flesh broke down, its unevolved innards going amorphous.

It was being destroyed, one piece at a time; an assassination of detail. Alan turned the fire up higher, relishing the liquidation of each bit and piece. He sat cross-legged, after tossing in the final episode and watched the Creature as it shook and cried, unable to fight the horrible ruination; the foreclosure of self.

It extended a hand to Alan.

"... please ..." Its voice was unprotected; frightened.

Alan looked into its eyes. In its vanishing features, he saw a fear he could remember. The way he felt on playgrounds when bigger kids would walk up with tough expressions and humiliate him.

The way he felt all through his life, when he couldn't please his father. The fear he felt when he stood by his mother's dead body and watched her bloodless face, that he loved with all his heart, as she went away forever, abandoning him.

"... please ..."

Be careful what you wish for.

Alan kept running the phrase through his head as he watched the Creature losing life; diluting into nothing. The only meager thread it clung to was Alan and it stared at him, terrified.

But he did nothing to help, despising it.

Feeling no sympathy or compassion; relishing the things he had, it didn't. He felt no pity as it writhed, its life seeping away; its skin translucent. He could feel his mouth watering as its eyes filled with tears and its pleading voice grew thin; inaudible. It was a fucking piece of shit and it deserved to suffer and feel all the hideous pain it had brought.

But he knew he was lying to himself, again. Knew it would never die. Somehow it would achieve life, again. He would simply find new ways to create other creatures that could embody the menacing thoughts and poison conclusions he carried within himself. Creatures with other names, which did other things. But they would all be that side of himself trying to cut its way out; seek oxygen.

Find light, that it might be nourished and grow. And he would be returned to where he was now, trying to escape it; trying to save himself from himself. Feeling terrified of what was inside him.

The only way to kill the Creature was to kill himself. He knew he was no better than what it was. He just had another side. A better side. The Creature wasn't the monster. But what he could never admit about himself might be. More than all the Jordans and Feiffers and Andy Singers put together. At least they were honest about their monstrous needs. At least they didn't hide behind polite walls, as Alan always had.

As it curled into a fetal ball and wept softly, Alan moved closer to it and noticed it was bleeding. *Bleeding* . . .

Becoming real, just as it was dying.

He looked at it, as it struggled to keep its eyes open, and realized he needed it. Needed it to express the constant anger he felt. Megatons worth, festering at the bottom of Alan's own silos, anxious for release.

Be careful what you wish for.

"You can be anything . . ." It's what they'd all told him. Everyone.

He sat there, hearing the gunfire between the two sides of himself, and watched the film burn. Rain fell harder and he felt like he was being buried alive.

ten months later

epilogue

Palm Springs was an ice-machine.

It was Christmas and twinkly lights covered the houses; elf jewelry. Forty-degree winds blew golf courses and tennis courts and shook snowmen grinning everywhere; triple scoop, Styrofoam goons.

Streets were empty, shops quiet.

Bentley boys and their wrinkly babes hung in seven-figure igloos using ultraviolet, and weekenders nuzzled in front of roaring Mitsubishis warming their brains. The sky was cold blue skin, and gangs of sand chased you everywhere you went, trying to kick your ass.

Alan was alone making dinner.

He glanced at the clock, stomach in knots.

Last week, it had been days.

The blond daughter of some Supreme Court bass drum had been alone in a bar in Rancho Mirage. She liked the Creature's tie-you-down eyes. His scarred hands and arms. The dominant awkwardness of his healing jaw. She told him her husband was in the Bahamas and bought him four Coronas.

Alan didn't see him for two days.

It was getting a little better. But in some ways, the same. He didn't go out much; saving strength. Healing. Muscle tone coming back. Sunken eyes improving.

The Creature did what it wanted and though Alan tried to be casual, inside it terrified him. To think of it out there, loose, never coming back. Doing whatever it wanted. But it always did come back. Hungry. Sleepy.

On edge; ready to argue.

He stirred the browning vegetables and decided not to call his shrink; they'd been talking every day for three months solid. It was exhausting sometimes to go through it again. Over and over. The sifting. The interpretive hunt as they walked Alan's ocean floor.

Besides, he had to call his father, in France. Let him know how things were. That he was okay. That his condo was being well-taken care of. To say thanks for the millionth time. To see how Wanda was. If she looked fourteen yet. To wait for his dad to say he missed him and hoped he was feeling better.

To wait for just the right moment of satellite lag where silence and emotion wordlessly passed each other, miles above the earth, and it was safe to tell his Dad he loved him. Sometimes the lag never came. But Alan always waited. At times, it was all he wanted from the calls.

The moment.

His Dad always asked if Alan was keeping in touch with his shrink and Alan would fill him in, just enough to reassure. Tell him how the two were continuing to discuss Alan's breakdown; how he could realign his fragmented insides to avoid future ones. To avoid the tributaries of pain that washed out his world.

His dad always mentioned how impressed he was that Alan's shrink, Delchamps, had accompanied the ambulance attendants when they took Alan from his office at the studio ten months ago. Burt always repeated positive aspects of any story rather than slip into emotion. It was his shield.

His anesthesia.

He would tell Alan how things were going on the film in France and what a beautiful country it was and how the injuries were healing for him and Wanda but that Wanda still had awful nightmares about the rape.

And Alan would always fall silent.

Not able to tell his father everything. Not able to tell anyone other than Delchamps everything. He could only remain soundless; trapped in a place of profound shame and guilt.

Waiting for the moment.

Telling his dad he loved him. It always helped a little.

And they would hang up and Alan would stare out the kitchen window at desert mountains, their soft crag coastline. He would start to feel himself crying with self-hatred.

Then, it would pass.

Delchamps told him to expect this to go on for a long time. Maybe forever. He told Alan he'd never seen or heard of such an absolute breakdown; this extreme a form of externalization. The actual outward creation of the id. He told Alan he wanted to study it for the remainder of Alan's life. Tell no one. Keep meticulous records. Reveal what had happened at the proper time, when more was understood, when they wouldn't be laughed at; disbelieved.

Despised by those Alan had hurt.

He told Alan what he'd gone through could help others. To realize that frustrations and feelings had lives; literal selves. And that when left unchecked long enough, they had the power to physically escape, not merely seep. Delchamps smiled when he asked Alan what the initials in A. E. Barek's name stood for and Alan finally guessed "alter ego."

Alan agreed to be studied, if it were in secret. To do it any other way, revealing the data and conclusions before he was dead, would legally place him in prison.

The guilt over what had happened was grotesque enough; total imprisonment. He could never transcend the horrid, endlessly consuming ownership for the lives he'd taken and destroyed. Not him; but a part of him. Still, he could see no separation. In his heart, he had done these things. They were his crimes. His inescapable sins. The deaths and tortures were debts he could never settle.

As he and Delchamps talked more and more, he began to understand that had the creature never materialized, Alan would've destroyed himself; eaten himself alive. Feelings and frustrations buried deep had to break free in a coherent form. Delchamps even told him ulcers were like creatures that grew in the stomach. And Alan had carried, within, a lifetime of visceral rage. Lunatic impulses. Without release, they would've eventually drowned his mind. Alan found no relief in the explanation.

Monsters . . .

Alan had asked him if we all create something that expressed censored inner rage and frustration. Delchamps said yes; sometimes we were the monster we created, sometimes we made others the monster.

Alan said conversion of self was the plague that had no beginning, had no end. Delchamps told him it was an interesting comment.

A divided self.

It had always been there, in his life. As a little kid, he remembered having an imaginary friend who was stronger and unafraid, and always took care of him. He could even blame the friend when he did bad stuff and turn to him when he needed help or strength.

He'd asked for a ventriloquist's dummy when he was twelve and it became his mouthpiece; a way to lash out and make others laugh. A way to disguise the malignance. He'd even drawn a cartoon strip in high school with a cynical character who said outrageous things. And it grew, right along with the rest of him. He considered the likelihood these innocent hobbies had foretold the Creature. Even wondered if they were younger versions; its infancy. Its boyhood. Its own hobbies as it grew up inside him.

His insides had been its world. It told him that a few weeks back, not even realizing what it was saying. But Alan knew that world could never have been enough; too cramped. A dark cell beneath his skin. It had felt entombed.

Alan had taken to reading about primitive man during the months in Palm Springs he and the Creature lived alone together in the condo. He'd read how Jung said people needed to maintain connection with primal roots; the ancestors who danced around fires and believed in magic.

Despite countless years, they were us and we were them. Nothing changed. They just remained inside now, as the Creature had. Hiding. Unwelcome outside. Dislocated immigrants, hoping one day to breathe fresh air.

The fierceness had been bred out. Instinctive apes put in clothes, houses. Spontaneity and need domesticated. But nothing ever went away. It just needed something to help it bend the bars and get out.

"Your childhood took care of that," Delchamps had said and Alan didn't disagree.

The pollen of madness was everywhere in his family. Physical and emotional illness. Fear. Avoidance. The list had no end. He could leaf through its history, stop anywhere. Throughout was dysfunction that broke his bones, set them the wrong way.

Alan turned off the vegetables and heard a motorcycle outside. The engine was killed, heavy boots walked toward the front door.

A key rattled.

Alan took his multiple vitamins, the third time that day, rebuilding his system; he had gained fifteen pounds. The Creature had lost ten.

It came in, wearing a biker jacket, carton of cigarettes under its arm. Tossed a video cassette on the couch near the VCR and belched. Parts of its neck and forehead were slightly caved in; the burning negatives had taken a toll. But when Alan decided to let it live, he'd quickly salvaged what footage he could. In strong light, you could still see right through the Creature.

"Got you a movie."

"What?"

". . . one you've been wanting, that's always rented."

It raised an ugly smile, jaw slightly misshapen. Told him it got a porno for itself. It went to the fireplace, balled up newspaper, started a fire, using wood from the stack. Tore open the carton, a pack, lit a cigarette.

"Thought you were gonna cool it on the smoking . . ."

The Creature glared.

Alan said nothing more about it.

For dinner, the Creature had a burger and beer and Alan had his usual vegetables and rice. They spoke little. As the video cassette was loaded, the Creature flipped past the network and he and Alan sat in silence, watching some of a new "Mercenary" episode.

It was as bad as the one last week, and the ones for the last few months. Patrick Benson had been lured down from Portland, with a hundred grand a week, to take the reins of the series, and a new actor had been hired.

Viewers were told Barek had died in a raid on a Peruvian consulate, to free a congressman's daughter, and that his ex-cop brother had taken over for him as series regular. But the new actor, Steve Perito, was a bag of rocks, siphoned off one of the soaps and utterly lacked what Corea had. What the Creature had. The scripts had become stupid and graphic in a mimicking way, throwing in naked girls and shredded bodies everywhere they could. Alan realized Patrick had always been your basic fucking hack and should've stayed in Portland, where he could remain in a thick fog.

The ratings were sinking and Andy Singer's sitcom, "Roomie" was gaining on it. "Roomie" was followed by another Andy-launched project, "Dog Boy," and the hour of comedy was perfect counter programming. Ever since Andy had come out of the emotional oxygen tent and gone to work on another network, he'd made it his goal to topple "The Mercenary." He held it against Alan that he'd quit to go down to Palm Springs and "flake." He just couldn't understand. But that had never been Andy's strong suit.

". . . shit without us," was all the Creature said, watching the new actor struggling, tied to a burning car, flesh searing. It looked unconvincing, screams of pain like a faked orgasm.

"Yeah . . ." said Alan, depressed. Somehow relieved.

There was no resolution. There couldn't be; it got no better and never could. And now he just felt a hollow ache when he watched what he'd created. It was like visiting the scene of a murder after everything had been cleaned up. Something terrible had happened, yet on the surface little gave it away.

A lingering atmosphere.

Exactly like the one at the house in Malibu he'd quickly decided to sell, after the breakdown. The house that so perfectly paralleled and reflected his insides; a thing of meticulously cleansed savagery. A thing that hid its violent truths. Just as the show he'd created, its very state of inhumanity within entertainment reflected his insides. It all reflected his insides.

Maybe most things everyone did reflected their insides.

He suspected it. Didn't know anymore.

He was tired. The Creature had several beers and tried to start an argument and demanded Alan fight back. He didn't want to but knew it was best. Tonight he even raised his voice and threw a magazine and it made the Creature smile.

He was making strides, absurdly civil as they were.

He asked the Creature about where he'd been and the Creature indirectly allowed Alan to give him some advice about a woman the Creature was seeing; having sex with. He told the Creature to be more patient and it told him to get fucked and laughed at him.

But Alan could tell it had heard what he said.

Another stride. So small. So ridiculously subtle. But small steps, enough of them, over time, could turn things around. It was the reason he'd chosen to do it this way: live with the other part of himself, try to coexist with his other half; learn to live with it. Maybe it was working. He couldn't tell for sure; didn't trust his judgment anymore.

Still, as he acknowledged the Creature more, his color and vitals were slowly returning. But it seemed insane, living side by side with this vicious hemisphere of himself. Staying under the same roof. Having to listen to it say ugly, despising things. Watch the brutish behavior, every day, as it drank beer and reacted with impatient rage to the slightest thing. As it threw things and broke things and screamed.

It was a six-foot-two newborn. Demanding; unable to grasp not getting exactly what it wanted. Throwing horrendous tantrums, just as a baby "makes" its mother and others pick it up by screaming. By planting thoughts; like soft, pink grappling hooks. The Creature did the same thing; a conceptual infant. A beginning. A radio station playing one song: "ME."

Most of the time, Alan couldn't stand it.

He thought he should've just burned all the negatives that night, in his office. Saved none. Just destroyed this vile half man who belched and laughed at stupid things and went out every night on his motorcycle to get his rocks off. Sometimes Alan was even amused to see it doing the things he'd always felt the impulse to do. Drinking. Being sexual and bringing home whores, now and then. All the things Alan had been ashamed of.

Other times, it simply irritated him.

The Creature never seemed to totally comprehend what had happened. It understood they were connected and at times called Alan its best friend. But beyond that simplicity, Alan knew the Creature was too primitive to discern more.

When Alan had burned the later episodes, which gave the character greater intellect, it had reduced its mental ability. The Creature was now functioning on limited, primary reasoning.

Alan thought, again, about rewriting the character, as he had when he'd tried to alter Barek's behavior with rewrites. Make him nice; gentle. But if he was going to learn to live with himself, he wanted to do it purely. Directly. However infuriating. He even knew an angry reaction was proof things were changing. That he was getting better.

Sometimes he thought that. Most of the time, he was just scared.

Late at night, when Alan was too tired to read or watch TV, he would go to his bedroom. He would lie there and hear the Creature in the living room, drinking and watching porno movies, sitting by itself. At times, it would even call out. Ask if Alan needed anything. It was a huge step in sensitivity.

Then, he would hear it, again. Being crude, like something in a cave. But Alan was comforted by the familiar things it did; things he always felt the impulse to do but stopped himself from. He wanted so much to escape from barred thoughts. Alcatrazed impulses. To free inhibitions; let it out.

Perhaps in time.

Alan hoped eventually, one night, the Creature would awaken him by coming into the room and pulling back the covers. That it would get into bed, beside him, and the two would lie in darkness, side by side, and slowly move closer. Slowly, tentatively touch. Make soft, infant sounds of comfort and recognition. Warmly begin to embrace and in the womblike blackness of his own father's bedroom, as if in some embryonic stillness, melt into each other, a new life, made up of two selves.

A man. Created by himself, upon himself. A whole man who could finally, on levels impossible to estimate or seize, forgive himself.

Tonight, as he lay in bed, with the Creature asleep on the couch, the night took a big breath. Slowly, silently, Alan floated into his imaginary five-year-old body, the boy he once was, and told himself things.

He saw the room he grew up in. The pennants and hot-rod posters, exactly like those in Corea's room.

His dead sister, Ellen, was there in the next room, playing, singing. His mother was downstairs, baking. Laughing at a show on TV. Burt was listening to Mahler, in his study. It was *real.*

The little boy was under sheets, alone in the dark room, scared; crying. Alan sat on the bed beside him and whispered to him, like a gentle hand taking his.

He told him, softly, it was okay to imagine strange things in life without thinking they'd come true. He told him it was okay to ask questions if things scared him.

He told him he wasn't responsible for his sister's getting sick or dying. That he wasn't responsible for his parents not being closer. Or for his mother's happiness. Or her death.

He told him that he was just a little boy and that it was okay to be a little boy. There would be plenty of time to be a grown-up.

Then, he imagined holding himself and saying to the scared little boy that he would always be there to make it safe. To take care of everything. And that he loved him. The little boy smiled, in Alan's arms, and closed his eyes. And as Alan rocked the smaller version of himself, he too began to relax.

Soon, all three were asleep.

"Nothing changes until it becomes what it is."

Fritz Perls